SECRET WARS

To Steve & Sheila Barid
Enjoy
Gerard Reldan

By
Gerard Reldan

Garry Nadler

PublishAmerica
Baltimore

ISBN: 1-60813-831-3
PUBLISHED BY PUBLISHAMERICA, LLLP
www.publishamerica.com
Baltimore

Printed in the United States of America

Dedication

To my loving family who supported me throughout my life, showed me the importance of love and family, taught me life-long lessons about right and wrong, and encouraged me to challenge myself and follow my dreams.

Acknowledgments

Secret Wars is entirely a work of fiction, and bears no factual resemblance to any persons or set of events. My experiences as an engineer and attorney taught me that the characters depicted in this book *are not* typical of the thousands of dedicated men and women who work tirelessly in government positions, and consistently demonstrate only the highest ethics and sense of obligation and responsibility. I respectfully acknowledge their efforts, hard work, and service to our country.

SECRET WARS

CHAPTER ONE

Sarge slumped deep into the lush brown chair, his soft leather boots crossed at the ankle, bright red tie loosened, arms outstretched, hands clasped behind his head as he relaxed – a very unusual activity. The rest of the room was obviously decorated in a tasteful, but masculine manner. The history of this famous room was evident in many of the furnishings. In addition, there were the personal sports trophies, school banners and memorabilia adorning a small portion on one side of the room. The space opposite the massive desk held about a dozen photographs, each personally signed by the easily recognized celebrity portrayed. The desktop was neat and uncluttered. An arrangement of Family Photographs was on the right edge easily visible from behind the desk. The pencil cup embossed with the School Logo was to the left of the dark brown, obviously expensive leather desk pad.

Sarge smiled to himself as he watched Doc make changes to the speech he was scheduled to deliver in twenty minutes. Doc was arguably the most powerful man in the world – the President of the United States of America, and Sarge was his faithful and long-time friend and competent Chief of Staff.

Dexter Ogden Chandler, known as Doc to his closest friends and relatives, had just achieved the first major legislative victory of his 14-month-old administration. The latest series of Polls showed that the voters who elected him to bring about changes in the way government operates were very disappointed in his seemingly lackluster performance – until now. Politics inside the beltway are a harsh reality. This voter uneasiness made his Domestic Anti-Crime Bill a triumph of huge proportions. Promises to voters during the long Presidential campaign had not been kept – voters were angry and upset. This new legislation may have saved the credibility of his presidency, and offered hope for re-election to a second term, but that is far in the future in Presidential Politics terms. The bill included new modern high-tech approaches to crime prevention with much more severe penalties for crimes such as drug trafficking, violence against Federal or State Law Enforcement officers and officials, interstate criminal activity and habitual violent offenders. Realistic but fair gun control, particularly limitations on assault weapons was a major focus. Forcing Congress to authorize billions of Federal dollars in funding that would go directly to the States was a major coup. Lobbying by the NRA and their liberal supporters had been more fierce then even the Administration had expected. But Doc, Sarge, and other trusted Administration aides and officials used their substantial influence, called in a couple of markers, and twisted a few arms to finally get the crime bill through both the House and the Senate without having it watered down, limited in scope, or have its teeth pulled. It took firm commitment and over a year of intense pressure by the Administration, but they got it done, and were now justifiably proud of their accomplishment. The pending Press Conference announcing the Bill's passage was richly deserved.

This Press Conference was designed to congratulate the winners and send a peace offering to those who voted against the landmark legislation. Partisan bickering bordering on hatred of the other Political Party was miraculously held to a minimum. It was time to show true leadership, and reunite the American people, not to mention trying to reach across the isle in Congress and start to heal wounds inflicted by both political parties. Doc would also publicly announce the appointment of Harold R. Watkins, the current Assistant Attorney General as the Point Man for all new anti-crime initiatives. There was more that still needed to be done, and Doc wanted to seize the momentum while the American voting public was still aching for even more anti-crime measures and increased anti-terror initiatives.

The tragic events of 9/11 were never far from anyone's thoughts, even after several years. Combating World-wide Terrorism and the extremists who used it for their own warped purposes was in the forefront of every Americans' thoughts. There were sporadic successes here and there that the Public was aware of – but most of the anti-terrorism activities were kept secret for obvious National Security reasons. The general Public was not told, and did not really know how many serious attempts at mass murder and destruction both at home and abroad had been uncovered and foiled.

But, every poll showed crime as the major domestic issue facing this administration. People feared for their lives as gangs roamed and terrorized their streets. Home invasions by crack-heads and unruly thugs were at an all-time high. Rape, murder, armed robberies, and assaults touched everyone's lives. If you personally weren't a victim of a serious or violent crime, more often than not you knew someone who was. Almost every News telecast led with some new heinous crime and the inconsolable victims sobbing for loved ones and begging for help from their government. The public was fed up. The voters wanted an end to the violence, the fear, and the bloodshed. They wanted to take back their streets and neighborhoods. They wanted to live in peace in their own homes and communities. They demanded it – they deserved it. The voters had mobilized and would throw out any politician that didn't deliver. Doc lived and breathed this brutal political reality every day. Mid-term elections were less than a year way.

Doc had delivered hope with this new legislation. Soon the Federal Government would pump billions of dollars into State and Local Law Enforcement Agency coffers. The states could hire more police officers, purchase new and better crime fighting equipment, and give the communities back to the decent people all over the country.

Doc, being the pragmatic politician that he was, knew that his slide in voter approval rating would get a significant upward boost because of this legislation. And he knew what it meant to all communities around the country. Doc did have a genuine desire to improve the delivery of government services, but in some ways Doc was no different than any other past President; re-election was never far from his mind.

The plan for today's White House Press Conference was a little different. Brent Schofield, the hard charging Attorney General, would also say a few words to emphasize the importance of the Federal Government Law Enforcement Agencies working closely with the state and local governments and agencies to implement these far-reaching measures.

* * *

Sarge was the only person allowed to be casual while in Doc's presence, and he only did so when the two of them were alone. "Why're you changing that speech again?" Sarge chided.

Doc ignored him and made a few more notes. Doc and Sarge had been buddies for almost 40 years. Raymond James Corbett had been called Sarge since he was 9 years old in the rougher part of Miami. He always wanted to be in charge of everything. Of the five boys in their schoolyard "club" Sarge was the oldest, if only by a few months. And being the biggest by a long shot, Sarge generally got his way. Every one of his friends called him Sarge because of his bossy nature. But Sarge was a very likable kid, and proved many times what a good friend he could be. No bully ever bothered one of Sarge's friends – except for the first and last time when Sarge would send the bully to the school nurse with a cut lip or a black eye. Surprisingly, Sarge never got in trouble with School Officials for these acts of apparent violence. In every case Sarge and his friends were able to convince School Offials that "he started it – Sarge just tried to stop it." Sarge quickly became a nickname used out of respect by his closest friends.

In fact, all the kids in the club had nicknames. The youngest was called Junior. The overweight boy was Chubby, and the kid that was the poorest student was Day Dreamer. Doc got his nickname simply because of his real name. He was smart, so his initials seemed to fit. In fact, all five were unusually gifted and each excelled in their studies. Learning and earning good grades just came easier for Doc and Sarge. The other three had to study hard. Besides, what kid wants to call his friend Dexter? Getting caught by Sarge while Doc was playing "Doctor" with a cute red headed 5th grader sealed the deal. Doc became further indebted to Sarge when the Red-head incident became their little secret. Sarge was a loyal friend, not a snitch or a gossip.

"Have you checked with Mitch?" Doc inquired as he pushed his tired and aching frame from the Presidential swivel chair.

"Yeah." slurred Sarge. Another odd habit only he could get away with. Doc tolerated a lot from Sarge. Because of their longtime friendship, Doc overlooked habits and mannerisms displayed by Sarge that ordinarily would be viewed as disrespectful to the Office of the President or to the President himself. Sarge was very careful though, and was always respectful when others were around. Doc and Sarge loved the other as a brother, and the respect each had for the other was genuine and deep.

Doc and Sarge remained friends all through college, were in the same Fraternity, and were groomsmen at each other's weddings. Doc followed Sarge to Yale Law School. Sarge skipped the seventh Grade and was a year ahead at Graduation. He passed the Florida Bar Exam in 1974, followed by Doc in 1975. Doc took the more intellectual do-gooder route, and rose through the political ranks of local and Florida State politics earning a reputation as a competent and tough Prosecuting Attorney for Hillsborough County.

Twenty years in the Prosecuting Attorney's Office in Tampa shaped Doc's perspective on crime and it's victims. Tampa was notorious for its connections to mobs, Cuban criminals, drug trafficking, and all sorts of other horrendous criminal activity. Sarge was also an Assistant Prosecuting Attorney in Tampa, but remained in Doc's shadow. Doc handled the much harder mob violence, murder and rape cases. Inevitably, Doc became much better known than Sarge. Reports of Doc's anti-crime campaigns became regular features in the local newspapers, story lines on the TV news and radio talk shows. Doc was very popular, well respected and a recognizable personality.

Not so with Sarge. There was a weak side to Sarge – he had trouble dealing emotionally with that much violence, misery and hopelessness – he particularly felt for the victims. Instead, Sarge developed a reputation as a top-notch administrator, excellent organizer, and a stickler for details. Sarge was always well prepared, leaving nothing to chance. He handled many more "minor" cases than any other Assistant Prosecuting Attorney in the history of the office, but remained well out of the spotlight. In all the years as an Assistant Prosecuting Attorney, Sarge never handled a single case that got any media attention. That was fine with him.

In time, the movers and shaker in the Tampa political community convinced Doc to run for an elected office. He was well known, well liked, and had the right political image. Doc aimed right at the top, running for Governor of the State of Florida against a very unpopular incumbent rival – a former businessman from Miami.

"Criminals do not deserve rights that are superior to those of their victims!" Doc boomed to a screaming throng of followers during his 1st campaign. Doc was easily elected Governor and served two very successful terms. He was elected the first time because of his hard-nosed, no nonsense anti-crime stance. He was overwhelming re-elected to his second term because of the dramatic improvements he made in crime prevention, deterrence, punishment and the tough treatment of repeat offenders. Sarge ran both of Doc's election campaigns, and was immediately offered the position of Chief of Staff to the Governor of the State of Florida when Doc won the office. How could he refuse?

10:56 a.m.

Sarge smacked a buzzer near the door as he followed his boss to the Press Conference. They buttoned their expensive tailored suit coats and straightened their silk ties as they walked briskly through the private halls of the White House lower floor. The buzzer alerted the Press Secretary that they were on the way. The Press Secretary notified the Secret Service contingent of the impending presidential entrance.

The Press Conference was planned for the White House Garden. Because of the unusually warm winter and mild spring, the flowers were starting to bloom and made a perfect setting that just screamed "A new beginning." As usual, every detail was perfectly orchestrated by Sarge. The White House Press Corps was notified of the impending speech as soon as the final compromise measure cleared the House. Select, handpicked visitors and influential law enforcement dignitaries from around the country were personally invited to attend this monumental event. Over three hundred people accepted the invitation and patiently awaited the arrival of the President.

As with all outdoor public appearances of the President of the United States, security was carefully planned, with all contingencies identified and prepared for. Outdoor press conferences on the fairly secure White House lawn were no exception. Secret Service Agents were strategically placed in and around the garden area. The natural good looks of the male agents with carefully tailored suits were a sort of camouflage that concealed the massive firepower of each agent, and also allowed them to be somewhat inconspicuous amongst the crowd. The four female agents all wore smartly tailored pantsuits. They too had massive weaponry concealed in their clothing.

Some Secret Service Agents acted as Spotters with binoculars, and were located out of sight on the upper floors and roof of the White House. Whispered communications into hi-tech scrambled walkie-talkies between Secret Service team leaders and their teams was hushed, but constant.

A new type of surveillance device was being deployed for the first time. But this surveillance device really wasn't new. It was only new to the Secret Service. Shinny, almost silent Remotely Piloted Vehicles, called RPV's for short, had been used for years by the military to conduct battlefield surveillance and targeted bombing missions. Some large law enforcement agencies had successfully experimented with RPV's by using them to help with surveillance and monitoring of large crowds. The RPV's had proved to be quite effective. Their success caught the attention of the Secret Service who was always looking for new high-tech toys. Justifying a multi-million dollar research program that offered better protection of those in their charge was an added bonus.

* * *

An RPV is a miniature airplane. They can be large or small depending on their use. The surveillance types, like the ones being tried by the Secret Service, carry lightweight cameras, and have five to six feet wing spans. Those carrying heavy weapons or bombs for military uses tended to be much larger.

This particular surveillance RPV carried two miniature high resolution video cameras. One pointed forward so the pilot on the ground could see where the RPV was going. By looking at the Video Monitor, it was as if the pilot on the ground was actually in the RPV, much like a Fight Simulation Computer Game. The other camera had even greater resolution and was capable of displaying a video picture so clear that the license plate of a car could be read on the High Definition monitor. This camera could be rotated and tilted by the use of a joystick to look at anything the surveillance officer on the ground wanted to see. The zoom feature allowed for the extreme close-ups when there was a need to identify a particular person or feature. Everything was videotaped. The rack of Digital Recorders allowed for quick replays or closer scrutiny if needed.

RPV's were being heralded as one of the great law enforcement tools of the future, and a must for any law enforcement agency that expected to deal with crowds. The "Eye in the Sky" was the moniker used by the manufacturer to emphasize their intended use.

A small motor powered a specially designed propeller that pulled the RPV silently through the air; just fast enough to keep it airborne but slow enough to allow for a very good look at everything going on below.

Knobs, switches and levers in a tractor-trailer truck parked nearby remotely controlled everything on the RPV. If need be, the trailer could be concealed up to four miles away. For these RPV trials the trailer was located out of sight on the other side of the White House.

The RPV was purposely designed to be silent and nearly invisible. If you didn't know to look up and search the sky for them, you wouldn't know one was circling silently overhead. Sterling & Associates, the designer of this version proudly proclaimed them to be the new frontier in law enforcement.

* * *

The sun was bright for late morning in Washington. There were a few wispy clouds in the late Winter sky. The assembled crowd politely applauded the arrival of the President. Henry Grissom III, the Vice President and several aides followed Doc to the raised platform set up especially for this occasion. The Secret Service agents were already positioned. Two near-by agents were whispering into walkie-talkies while ten others stood around the garden and watched everyone else.

Sarge had already placed the repeatedly edited speech on the podium and was standing in his usual place about ten feet to the left and several feet behind the podium from where the President would be delivering his speech. The Attorney General and Harold Watkins fell in behind the Vice President as they leisurely strolled though the crowd shaking hands with friends and well wishers.

After a few hardy back slaps and making small talk with some of the better known law enforcement officials in the first row, the President walked casually to the podium. The small contingent that followed him into the garden stood behind him on his right. The President raised his arms to the gathering and the noise of the crowd dissipated.

The White House Press Corps was situated to Doc's left. Behind them were several dozen other reporters from all around the country. They represented various newspapers, magazines and special interest groups. The NRA was not invited, and not represented. The Network video crews were stationed on a specially constructed platform in the back facing the President. CNN was in the middle, with ABC and CBS on the right, NBC and FOX were on the left. Reporters with note pads and laptops clutched tightly and photographers with long zoom lenses attached to expensive cameras could be seen everywhere. Dignitaries and officials were seated on the right. This was a "happening."

Doc usually spoke from a podium and was most comfortable with both hands gripping the slanted edges. This speaking posture was a common practice of trial lawyers, and a holdover from his trial days as a Prosecuting Attorney. He took his familiar pose as the crowd quieted and started strongly without looking directly at his notes.

CHAPTER TWO

A Trailer Behind the White House
Washington, D.C.
Friday, Early March
10:22 a.m.

Richard was feeling sick to his stomach. He also had a slight fever and a pounding headache. His palms were sweaty and his forehead throbbed. The way you feel when you are not really sick, but you know you will be soon. Maybe he caught a bug somewhere. He couldn't think of any other reason to feel so bad.

Sterling & Associates skillfully convinced the Secret Service to allow a full-scale evaluation of their RPV under typical, but reasonably controlled circumstances. Everything was running smoothly from what Richard's keen observation could determine. He drank his usual two cups of coffee with Sweet N Low before 9:30, and didn't notice the attention Luis was paying to him and his steaming brew.

Richard's condition and obvious discomfort was apparent to Luis. "Why don't you just go back to the hotel and try to shake that bug? If you feel as bad as you look, you don't belong here. We've done this a hundred times. We can handle this little demonstration."

After all, Luis was Richard's friend and appeared to be genuinely concerned. Richard reluctantly agreed. His team had given dozens of hours of presentations to all levels of the Secret Service, including Carl Worthington, the director of the Secret Service. Even though this was the real thing and not just a Slide Show, this was a 1st Flight Demonstration without you. Richard knew his RPV-team, the one he personally assembled and trained would perform competently again, even without him supervising every step.

Richard was oblivious of Luis's secret desire to get him out of the way and out of the trailer. His unfortunate illness was a direct result of Luis's tampering with his coffee. Richard was in the way there, and "The Plan to fight the Secret War" could not be carried out unless Richard was out of the trailer and away from the action. Besides, in his condition, Richard realized he could actually do more harm than good at this point if he stayed.

"You're right. I feel like crap. Must've picked this up from my wife. She was really sick all last week with the same symptoms I've got."

How convenient mused Luis. "You look like crap. Go back to the hotel. If you want, I'll take you," offered Luis knowing full well that Richard would decline his offer. Luis was shrewd, and he prided himself in planning ahead. He knew Richard would insist that Luis stay and take over the demonstration. Luis was second in command of the demonstration team, and arguably the next-most experienced. Richard would never allow both he and Luis to be absent during any demonstration, especially one as important as this.

Luis was right. His Secret Plan was working. Richard insisted Luis stay. True to the Plan, Luis ensured his boss that he could manage on his own.

The fresh air and brisk Washington wind helped Richard's condition. The trailer where the Sterling & Associates team was housed was cramped and stuffy in spite of the massive oversized air conditioning system needed to keep the equipment reasonably cool. The tons of equipment, two self contained gas powered electrical generators, and nine people plus himself were more taxing on the air conditioning system than expected. To make matters worse, Richard wouldn't admit it, but his giving commands like the director of a live sports telecast and the non-stop activities that resulted, was no match for even this air conditioning system. Richard made a mental note to have this AC problem checked out and improved when they returned home.

Richard hailed a cab a block from the White House and instructed the cab driver to take him to the Holiday Inn Crown Plaza. The five-minute ride with the rear window open helped clear his head and cool his fever.

Richard ignored the bellman holding the door open for him and headed straight for the elevators, where he repeatedly smashed the UP Button – the way impatient slobs do when only a gentle touch is necessary. When the doors silently opened, Richard rushed inside and again repeatedly mashed the button for the twelfth floor until the elevator door closed silently behind him. Maybe the cool outside air wasn't helping after all.

Richard almost fell out of the elevator when the doors opened. He stumbled down the hall to his room. Fumbling several times with the magnetic card key. Dropped it. Bent over to retrieve it and almost fell over. He jabbed the key at the slot until he finally got the door opened. He flung his windbreaker on a convenient chair, kicked his shoes off into a corner, and quickly unbuttoned his shirt. Richard flopped exhausted onto the neatly made-up king-size bed. He didn't bother to take off his slacks, pull down the covers or even turn on a light.

He laid there in a stupor somewhere between awake and asleep, not knowing, not caring for what seemed like an eternity drifting in and out of twilight land. Two hours and thirty-five minutes passed before he was startled awake. He didn't hear anything. No bright lights were shining into his twelfth floor window. He just had a feeling – a really bad feeling. He sensed something had happened, but didn't know exactly what it was. He was not afraid that something had happened to his wife, but he knew that whatever it was, it was not good.

Holiday Inn Crown Plaza
Washington, D.C.
Friday, Early March
12:57 p.m.

The clock radio blinked a hazy green 12:57. As a diversion while trying to figure out what to do, Richard grabbed the TV remote control from its holder on the nightstand and clicked on the TV, which automatically starts on Channel 2 – the Hotel propaganda Channel. Click…! An afternoon soap opera. Click…! A 1970's Andy Griffith in Mayberry show. Click…! Nothing any better. Click…! Click…! "Where the hell are the networks?" Click…! CNN. Finally. Good choice, maybe a recap of the President's speech would be on.

Instead, a harried looking reporter was detailing what little was known about what appeared to Richard to be a bombing or plane crash. From the looks of the decimation behind the reporter, and the few pans from the cameraman, there must have been an explosion somewhere. Maybe a train wreck.

The reporter's white knuckles clutched the microphone with the bold CNN logo attached and spoke in a strained tone. His voice was weak and broken, but he was a pro – he kept going. "We just got word that the President is uninjured. I repeat, the President was not physically injured. Unfortunately, we must sadly report the tragic death of the Vice President. The doctor at Georgetown Medical Center put the time of death at 11:25 a.m. That puts the total number of deaths at 14. Two top-ranking Cabinet Members, the Vice President, two Secret Service Agents, eight Law Enforcement Officials and one civilian guest are now officially confirmed dead. Officials have not released all the names because their families have not all been notified. There is no accurate count at this time of how many were injured or wounded. Initial estimates by hospital and police officials were as high as 35. We're still checking. We are trying to arrange interviews with the triage doctors and the hospital spokesperson and will bring those reports to you as soon as we receive the footage." Obviously a hastily prepared, non-scripted report.

Ron Marshal, the reporter, looked away from the camera and nodded his head in agreement to an unseen associate. Looking back directly into the TV camera lens, he regained his composure and spoke in his customarily distinguished voice. "We now have a composite of unedited taped footage of the President's speech and the ensuing assassination attempt. Roll the tape Bill."

Richard slumped with his mouth agape. His heart pounded. His pulse raced. He could feel the heat of his own blood as it surged throughout his numb body. Utter disbelief. What the hell was going on? How could there be an assassination attempt on the President? His RPV was there specifically to prevent such an attempt.

An obviously unedited tape showed the beautiful White House garden, and the President and his entourage ascending to the podium. Then the scene of the President stopping to shake hands, chatting and backslapping old friends. A few seconds later, the President was at the podium, he placed his hands on the sides and comfortably started speaking.

"My fellow Americans and honored guests, I stand before you today on this auspicious occasion to commend both Houses of Congress for their hard and diligent work on the most far reaching anti-crime legislation ever passed. It is now time for all Americans, regardless of political party affiliation, to pull together to once and for all finish the job and bring crime to its knees. This legislation is only a tool to. . . ." His voice trailed off as he looked up and slightly to his left.

Another camera angle was cued showing a miniature airplane with wobbling wings diving right at the President. A third camera angle showed the Secret Service Agents whipping out their Uzi's, seemingly from nowhere, and frantically firing loud, long bursts at the small plane. Richard immediately recognized the plane as his RPV. Two Secret Service Agents dove at the President, knocking him backwards off the raised platform onto the damp garden lawn, and then totally shielding his body with theirs. The incessant machine gun fire caused the RPV to explode into a fireball within 50 feet of the presidential platform. The crowd was screaming and scattered in a wild panic in all directions. The Secret Service agents protecting the President took repeated direct hits of razor sharp shrapnel. They died instantly.

The UZI blasts were just like in a James Bond movie. But this was not James Bond, and this was not a carefully staged movie stunt. This was very scary. This was very real.

The well-prepared Secret Service Agents not assigned to shield the President stood firm. Some fired at the RPV, while others pushed guests to the ground. Bedlam, fear and panic were evident everywhere.

Ron Marshal's face was back on the TV screen. Richard watched transfixed and in shock. "The FBI has entered the case and their agents are assisting in the investigation of who is behind all of this. For more on the RPV involved in the attack, we have Lois Winters. Lois."

A fade to black. Then a pretty young women's face appeared on the TV screen. "Thanks, Ron. I'm Lois Winters, reporting from just outside the trailer where the crew from Sterling & Associates was housed. "The camera panned to show the side of a very large stark-white tractor trailer with the name Sterling & Associates painted across it in fancy bright red letters. "According to the most recent reports, everyone inside the trailer is reported to be dead. Obviously, the investigation into this tragedy has just started. But, it is possible someone at Sterling & Associates masterminded this entire tragedy. It is speculated that part of the plan to assassinate the President might include the mass murder of the Sterling & Associate team. But that has not yet been confirmed. There were reportedly nine Sterling & Associate employees inside the trailer. Eight are dead, possibly from some sort of poison or gas. Autopsies are scheduled to begin later this afternoon to definitively determine the cause of death. Authorities should know the exact nature of the toxin, if there was one, within 72 hours. There is no indication at this time of a suicide, or murder-suicide plan. The ME will establish the cause of death for those poor Sterling & Associate workers. The investigation into this tragedy has only just begun!"

File footage of the Sterling & Associate facility in south Orlando popped onto the screen as Lois Winters continued. "We don't know a lot about the attempted assassination, but we do know about the RPV's. The RPV used in the attack was designed and built in the Sterling & Associate facility on Orlando, FL. A preliminary check of Sterling & Associates, and of the owners and key corporate officials shows nothing out of the ordinary. But, we do know that it was a Sterling & Associate employee at the controls of the RPV, and only Sterling & Associate employees had access to the RPV prior to its launch and use this morning. And we know eight people inside the trailer are now dead from a mass, apparently pre-planned, murder. The FBI won't speculate as to whether all eight died the same way, but it appears that way at this time. All of these facts and theories are being checked and rechecked by the joint investigating team composed of Homeland Security, FBI, CIA and Secret Service Agents."

Lois looks to her right and reaches off-camera. She takes a few pages from an unseen producer and scans them quickly. "I have just been handed some new information. The FBI reports there was a note found inside the trailer. The exact contents were not made public at this time, but the Sterling & Associate Program Manager in charge of this project, a Mr. Richard Feinstein, was not found in the trailer. An All-Points-Bulletin has been issued on him. The FBI will not say whether or not he is a person-of-interest or a suspect in what is now being called the Crime of the Decade. Terrorism has not been ruled out, but Officials are not saying anything along those lines at this time."

Richard gasped and stared at the TV. His eyeballs nearly popped out of his head. A grainy picture of him flashed on the screen. It was the same picture as on his security badge.

"Anyone having any information about the whereabouts of this person is instructed to call the local authorities or the FBI." Toll-free numbers appeared on the screen.

Richard collapsed onto the bed. He gagged and couldn't breathe. He wanted to throw up – or die.

CHAPTER THREE

Holiday Inn Crown Plaza
Washington, D.C.
Friday, Early March
1:04 p.m.

Richard sat up on the bed stunned. His stomach churned uncontrollably. Searing hot blood surged through his veins. Eyes wide as saucers, as he stared blankly at the TV but not actually seeing anything. He tried to think. Did he actually do this – was he a murderer? An Assassin? A Terrorist? What should he do? Turn himself in? Run? Run where? Hide? Hide where? How can he hide when the whole nation, and probably the whole world, saw his face on CNN? If this coverage was on CNN, every network was also flashing his face across their screens and teletypes. This was a big story – very hot. He was nauseated. He visualized his face plastered in living color on the front page of every newspaper, shown on every TV news show, hung with the "Top-10 most wanted" posters in black and white in every Post Office across the country – probably the top Most Wanted.

What could he tell his wife? Oh God, Sherrie!! What was she thinking right now? Could she be in as much danger as he knew he was now in?

Richard did not yet realize, or even suspect he had been drugged, and enough time had passed for the effects of the drug to wear off. Richard had never been in trouble with the law; he'd never been arrested; he'd never even marched for a cause as a college student. For God's sakes, he had a Top Secret Clearance. His government trusted him with its most secret information. So why was he under suspicion now? He didn't attack the President or anyone else. He just couldn't have done anything like that. What the hell was going on? Why? And most importantly – why did the authorities think he had anything to do with this nightmare?

He had no answers. He collapsed on the bed and covered his eyes with his arm trying to think. Then he sat up with a jerk.

I've been set up. Framed! Now he realized the real seriousness of his predicament. He was in really big trouble. Trouble probably caused by experts that carefully planned and calculated all possibilities. He was an on-and-off fixture around the Holiday Inn and the White House during the past three weeks. Hundreds of people had seen him. He started to panic. Wild ideas raced through his muddled brain. He thought out load "The police were probably coming up the elevator at that very moment to arrest me, if they don't shoot and kill me first." His panic intensified. He could never explain what happened – he didn't have a clue. No one would believe him anyway. He wasn't even sure that the police would give him a chance to explain. Shoot and ask questions later. Killing him under these circumstances would be a sort of police justice. If they didn't kill him out-right, he would be sent to prison for life – more likely to the gas chamber!

"Shit!" was the best he could come up with at that moment.

Richard's analytical mind took over almost subconsciously. He forced himself to review his choices quickly. He knew he needed time he didn't have. Run! Run and Hide! That might buy time. He headed for the door as he snatched his windbreaker from the chair. Gripping the knob, he paused. Running would certainly incriminate him even more. Everyone would ask, "If he wasn't guilty, why was he running and hiding?"

"Hell," he muttered to himself, "Everyone already thinks I'm guilty anyway. Running wouldn't add to that impression."

But he couldn't just run. He would be spotted too easily. Richard turned quickly from the door and yanked open a dresser drawer. He rummaged through it, flinging clothing around the room. Not finding what he was looking for, he slammed it shut and opened another.

There they were! The only things he had not worn at least once during the past two weeks. He ripped off his red Polo shirt with the Sterling & Associates Logo and quickly put on the white Oxford cloth button-down dress shirt, a red and blue striped necktie and a baseball cap sporting the Washington Wizards Logo. Not much of a disguise, but it was the best he could do.

His brain was racing now. He had to get out of the hotel without being seen or detained, and then get to some safe place to map out the rest of his strategy. What strategy? He was scared out of his mind. What was he trying to prove? What could he do all by himself against all the Federal and State law enforcement agencies – not to mention whoever was behind this frame-up.

Ignoring those negative thoughts that numbed his mind, he peeked out the crack in his door. The hall was empty. Cautiously but briskly, he walked to the elevator area, his eyes darting in all directions. He jerked open the stairway door just as the elevator dinged its arrival. Close call, but he wasn't seen by any of the five Washington, D.C. SWAT Team officers in full riot gear that strode off the elevator with guns drawn, obviously looking for him.

He shivered in the damp cool stairwell as he descended the twelve floors. He wasn't really cold, just terrified to the point of shivering. He tried to steady himself and regain his composure. He knew he had to. He paused on the fifth floor landing panting, and wondered to himself as he looked back up the stairs. Luckily no Cops. It seemed to be as hard climbing down as he imagined it was climbing up those steep menacing concrete steps. As he trudged from one floor down to the next on the zigzagging staircase, he wondered again why he was running and to where he should run. Then it struck him like a bolt from the blue. The little synagogue two blocks away where he went to say Kaddish, the Jewish prayer for the departed, last Saturday morning for the anniversary of his father's death—his father's Yartzeit. The Rabbi was a nice middle-aged man whom Richard took an immediate liking. The Rabbi and Richard talked leisurely for over a half hour during the

Kiddush Lunch provided by the sisterhood. The Rabbi would help him decide what to do.

A surge of newfound energy propelled Richard to almost race down the last three flights of stairs only to be stopped short by the closed door boldly marked "1st Floor." There was no window in the door, and Richard had no way of knowing if anyone was on the other side, or waiting near the bank of hotel elevators a few feet away.

Richard knew he had no other choice. He hesitated for a few moments, straightened his tie, sucked in a deep calming breath, pulled the beak of his cap down farther over his face, and with fake confidence and a racing heart flew open the door and exited the stairway into a nearly empty lobby. His sigh of relief was imperceptible. But he knew his luck was holding. The few people standing around were engrossed in the lobby's huge Plasma TV tuned to the MSNBC reports of the assassination attempt. No one noticed him – the prime suspect in the flesh, right under their noses and no one saw him.

So much for the people getting involved to stop crime and get criminals off the streets. The irony momentarily amused him as he scurried out a side entrance onto the narrow shaded side street.

Beth Shalom Synagogue
Washington, D.C.
Friday, Early March
1:26 p.m.

The Shul, Beth Shalom, seemed deserted. No one should be around in the middle of the afternoon. Richard tentatively turned the bronze knob and poked his head inside the small entryway. The lights from the Rabbi's Study shown like a beacon. What a relief. The Rabbi was in.

Richard walked nervously inside and knocked politely on the open door frame announcing his presence. Rabbi Meyer Teitelbaum looked up from his papers and smiled warmly as he immediately recognized Richard. Rabbi had a knack for remembering names and faces – that was also part of his job. The Rabbi didn't seem to mind that his tie was loose and his shirt wrinkled, nor that his pleated trousers were too baggy to be fashionable. "How are you Richard?" he said as he rose and stuck out his pudgy hand. He mentally searched his mind for some details about the new arrival.

Rabbi Teitelbaum was a short, stocky man. He rose to his full 5'-7" as Richard leaned forward over the desk to grip the Rabbi's hand with his customary firmness. "Not so good Rabbi. Have you heard the afternoon news?" The Rabbi didn't comment or appear to acknowledge the sweaty handshake.

"No, I haven't. I'm here alone today working on my Friday evening sermon, just like I do every Friday. What happened? You look pale. Frightened. Can I call a doctor?"

Richard didn't know how to explain, or even where to start. Finally, after a few awkward moments of hesitation, Richard let go of the Rabbi's hand and blurted out, "Thanks Rabbi, but I don't think a doctor can help me." Richard hesitated again, and then began in rapid whispered tones, "There was an assassination attempt on the President earlier today. A lot of people were killed and many more injured. The reports say the President is uninjured. The Police are looking for me because they think I was the mastermind behind the whole scheme." Richard took a deep, loud breath as he refilled his lungs with oxygen and waited for some response.

Rabbi Teitelbaum fell back into his old swivel chair and stared at Richard trying to comprehend what he just heard.

After several moments of eerie silence, Richard added, "I didn't do anything! I swear on my father's head. I've been framed. I need your help, Rabbi. I don't know anyone else in Washington, DC I can trust. You're the only one I could think of who can help me."

More silence as Rabbi Teitelbaum realized his mouth was gapping open and quickly shut it as he tried desperately to regain his composure, make sense of and digest the enormity of Richard's outburst. But nothing made sense.

"Richard, what are you saying?" was his initial, non-rabbinical response.

Richard stuttered as he repeated his short description of the assassination attempt, but added, "I've been working on these RPV's to help the Secret Service protect the President. Just before the President's address today, I got sick – maybe I was intentionally drugged, I don't really know for sure, and I went back to the hotel because I just couldn't function. I was totally out of it for over three hours. During that time the assassination attempt was made using the RPV provided by the company I work for. I just heard about it on CNN a few minutes ago. I swear I had nothing to do with the attack."

More silence. More dagger stares from Rabbi Teitelbaum.

Richard spied the small TV tucked away behind a stack of books in the corner. Pointing to the TV, Richard queried, "Does that work?"

"Uh. Well, I think so. I never have time to watch TV, but it was a gift from Sam Rothman several years ago, so I keep it around." shrugged the Rabbi.

"Where's a wall outlet?" Richard scanned the walls for an electrical outlet.

Rabbi Teitelbaum also looked around his office, and finally pointed to a far wall. A straight-back wooden chair lovingly holding his Rabbinical Robe and Tallit Bag concealed the elusive outlet. "We're not wired for Cable in my office, and I don't use a computer here" Rabbi said almost apologetically.

Richard carefully moved the books from in front of the TV, picked it up and carried it the few steps across the room. After setting the TV on the floor near the chair, he plugged it in and fidgeted with the rabbit ear antennas. He then adjusted the volume and channel selector knobs until a clear picture with sound came through.

"What channel is CNN on?"

"Eight, I think. But that's on Cable. I really don't have much time for TV," the Rabbi repeated in defense of his apparent ignorance of the local TV stations.

Richard spun the dial through the channels waiting just long enough for a picture as he hesitated on each. Finally, on Channel 6 was Ron Marshall, still reporting from the same location. This time, he was reading from a clipboard.

"The FBI has confirmed that a type-written, unsigned note was found in the Sterling & Associates trailer implicating Richard Feinstein as the mastermind behind this terrible crime. The FBI Agents believe the note was a deathbed confession by one of the eight Sterling & Associate employees, all of which died moments after the attack, but before law enforcement officials arrived at the trailer."

Looking up into the camera with a somber face, he continued, "Facts are still a little sketchy, and the motive has not yet been established, but the FBI officials I spoke to want very much to find Richard Feinstein. They will not divulge how much they know about him and what they want to question him about. They will not confirm that he is a suspect, but every indication suggests that Richard Feinstein is their only suspect."

The same employee badge photo covered the small screen as the voice of Ron Marshal continued. "Anyone with information on the whereabouts of this man is urged to contact their local law enforcement agencies, or the FBI. The Police urge you to use caution. Do not attempt to apprehend this man yourself. He may be armed. And he may be responsible for the most vicious crime of this decade, and should be considered extremely dangerous."

Richard pushed the "Off" button and swung around to Rabbi Teitelbaum. "You see! Everyone already thinks I'm guilty. I'm considered extremely dangerous. Can you believe that? You've got to help me, Rabbi. If the police, or God forbid, a gun crazy vigilante finds me, they'll shoot first and not ask any questions later. I'm as good as dead."

Richard leaned far across the expansive cluttered desk, looked Rabbi Teitelbaum right in the eye and pleaded, "Will you help me? I'm afraid for my life. I can't even imagine what my wife is thinking right now. Please, Rabbi! Please help me."

Rabbi Teitelbaum prided himself on his compassion for the underdog and in helping those in need. He leaned back in his chair and rocked slowly as he pondered the plea for help from a man he liked, but knew so little about.

The two men stared deep into each other's soul in silence, each waiting for a response from the other. Neither made a sound, nor moved a muscle for several minutes.

CHAPTER FOUR

The Oval Office
Washington, D.C.
Friday, Early March
2:43 p.m.

"This is a domestic crime committed on US soil. My men found the note in the Sterling & Associates trailer. The FBI should be in charge of this investigation."

"The President was attacked for Christ sake! The Secret Service is responsible for his safety. This is my case. I'm in charge here." Voices were loud; the arguing intense as each side struggled for an advantage.

Timothy Jenkins, Director of Homeland Security shouted, "This is a Homeland Security matter. I should coordinate all the intelligence gathered by law enforcement."

President Dexter Ogden Chandler could no longer keep his silence. He had been listening to the bickering between Gordon Krump, the Director of the FBI, Timothy Jenkins the Head of Homeland Security and Carl Worthington, the head of the Secret Service. Doc couldn't take any more.

"Shut up! And I mean all three of you!" bellowed Doc as he sprung from his plush chair and charged across the office.

Sarge leaped to his feet, bolted across the room and flung an arm around Doc's chest, stopping him dead in his tracks.

Doc spun around to glare at Sarge in a fit of rage "God Damn it! I was almost killed. Henry was. And these Bozos are arguing over who is in charge! I don't give a rat's ass who's in charge. I just want this thing solved. Catch that Feinstein character and string him up by his balls."

Spinning to face Timothy Jenkins, the President demanded, "Every morning you come into this office and tell me how well the Intelligence gathering by all the agencies is being shared and used to make us all safer. Bull shit! We are not safe, damn you. Have you told me anything that's true? Is it accurate? Is it complete?" Timothy Jenkins just hung his head. He knew better than to respond.

"We all understand how upsetting all this must be for you, but you know as well as I that nothing would ever get done if there is no clear chain of command," calmly offered Sarge as he firmly held Doc's arms just below the shoulders. The President was trembling slightly, but settling down.

Good old Sarge. He had become the consummate diplomat. Always there to protect his friend, his President, the President's image, and whatever else needed protection.

No one had ever seen the President act like this. Sarge immediately went into damage control mode. Turning to the small gathering almost cowering across the room, Sarge spoke in his normally authoritative manner. "Gentlemen, and ladies. This has been a very trying experience for the President, and for all of us. We can be of most help to our country and our President in this time of grief and mourning by postponing this meeting for two hours. At that time, we will all meet back here. Each Agency has important, unique and critical capabilities. All your best efforts will be needed when all is said and done. Within one hour, all Agencies will present to me a written brief for the President outlining and substantiating with precedent, the organizational structure you believe is required to best conduct this investigation and solve this case. Any questions?"

The group rose in unison, some murmuring, "No! No questions" and politely left the oval office. Sarge closed the door softly, but firmly behind them.

"I can't believe I appointed every damn one of those grandstanders. What the hell was I thinking?"

"Come on, Doc. Don't be so hard on them, or yourself. Other than 9/11, this is the biggest crisis to hit Washington since the Kennedy assassination and Nixon's disappearing act. Maybe we can throw in Clinton. Each of these guys wants to be a major player in this scenario. With Kennedy, there were no incriminating notes pointing directly at Lee Harvey Oswald. It took good police work to nab his sorry ass. Then the Warren Commission was convened to fake out the public. Nixon was a con artist—guilty as hell, but harder to prove. Impeachment, with all the public hearings would be disastrous for the country. Clinton was too popular and no one gave a damn. This case is so simple. Everyone wants to be in charge to grab the credit for themselves."

"Yeah. Yeah, you're right." Reluctantly agreed Doc as he slumped lower into his chair.

As usual, Doc forgot to thank Sarge for taking charge and clearing the room, but Sarge was used to that. He knew Doc appreciated all that he did.

The two men sat quietly, each deep in their own thoughts. Doc thought about his friends that were killed in the attack, and cared only about finding and convicting Richard Feinstein. Sarge planned strategy. How could he control the powerful Agency heads? There had to be a way.

4:56 p.m.

It is rare that meetings of more than a few people ever take place in the Oval Office, so the Situation Room down the hall was mobilized. It had a very large conference table in the center that could accommodate 20 Senior Officials. An additional 45 chairs encircled the walls for lesser staff members.

The room was buzzing with the din of small talk between the various Agency heads and their senior staffers. Twenty men and eleven women, conceivably the most powerful group of people in the entire world, waiting for their leader to discuss the most unusual, if not the most serious attack on a US president in the history of the nation. But this time, everyone in the room knew the case was already solved.

Each person had a briefing file. Each file, identically arranged and collated, had the latest report from the FBI, the Secret Service, Homeland Security and the Washington, D.C. Police Department; a list of the names and a brief profile of the eight people, now all dead, found in the Sterling & Associates trailer, an up-to-date list of the other casualties and fatalities, and an extensive dossier on Richard Feinstein. The top sheet of each file was a hard-to-read copy of what appeared to be a hastily typed, but undated and unsigned note naming Richard Feinstein as the mastermind of the attack. The folders were made of bright red heavy-grade cardboard stock, with a printed label in the middle. The label read:

TOP SECRET

PRESIDENTIAL ASSASSINATION ATTEMPT
BRIEFING FILE

SPECIAL CLEARANCE REQUIRED
SENIOR STAFF ONLY

TOP SECRET

The folders were embossed with the Presidential Seal and handed out by the President's personal Secretary as each entered the Situation Room. Receipt was noted with the signature of the owner of the numbered file folder. Some of the Senior Staffers were busily skimming the documents inside their folders as the President, followed by Sarge, entered the room from the side door.

"Good afternoon." acknowledged the President as he moved swiftly to his chair at the head of the long table. The President menacingly leaned forward toward the group as they hastily took their seats in their assigned places. Everyone was now seated except the President. He now had their full attention. He placed his palms flat on the table, and began in a slow but determined manner. "I have carefully reviewed the briefs from Homeland Security, the FBI and the Secret Service. As pointed out in each of those briefs, as President, I have the authority to appoint whomever I select to head special investigative committees. This investigation requires just such a special committee. In exercising my authority as President of the United States, I appoint Mr. Colbert, my Chief of Staff, to head the Special Committee on this Presidential Assassination Attempt. An Executive Order to that effect is being drafted as we speak. An Assassination Attempt Committee, with sole and complete authority to coordinate the investigation of the attempted assassination earlier today is needed. There will be no more squabbling about who is in charge, who has what information, or any other damn aspect of this investigation. We will do this before Congress gets its act together and starts their own Investigations. This is not a matter for the DC Police either. Both the FBI and the Secret Service have outstanding investigators and immense investigative powers. Homeland Security has the tools to allow everyone to communicate with each other. All Agencies will work together and share all, and I mean all, information with the other agencies. The FBI will concentrate on locating and bringing Richard Feinstein in alive for questioning. I repeat, every attempt will be made to capture Richard Feinstein alive. If he is harmed or killed, those involved will find themselves under investigation. No matter how heinous this crime, the American Public deserves a full, open and honest investigation. History will be judging us ladies and gentlemen. Let's do ourselves proud. The Secret Service will scrutinize Sterling & Associates and all of their employees, living and dead. I want to make damn sure that Feinstein acted alone. I don't want there to be any questions raised twenty or thirty years from now criticizing how we handled this. Hell, the talking heads are still discussing the Kennedy assassination after all these years, and we still don't know everything about that fiasco. Do we all understand how this investigation will be conducted?"

Sarge and Doc looked at each person in the room individually, and waited for a nod of agreement, or some other sign of acceptance of these terms before the President continued to the next person. A slow, but necessary process.

"Anyone who tries to circumvent these orders or leaks any unauthorized information will be summarily discharged. That person will not even have time to clean out his or her desk. The Marine MP's will immediately escort them out of their office building, and their personal belongings will be boxed and mailed to them. They then will face the wrath of a Special Prosecutor. Jail time is a reality. Is that clear?" The President banged his fist on the table for emphasis. He was clearly back in control.

Again Sarge and Doc performed the head nodding acceptance ritual with everyone in the room. No negative responses.

"Good! I knew you good men and women of reason would quickly realize the importance of the situation we are faced with, and will willingly cooperate with Mr. Colbert and each other." In politics, sugar coating always helps—something Doc was well aware of, and very good at doing.

A good approach, but not really convincing. The limelight-seeking Agency heads and their up-and-coming yuppie staffers would agree to anything, then merrily go on their own way and do whatever was in their own best interest. Leaks, backstabbing and outright disobedience was common in Washington's power circles. Each knew that their future, and the certain riches that followed, depended on their individual names being directly linked in a positive way with big, important issues and situations such as this.

The President had threatened immediate firings for leaks to the press and commission of various other distasteful or embarrassing misdeeds in the past, but cowardly, although skillfully backed down using a variety of self-serving excuses. He wasn't sure himself what he would if faced with a leak by someone in this room. He had no choice but to accept their positive responses.

"All right then, I'll turn this over to Mr. Colbert." declared Doc with a grand gesture.

Sarge leaned forward and scanned the room until everyone was staring only at him. "The first thing we need to do is share all known information. Carl, your guys at Secret Service have been working with Sterling & Associates for quite a while on this RPV project. Briefly fill us all in on the history of the program, who and what Sterling & Associates is, and anything else we should know about them."

"Well, Mr. Colbert, I'm not as familiar with the details of this program as Lindsay is. I keep up with the status and have a broad general knowledge of what is going on, but Lindsay is the real expert. She heads the Secret Service RPV study team, and works, or rather, did work closely with the Sterling development team. Except for Mr. Feinstein, they are all now dead. I'll let her provide the details."

Lindsay Hawthorn is a petite attractive young woman. She graduated third in her class at the Wharton School of Business, and fifth in her Michigan State Law School class. At age 29, bright and ambitious, she is typical of the young women attracted to, and hired by this administration. As head of the RPV development project for the Secret Service, she demonstrated her skill as a manager, negotiator, and point person. Her quick, keen mind easily grasped both the technical and the conceptual details and issues associated with the RPV Project.

Lindsay was confident of her knowledge and position, and very capable of briefing this illustrious group without fear or anxiety. Still seated, and without referring to her thick, well-organized notebook, she began. "Sterling & Associates is a small technologically advanced company with headquarters in Orlando, FL. They specialize in RPV's. RPV is an acronym for Remotely Piloted Vehicle. Sterling has sold dozens of RPV's to large law enforcement agencies in California, New York, Florida, and a few to police departments in Denver and St. Louis. The Military, particularly the Army and Air Force have used RPV's for various purposes for years. But no Federal Agency other than the Secret Service until late last year, had any actual hands-on experience with Sterling & Associates, or with RPV's. The trial this morning, or as we prefer to call it, a demonstration, is the first real-life use of RPV's by a Federal Agency under actual non-choreographed situations."

Gordon piped up. "Lindsay, doesn't it seem strange to you that the very first time an RPV is used to supposedly protect the President, that he is almost killed, and we are facing the worst assassination attempt since Kennedy? Didn't the Secret Service drop the ball here?"

B. J. Mathews, a more senior, but not more important staffer at the Secret Service leaned over to Lindsay, and blocking his face with the back of his hand, whispered in her ear, "That's exactly what I warned you about. That bastard will do or say anything to cut us down and pump himself up."

Before Carl Worthington could speak, Lindsay responded undaunted. "Mr. Director, or may I call you Gordon?" she smiled her cute, innocent, come-and-get-me smile while now waiting for Gordon to reply.

Gordon looked around sheepishly. Loosened his tie and cleared his throat. "Well, Uh. Yes. We're all friends here, and these intelligence-sharing meetings are usually informal. Sure, call me Gordon." He tried to smile, but couldn't even fake it.

Point One for Lindsay. "Thanks, Gordon. My team has worked very closely with the Sterling team for over six months. We have been in each other's homes, had dinner with each other's families. DOD checked out all Sterling Employees in advance, just like everyone else that gets a Secret or Top Secret Clearance. I've personally met Sheila Feinstein, Richard's wife, who, by the way, is about seven or eight months pregnant with their first child. We had no warning, no indication at all that there would be any problem what-so-ever with this demonstration. The Feinsteins are very decent, nice people. They belong to a small synagogue in Orlando, and neither of them has any kind of criminal record or links to terrorism. Certainly there has been no indication that Richard Feinstein was any kind of a threat to the President or to anyone else. He, and everyone else at Sterling & Associates got a full clearance after the people at DOD, and I presume the FBI, checked each of them out thoroughly." Lindsay could afford a little smirk here as she drove the knife deeper into the heart of the FBI and twisted it.

Lindsay paused for effect, and looked at Carl who nodded approvingly before continuing. "I, personally, have trouble believing that Richard Feinstein had any involvement, much less masterminded this. I admit I have nothing to substantiate my personal feelings. Just an instinct."

"Well, girlie, you keep your instincts, high falutin' women's lib crap, or woman's intuition, or whatever the hell you call it, to yourself and leave the detective work to real men who know what they're doing." snapped Gordon. He lost his cool, just as Lindsay had expected.

Lindsay was ready with her practiced stereotypical retort. "How dare you talk to me like that, you pompous, overstuffed male chauvinist pig." A cliché, but effective here – Gordon was goaded even further as he sputtered and wiped spittle from his lips with his sleeve.

Carl Worthington tolerated Lindsay only because he had to. She was not one of "them," but had done a reasonably good job with the otherwise low-key RPV program. There was no reason to support her now that the RPV program was going down the toilet.

Everyone forgot where they were and why they were there. The Situation Room in the White House should be a place for mutual respect and common dignity. Today it was nothing like that. The room erupted with name-calling, finger pointing and general chaos. Everyone was yelling at once. Some folks nearly came to blows. The FBI side against the Secret Service side against the Homeland Security side. Nothing would get accomplished this way. Doc buried his head in his hands, closed his eyes, and waited for Sarge to restore order.

CHAPTER FIVE

Beth Shalom Synagogue
Washington, D.C.
Friday, Early March
1:43 p.m.

Richard was the first to break the silence. "Rabbi, I swear to you... No, I swear on my Bar Mitzvah Sidurim that I had nothing to do with that attack. You must believe me. I have nowhere else to turn for help. Please help me."

Rabbi Teitelbaum was again lost in thought. He carefully contemplated his response. "It doesn't matter whether or not I believe you. You have few choices. I believe that your best choice is to go to the police. Turn yourself in. If you're innocent, then they'll let you go. This is America, not some dictatorship where you have no rights. Is that not so?"

"Sure, we're in America. But Washington is full of trigger-happy lunatics. The murder rate here is sky high. I've already been convicted in the eyes of most Americans. My life isn't worth squat if I'm seen on the streets. Those bible-thumping, gun toting ass-holes, will shoot first and ask questions later. Pardon my language Rabbi. Maybe, so will the cops. I just can't take a chance like that. What else can I do, Rabbi?"

Rabbi thought for a few more agonizing moments, and offered,

"What if I get you a lawyer and he handles the details of turning yourself in. Surely, he can make some arrangements for your safety."

Richard looked up. "Why didn't I think of that?" he thought to himself. "OK. I'll talk to a lawyer. But, it must be here, and he can't know why he's coming here until he arrives. I can't take a chance the cops get tipped off."

"Well, I don't know about that. I'll call him and see what can be done."

Rabbi Teitelbaum pushed some files aside, flipped through his Business Card Case he used as an Address Book and pulled out a card. "Ah, here it is," he exclaimed with meaningless triumph. "I'll call him right now at his office."

Rabbi punched in the number and then cheerily greeted the receptionist on the other end. "This is Rabbi Teitelbaum. Is Mr. Weissman in?" he inquired. A short pause, then, "I'll hold. Thank you."

Rabbi unconsciously covered the mouthpiece and turned to Richard. "Harvey Weissman is just getting off the other line. He's always on the phone. His receptionist said it would be about 2 or 3 minutes"

The two men waited for over 3 minutes, which turned into 4 and then 5. Rabbi rocked rhythmically in his chair holding the receiver to his ear patiently waiting for a voice on the other end. Richard played with a pencil on the desk during the agonizing silence. Drummed his fingers. Looked around the room. Neither man spoke. There was only silence except for the sporadic noised Richard's uneasiness evoked.

Finally, Rabbi sat up and spoke into the receiver. "Harvey. Hi. How are you doing? Rabbi Teitelbaum here. … Good. Glad to hear it. … Listen, Harvey, I need a favor for a friend. He is in a bit of a jam with the police, and needs a good attorney. You still do criminal work, don't you? … Good. … No, he can't come to your office next week. He really needs help right now! Today! … Harvey, please, you have to trust me on this. He really needs help immediately. … No, I can't tell you the exact nature of his problem over the phone. Please, Harvey, just come to the Shul this afternoon. He will be here waiting for you, and you can ask him all the questions that you want. … OK. We'll see you at three. Thanks. I really appreciate this, Harvey."

Rabbi recapped the gist of the conversation as if Richard hadn't heard anything. Richard, keeping his nerves in check, and trying to maintain what little sanity he had left, simply nodded and mumbled his thanks.

Rabbi Teitelbaum went back to his sermon leaving Richard sitting in the room with absolutely nothing to do.

The next ten minutes seemed like ten years to Richard. Finally, he blurted out, "Can I borrow this?" as he shoved a blank pad of paper under Rabbi's nose.

"Uh, sure. If you need more, just ask. Do you need a pen or pencil?" replied Rabbi somewhat startled, but trying to be helpful.

"Thanks, but I've got a pen." He replied absently as he pulled one from his pocket and showed it to Rabbi Teitelbaum.

Richard started slowly, but gradually outlined everything he knew. He listed all the people he worked with at Sterling & Associates, a chronology of events starting with his first interview with Sterling, his being hired, his first few assignments, his promotion to Project Leader of the RPV project, and then concluded with the first meeting with the Secret Service. He then listed a more detailed chronology of his contacts and the major events pertaining to the Secret Service Project known at Sterling & Associates as Sky Hawk. He figured these notes would come in handy when he tells his story to the attorney, and eventually the authorities. He wanted to be sure his facts were straight.

3:22 p.m.

A soft knock on the door announced the arrival of Harvey Weissman. "Hello, Rabbi. Good to see you again. Sorry I'm a little late, but my phone wouldn't stop ringing this afternoon."

Rabbi looked up for the first time in over a half hour. Richard swiveled around in his chair to ease his curiosity about this unknown, at least unknown to him, attorney who would become his savior. "He doesn't look like the savior, Jesus Christ to me," he mumbled inaudibly to himself. Richard was never short of sarcasms when he was upset or tense.

"Harvey. Good to see you too, and thanks for coming. Especially under these strange circumstances," greeted Rabbi Teitelbaum, sticking out his hand as he rose.

Harvey offered his own firm grip and stared directly at Richard and then continued. "Now what's all this secrecy about, Rabbi?" There was a spark of recognition, but nothing he could put his finger on.

Motioning towards Richard, even though Harvey was looking the other way at Richard, Rabbi continued, "Harvey, this is Richard Feinstein. You may have heard about him on the afternoon news."

"You're kidding ... No. No, you're not kidding," as he looked back at the smiling Rabbi Teitelbaum. "I've got to sit down," as he backed into a chair in what otherwise would be called a drunken stupor. "Now I understand all the secrecy."

"Oh, great. Just great. A hot-shot attorney scared of a name." Muttered Richard under his breath again. More sarcasm from Richard, not realizing he was getting off to a very bad start.

"I'm sorry. All this took me by surprise. I envisioned all sorts of crazy scenarios while driving over here. A husband accused of wife beating. A rapist who didn't want to be identified. An accused child molester. Some famous Politician. Even a victim of gang warfare. But never this." Harvey just shook his head in disbelief.

Rabbi interjected. "Harvey, can you help Richard?"

"Help him? How? From what I hear, he tried to assassinate the President of the United States. Last I heard he killed eight of his co-workers. God knows how many others at the White House. Even if I represent him, I probably can't keep him from the gas chamber." Harvey spoke as if Richard wasn't even there.

"What if he told you he was innocent? That he was framed?" chided Rabbi, trying to goad Harvey into reconsidering.

"What? Innocent? Framed? Let's start over here."

"OK. OK, I understand how you can be skeptical." offered the Rabbi in an attempt to keep Harvey from bolting the room altogether.

"Richard tells me he is innocent. I don't know enough about what did or didn't happen to believe him or not, but I know him well enough to give him the benefit of the doubt. As an attorney pledged to protect the innocent, you should too."

"That's preposterous! Anyway, I make it a practice never to even ask if my clients are innocent or guilty. I don't want to know. Guilt or innocence is for a Judge and Jury to decide, not me."

"Then how can you represent thieves and criminals?" queried the Rabbi with genuine surprise mixed with a tinge of curiosity.

"That's easy. I, and 99.999 percent of other defense attorneys are protecting the American judicial system, not just the Defendant. We use facts, just like the Prosecutors do, only we sometimes interpret those facts differently trying to raise alternate theories about the crime to create reasonable doubt. Our job as defense lawyers is to ensure the defendant gets a fair trial. The defendant's Constitutional rights must be protected. Which translates into protecting the rights of the accused to get that fair trial. Some people with preconceived notions about the guilt of a particular person think the accused has more rights than the Victim, when in reality they only have different rights that are designed to protect against false accusations. It's a matter of ignorance or of perception. Our job is not, and I repeat,...not...to always get the defendant off. Thousands of guilty criminals go to jail every day around the country, but only after receiving a fair trial where the facts were used to convict them of the crimes they were charged with. Good attorneys can use persuasion and skill to plea-bargain a lesser sentence – and that is a form of winning for the client, but still within the Constitutional rights of everyone. Plus, our legal system through Defense Lawyers forces the Government to follow their own rules of Due Process. The Defense Attorney makes them do that as best we can."

"Haven't you ever defended anyone you believed was really innocent?"

"The American judicial system presumes the defendant is innocent until proven guilty beyond a reasonable doubt in a court of law, usually by a Jury of their Peers. Based on years of experience defending the accused, I personally believe most defendants are probably guilty of something. If not the crime for which they are charged, than for something else – something possibly even more heinous, only the police and prosecutors haven't figured out what yet, or don't have enough factual evidence to prove it. It is very rare that the police chase down and arrest a truly innocent person. In the vast majority of cases, the police have some pretty compelling reasons to accuse and arrest someone. Some actual evidence pointed them in that direction."

"You, of all people, can't mean that. How can you not care about the innocent people that get caught up in the legal system?" Rabbi Teitelbaum respected, even admired Harvey, but this attitude really bothered him.

"Rabbi. Please, I have practiced criminal law for 18 years; six as a prosecutor. I haven't seen many defendants in front of a judge that weren't guilty — even if they were acquitted on what you would call a technicality. And they usually were guilty of whatever they were charged with. Let's not be idealistic here."

"Harvey, but some people who go on trial really are innocent, aren't they?"

"Rabbi, save your breath. Mr. Weissman isn't interested in helping me, or probably anyone else. He looks and acts like all the other greedy little lawyers. They tolerate the clients who pay their monstrous fees only because they have to if they want to get paid. Without those unfortunate clients, the lawyer-leeches couldn't make the payments on their BMW's." Richard was livid, and didn't care much about what he said, or who heard it. All he could think about was how his life was going down the crapper, and no one would lift a finger to help him.

"Rabbi, thanks for trying. I'll just take my chances on the street. Mr. Weissman probably couldn't help me anyway. And if he could, I don't have enough money to peak his interest."

Richard rose slowly and shuffled toward the chair where his windbreaker was awkwardly hung. Rabbi Teitelbaum watched with sadness. Harvey watched with indifferent eyes.

As Richard exited the Rabbi's study, he hesitated momentarily, and then turned back.

"Rabbi, could I ask one more favor from you before I get out of your life completely?"

"Sure, Richard. What is it?"

"If I give you my telephone number in Orlando, will you be so kind as to call my wife and tell her I love her. Also tell her that no matter what she hears on the TV or reads in the papers, I did not have anything to do with the assassination attempt. She knows deep in her heart that I could never do such a horrible thing. We have never lied to each other and I'm not about to start mow. She trusts and believes in me. Will you do that for me, Rabbi?"

"Certainly. What's the number, and what is your wife's name." Rabbi said calmly, desperately trying to ease Richard's despair.

Richard was near tears. Through trembling lips that slurred his speech, he responded. "Area code 407…555-1336. Her name is Sherrie. Thanks Rabbi" sobbed Richard as he broke down completely, trembling with fear and desolation.

"Richard. Something can be worked out. If you're innocent, and I for one…" a stern glare at Harvey then back to Richard, "believe you are. The Police are men of honor and integrity – they are reasonable people. Tell them the truth. It will all work out OK."

"How can it, Rabbi? I don't know the truth. All I know is I got sick, possibly drugged just before the president's speech, but I didn't know it at the time. I went back to my hotel room, passed out and woke up in the middle of this nightmare. I was lucky to get here without some gun-crazed whacko recognizing and killing me on the spot."

Harvey piped up, but a sincere gentleness was evident in his voice. "Are you telling me that you really are innocent? That you had nothing to do with the attack? You're not just saying you're innocent to get me to help you? None of this is made up just to bamboozle us?"

"Yes, but what the hell does that mean to you? You said it yourself – you don't care." sneered Richard.

"I never said that. Look, I tend to be very harsh on people that lie to me about the facts and then claim they're really innocent. Most of them are putting on an act. You're telling me the truth. You're not acting, are you?"

"No!" Richard was glaring at Harvey. "I'm not putting on an act. This friggin' nightmare is really happening to me exactly as I told you."

Turning back to Rabbi Teitelbaum, Richard continued as Harvey pondered. "Tell Sherrie that I will try to contact her as soon as I find some safe place to hide, if there is such a thing. Tell her I'll call just before the baby is due, to see how she is doing. And don't forget to tell her that I love her."

With Richard's honest love and a display of real tenderness for Sherrie, Harvey was convinced. "Richard. Try this on for size. You tell me everything you know about the assassination attempt, and if you're telling the truth, aren't holding anything back, and tell me everything, and I mean everything, then I'll consider representing you. That's the best I can do. How about it?"

"Why now? After that big pompous-ass speech about no one's ever really innocent," he mocked.

"There's just something different about you. You're not like the other people I represent. I don't know. And I trust Rabbi Teitelbaum's judgment about you."

"I'm different because I'm innocent!" snapped Richard.

"OK. Maybe I was too hasty. Maybe you are innocent. Maybe you were framed. Let's talk. Then I'll see what we can do."

"Mr. Weissman, I will tell you everything I know, but if you take my case, I can't afford much. We only have a few thousand dollars saved, and most of that is for the medical expenses for the delivery."

"We'll discuss my fee later."

Rabbi Teitelbaum smiled as he folded his arms triumphantly across his barrel chest.

What went unspoken was Harvey's shrewd mind telling him that book deals and movie rights would be worth a hundred times his normal capital offense fee of seventy-five thousand dollars. Maybe this wasn't such a bad idea after all. If Richard is innocent, and he could get him acquitted, what a publicity coup that would be. Rich and powerful clients would flock to him in droves. He could even raise his fees if this worked out. What luck.

Even if Harvey wasn't such a generous and compassionate man, at least he was honest with himself.

Rabbi Teitelbaum showed the two men into the small chapel used for the morning minions, the daily prayers recited by observant Jews. Harvey maneuvered one of the metal folding chairs in front of another, using the seat of the first to form a sort of table. Sitting down, he motioned for Richard to sit directly across from him in a 3rd chair. Harvey opened his briefcase, pulled out the obligatory yellow legal pad and his silver engraved pen.

"OK, Richard. Let's start with some personal details. Spell your full name."

CHAPTER SIX

The Feinstein Kitchen
The Northern Suburbs of Orlando, FL
Friday, Early March
12:03 p.m.

Sherrie casually performed her normal noontime routine. She flipped on CBS, the Channel 6 noon news show, trudged in her flowered maternity house dress and fuzzy slippers to the refrigerator, opened it smoothly and retrieved a glass bottle of orange juice. She loved Florida Orange Juice, especially the pulp-free Tropicana juice. Knowing that good nutrition for her translated into a healthy baby didn't hurt. She poured herself a generous portion as she absently listened to the frantic reporter.

"As we reported earlier, the Vice President is dead, and at least 10 others at the scene are reported dead at this time. Dozens are injured and according to officials the fatalities are expected to rise. The President, we are happy to report, is uninjured." The pretty young noon anchorwoman, Heather Reinhart, was obviously distressed as she reported this story.

Sherrie turned to look over her shoulder and to listen more closely to what appeared to be a breaking major news story. Being a Political Science major at the University of Florida, her natural curiosity was peaked. A Political Junky. She loved government and politics and devoured newspaper and magazine articles about anyone and anything that had to do with either. Among her friends and acquaintances, she was the resident expert on politics, and sparked many lively discussions, debates, and more than a few emotional arguments, over various government policies and the antics of our leaders. The infamous extramarital exploits of now-discredited politicians were a favorite topic – and the Political party didn't matter. Sherrie told everyone she was a Democrat, but in reality she voted more as an independent.

Sherrie shuffled a little more rapidly to the sofa with her juice as she intently stared at the harried reporter.

"The FBI and the Secret Service are investigating the attack on the President. Homeland Security is actively involved. There is no confirmation of a Terrorist connection, but that has not been officially ruled out. Little has been released yet about who might be behind this horrible act. It appears that employees of Sterling & Associates, a small R&D firm right here in Orlando, FL may be involved."

Sherrie stopped drinking in mid-gulp and sat up straight on the couch. Her skin crawled, large goose bumps formed all over her body, her stomach flipped over as she braced herself for the worst. The hairs on the back of her neck felt like they were jumping off her body. Instinctively she wrapped her free arm around her bulging belly, subconsciously trying to protect her yet unborn child.

"For more on the Sterling & Associates angle, we switch to our national affiliate in Washington." The camera zoomed out and panned slightly to the left to show both Heather and a large video monitor on the wall behind her newsroom desk. Heather turned to the monitor, which showed a full-length view of Harlan Montgomery standing nervously with a microphone in one hand, with the other hand pushed against his earpiece. He was in front of some nondescript government building. As he impatiently waited for a cue or a question over his earpiece, he looked at his shoes, to his right, to his left, then again at his shoes. All the while, he shuffled from foot to foot, giving an eerie rocking motion to the image on the monitor. He was unaware that he was on live TV at that very moment. His experienced news crew was too caught up in the excitement to perform in their normal professional manner – no cues from his video team or producer. The result was dead air.

A frantic off-camera producer finally motioned erratically at Harlan. Suddenly he looked up and stared directly into the camera. The rocking stopped as he waited for the questions from Heather.

Heather spoke to the image on the screen. "Harlan, what can you tell us now? Are there any new developments? Do you know any more about the attack?"

"All I can tell you at this time is that the Secret Service and the FBI have sealed off the area. No one is allowed in, not even the press. The uninjured reporters and video people who were there when the attack occurred have all been asked to leave and were summarily escorted out. Their raw video, still photographs and any audiotapes have been confiscated as evidence to help in the investigation. A news conference has been scheduled for early this evening. The exact time has not yet been released. There are uncorroborated indications that the President will address the nation personally later today."

"Any more casualties?"

"Yes, unfortunately there are."

"What can you tell us about them?"

"The latest casualties were not actually at the site of the attack. That is, they were not at the garden where the President was speaking. According to preliminary information from the Secret Service, all eight people inside the Sterling & Associates trailer are dead."

Sherrie froze. One hand subconsciously sprung to her mouth to drown out the silent scream, the other clutched her extended belly.

"As you know, Sterling & Associates is headquarters right here in Orlando. What have the authorities told you about Sterling & Associates? What did they have to do with the attack?"

"We don't know very much at this point. The Secret Service is being very tight-lipped about all this. That is quite understandable. But we do know that Sterling & Associates was working with the Secret Service on some kind of experimental surveillance aircraft. Those experimental aircraft are called Remotely Piloted Vehicles, or RPV's for short. That was what the trailer was for. Apparently, the people inside the trailer controlled the RPV's and collected surveillance information. The surveillance was for the purpose of protecting the president. In this tragic case, they almost killed him."

"Do you know how the people inside the trailer died, or anything else about their deaths?"

Sherrie almost fainted. She slumped into the soft couch, almost spilling the juice in her lap. Her eyes were like saucers, yet she saw nothing. She heard nothing for what seemed like hours, but was actually only a few seconds.

The fifth ring of a telephone that sounded like it was a hundred miles away, jolted her upright again. She blinked the fog in her brain away as she tried to remember where the telephone was located. She gingerly picked up the receiver slowly after the sixth ring, but before the answering machine took over.

"Sherrie!! Have you heard the news?," bellowed Jennifer Cohen, a usually loud person anyway.

"I can't talk right now, Jenn. I'll call you back." Sherrie was in Never-Never land. Her senses defying her to jump back into reality. As she slowly started to replace the receiver in the cradle, Jennifer's shouting was still very audible, so Sherrie put the receiver slowly back to her ear. Every move was an effort.

"Sherrie, the FBI is looking for Richard. They say he tried to kill President Chandler."

Sherrie was confused. She looked at the receiver as if it, not Jenn, was talking.

"Sherrie! Where is Richard? We've got to find him before the police do."

"Jenn. What am I going to do? Richard's dead."

"What are you talking about? The reporter said the entire FBI, Secret Service and the Washington, D.C. Police department are looking for him. If he were dead they wouldn't be looking for him, would they?"

"But the news report I just heard said everyone inside the trailer were found dead. Richard would have been in the trailer," whined Sherrie. "He's dead. What am I going to do?"

"Sherrie! Get a hold of yourself. Look, I'll be over there in fifteen minutes. We'll make some phone calls and get this whole thing figured out. You just sit tight. I'll be right over." The phone clicked and fell silent.

Sherrie replaced the receiver with what seemed like the most effort she had exerted in years. The TV was still on. Dazed and confused, Sherrie reluctantly turned back to watch.

Heather was talking again. "Harlan, what do you know about Richard Feinstein?"

"The FBI released a photograph of him just a few minutes ago. I think we have it."

Richard's expressionless face stared back at her. She immediately recognized the photograph as being the one she looked at every day on his Sterling & Associates ID Badge.

Sherrie's mind alternated between racing with wild thoughts of Richard's death and going numb with fear of what would happen next. Large tears rolled uncontrollably down her now red swollen cheeks. Her eyes welled up with more tears and her nose was running. Dabbing at he face with a sleeve didn't help. She just sat there, totally motionless. She heard and saw nothing more until the banging on the door and Jenn's shouting invaded her private stupor.

Jennifer barged in as soon as Sherrie opened the door. "God, Sherrie. What the hell is going on?"

"I don't know. I'm so confused. Richard would never be involved in something like this. He's such a nice person—how could he be?" Sherrie's words were slow, and slurred by the overwhelming desire to cry and moan.

"Of course he wouldn't. We have to think positive thoughts." Jenn held her gently, taking care not to press on her stomach. Sherrie shuddered and broke down again. It was all Jenn could do to hold her on her feet.

Jennifer really didn't know what to think either. All she knew was that her best friend's husband was the object of the biggest manhunt in the United States since Kennedy was shot. She also knew Sherrie very much needed a friend right now. Above all Jennifer was compassionate and cared deeply about her friends.

Jennifer broke the silence after several awkward moments. "I heard on the car radio coming over here again that the authorities are looking for Richard. He can't be dead if they are looking for him, can he? He's alive, Sherrie. You must think positively." Jenn kept trying to reassure Sherrie that Richard was alive. She personally was not quite so sure. She heard about murder-suicides every week or so on the news but was wise enough not to say anything now.

Jennifer's attempt at consoling Sherrie wasn't working.

The phone rang. Sherrie picked up the receiver and with great effort said, "Hello."

The voice on the other end identified himself as a reporter for the Orlando Sentinel, and he wanted to interview Sherrie Feinstein over the phone

Sherrie's voice quivered. "I can't. Not now." And she hung up.

Jenn prodded Sherrie out of motherly curiosity to find out who had just called. As Sherrie explained the gist of the call to Jennifer, the phone rang again. The same reporter was very polite but persistent. He wanted permission to schedule an interview for later in the day. Sherrie stood motionless, unable to talk. Jennifer sensed Sherrie's conflict and took charge by grabbing the phone.

"Listen Mr. Reporter. Whoever you are. Mrs. Feinstein has nothing to say to the press. Not now, not later, not ever," and slammed the phone down.

Jennifer was a big fan of old movies. She'd seen that stunt pulled a hundred times and always wanted to do it herself. She smiled at her accomplishment. Jennifer was also a very strong-willed lady. She heroically endured the loss of her first husband to bone cancer after only three too-short years of marriage. Now at the mature age of twenty-nine, and remarried for two years, she was both tough and smart. Her natural instinct to take charge sprang forward. She must help her friend, even if she didn't exactly know how to do that under these very strange circumstances. She was confident she would figure it out as time went on.

"Don't answer any more calls. I'll do that. You're in no condition to talk to anyone. Let me handle this until Howard comes home from his business meeting. He's driving back from Boca Raton and should be in Orlando by 5."

Sniffling and in pain, Sherrie tried to smile, but couldn't. "Thanks Jenn. I'm so glad you're here. I really couldn't handle this by myself." whispered Sherrie as she again slumped deep into the soft couch sobbing almost hysterically.

3:58 p.m.

"How do these guys get your phone number so fast?" sneered Jennifer as she hung up the phone for the twelfth time in an hour and a half.

"I don't know? All I know is I'm going crazy. My husband is wanted for murder, the press is hounding me, and I don't know what to do. For all I know Richard could be dead." Sherrie started sobbing again. It had been over fifteen minutes since the last crying episode and Jennifer had thought they had stopped. Obviously she was wrong.

The phone rang again.

Jennifer sprang for it. The fire in her eyes revealed the anger she felt as she beat the caller to the punch. "Listen you miserable leeches. Mrs. Feinstein will not speak to anyone. Got that?"

A surprised, but comforting male voice simply said, "Are you Mrs. Sherrie Feinstein? I'm sorry if I disturbed you, but I have a message from Mr. Feinstein." Jennifer's jaw dropped two inches as she listened motionless. Her eyes glazed over. Then she dropped the phone.

Sherrie looked inquisitively at Jennifer, who could only point to the dangling receiver.

Sherrie cautiously picked up the phone. "Hello, this is Sherrie Feinstein. Who...who is this?" She was still choking back tears.

"Hello. I am a Rabbi in Washington, D.C.. I can't tell you my name. Your husband, Richard asked me to call you and give you a message."

Surprised and excited Sherrie stammered, "Rabbi, is my husband all right? Can I talk to him?" The tears flowed freely again. Sherrie sobbed with excitement, panic and fear.

"Mrs. Feinstein, I assure you he is physically OK. Naturally, he is a little fimmished. You know, Yiddish for shook up. He wants me to tell you he loves you and that he will be in touch with you as soon as he can."

"Where is he?"

"Maybe I've told you too much already. The phones may be tapped. I contacted an attorney to help him. The attorney told me to make this call very brief, and not to reveal anything more than I've already told you. I'm sorry."

"Please, Rabbi. I'm so scared. Let me talk to him, or at least tell me where he is"

"For Richard's sake, I have to hang up now. Someone will be in touch. Good by, Mrs. Feinstein." Rabbi Teitelbaum was as gentle as he possibly could be.

The phone went dead. Sherrie was stunned. Jennifer was in a daze. They stared at each other for what seemed like an eternity until Sherrie flung her arms around Jennifer's neck and the tears flowed freely again.

Jennifer regained her composure first and tenderly pushed Sherrie away. Holding her by the shoulders and looking Sherrie squarely in the eye, she inquired, "OK. Enough of this crying. What did that man say to you?"

Through her sniffles and sobbing, Sherrie replayed the message from the Rabbi. Jennifer nodded as she reinforced the grave seriousness of the situation.

"I'll call Howard. Maybe he's home early."

Jennifer dialed her home phone number and patiently waited through five rings, until a panting voice softly, but with great effort whispered. "Hello, Jennifer is that you?"

"Thank God you're home, Howie."

Howard wheezed as he tried to catch his breath. "I heard the news on the car radio coming up the Florida Turnpike. The phone was ringing as I drove up, and I rushed into the house to get it. We need a cell phone, you know—we'll talk about that later. I figured it was you. What's going on?"

"I'm over at Sherrie's running interference with the press. They won't leave her alone."

"How did they find her so fast?"

"I don't know. They must have very good researchers though."

"Is she OK?"

"She's all right, all things considered."

"You stay there, I'll be right over. Don't open the door for anyone but me."

"Howard. We got a message from Richard."

Silence. Then, "What did he say?"

"It wasn't Richard himself, but a Rabbi he contacted in Washington."

* * *

A Van Near the Feinstein Home
4:23 p.m.

"So he's contacted a Rabbi in Washington. That should narrow the search. Hey, Mike, call the Captain. I've got to give him this information immediately."

The emergency secret wiretap bore fruit within the first hour.

Secure phone lines hummed as the newly gained information about the whereabouts of Richard Feinstein made its way electronically encrypted to the Secret Service high command. Carl Worthington was pleased as the news was relayed to him through his top aides. The nest step seemed simple: find the Rabbi, make him divulge Richard's whereabouts and complete the arrest. How many Rabbis can there be in Washington, D.C.?

CHAPTER SEVEN

The Chapel at Beth Shalom Synagogue
Washington, D.C.
Friday, Early March
3:45 p.m.

Harvey Weissman started slowly with the personal details—the standard name, rank and serial-number routine. Richard Feinstein was immediately annoyed, and didn't understand the need to provide these trivial details now, before getting into the meat of his very serious problem. His life was at stake for G-d sakes.

Richard tried his best to stay calm. "Mr. Weissman, can't we skip this part for now? I'm in deep doo-doo here, and I'm sure you want to know about my involvement...," a short hesitation, then "...actually my lack of involvement in the assassination attempt." This was more a statement expressing his frustration than a real question.

Harvey stopped writing and looked up from his legal pad with his best lawyerly smile. "Call me Harvey. I imagine we'll become very close real fast."

"Sure, Harvey. But shouldn't we get into the events of today? I mean, there is so much I don't understand." Richard looked down at his brown loafers sheepishly. "I don't even know what the hell I'm saying."

"Look Richard, this may take a few hours. Then I'll start my investigator on whatever we find. But the most important and immediate problem is your safety."

"No shit! Pardon my French."

"Richard. Get a grip on yourself. We haven't even started and you're grumpy and angry. You must clear your head. Gather your thoughts. We have to work together. You, and only you, can provide the information we need to save your skin. We'll take it slowly—step by step. I have a lot of information that I must digest before I can even begin to help you. When we're done with the facts surrounding the assassination attempt and your involvement, or lack thereof, in it, we'll work on what to do about your personal safety. Okay? And don't worry: we're safe here for the time being. My office doesn't even know where I am."

"I have no involvement in the assassination attempt!" denied Richard sternly.

"I didn't mean to imply that you did. But, you did work for Sterling & Associates, and by the authorities identifying you as being the supposed mastermind, they must have some evidence of your involvement or they wouldn't have identified you. Do you understand that?"

"Sorry. Yes, of course I understand. Someone has gone to a lot of trouble to make it look like I was involved. I apologize for my behavior. I don't get this flustered normally." Silence as Richard took a deep breath, exhaled loudly and tried to calm his churning stomach. "OK. Where should we start?"

Harvey returned to his legal pad. "Tell me about the RPV Project and your role in it."

"OK." Richard took another deep breath, exhaled slowly, but silently this time. Collecting his thoughts he began his explanation of the facts he was sure about.

"RPV's are the main product line of Sterling & Associates. The entire business was built on the premise that RPV surveillance was the wave of the future in law enforcement. They fill a need so to speak. I joined the company about a year and a half ago; right after the Orlando office was opened. The marketing guys at Sterling got our foot in the door with the Secret Service, but were politely told to butt-out so the Fed's could talk directly to the project team. The higher up's at the Secret Service couldn't stomach the hype and bullshit the marketing guys kept throwing at them. The Fed's simply wanted to know exactly what the RPV's could and could not do. They could care less about the marketing drivel they were hearing. They were only interested in actual, provable performance information."

"Such as?"

"Typical flight characteristics; like speed, endurance, cruising altitude. They also were interested in video resolution and the distances from an object at which video could be taken, and how far that picture could be transmitted back to the ground teams. Stuff like that. They needed very precise surveillance for at least four hours duration. They needed to be able to survey a site up to six miles away from the remote trailer with video that could read a type-written letter from 1,000 feet away."

"Wow. That is impressive stuff. Could your RPV's do that?"

"Yes; not really difficult technically. We already have satellites that can relay readable video of road signs from 200 miles in orbit. This is classified information – you understand. If you reveal any of this, I'll have to kill you." joked Richard trying to lessen the tension. Harvey simply looked up, raised his eyebrows, and then returned his attention to his notes.

"Oh, really. Where do you fit in?" Harvey ignored the classified part.

"Upper management finally got the hint about the interference of the marketing guys. I was the team leader for the flight control system development effort. Since an operator on the ground controls the RPV, the Secret Service was very concerned about how it would really be controlled. You know, does it fly like a real airplane? How does the pilot actually see where the RPV is going? How hard is it to actually make the RPV go where you want it to go? What is its current speed and altitude? Those sorts of questions."

"How do you know all of this about Sterling Management and the decisions they made? Were you involved with any of the decision making process?"

"You hear things. Other people talk. You know." Richard shrugged as he sensed his knowledge of the facts might not have come from reliable sources.

"Okay. So how were you involved exactly? What was your role in the program?"

"I'm getting to that. Sterling & Associates promoted me to Project Leader so I could interface directly with the Secret Service. That was about seven months ago, and a few months into the project with the Secret Service"

"How many members were on your team? Did they report directly to you?"

"I directly supervised nine people, so there were ten technical people officially assigned to the RPV Project from Sterling & Associates— including myself, of course. The crew that actually assembled the RPV was composed of assembly line workers who probably did not know exactly what they were assembling – they certainly did not know its full capabilities or what it might be used for. There were probably 12 - 15 of them over the course of a year. Technicians, inspectors, machine shop workers, and the Quality Control guys. None of them were in Washington for this Demonstration, only my Team"

"OK. Let's ignore the assembly workers and the Quality Control types for now, and concentrate on the technical guys you supervised. Who were they and what did each of them do?" queried Harvey as he made rapid notes in a scrawl mostly decipherable only to himself and his long-time secretary.

Richard was finally calming down enough to think in a more rational manner. "Let me get the list I made while I was waiting for you."

Richard rose and walked casually to his windbreaker to retrieve the poorly folded sheets of paper. He was still deep in thought. Something seemed strange but he couldn't put his finger on it. There was a gnawing in his gut that what he thought he remembered didn't add up just right. It just wasn't kosher! He forced himself to concentrate harder. Then he paused in mid step, closed his eyes, tilted his head backward and arched his back as if seeking divine intervention.

He looked down eventually as Harvey watched patiently. Richard finally came over and took his seat opposite Harvey. Scanning the pages and flipping them as he gazed, he responded with measured tones as his misgivings nagged at him. "Right after I became team leader, I organized the ten man technical group into sections. I had three people devoted to the flight control system. They dealt with the responsiveness of the ailerons and rudder, the speed controls of the propeller, the stability of the actual flight, and other flight control issues. Four others were strictly in the surveillance area—cameras, radio relays, optics, clarity, magnification and such. One other guy was the Mechanical Designer, and the last was my assistant and Systems Engineer, Luis Ramirez. He was a sort of overseer—the de-facto supervisor since his work involved dealing with al the other guys. After my promotion, I spent most of my time as a diplomat. My time as an engineer was greatly restricted. I did very little engineering work these past six or seven months, but I did review all the technical work and approve everything on the Project. The nine of them, Luis and the other guys did all the technical stuff first. I only reviewed and approved it before we said anything to corporate or reported to the Secret Service guys."

Glancing up from his notes, Richard interjected, "The Secret Service team leader was actually a very nice lady lawyer by the name of Lindsay Hawthorn. We had her over for dinner a few months ago."

No response from Harvey, who immediately went back to his notes. "Of the nine members of your team, who was in the trailer?"

"I told you before that there were ten of us, not nine. We all were in the trailer. All ten of us." Richard paused monetarily as the gnawing in the pit of his stomach returned with a vengeance

Pressing on in spite of his uneasiness, "We each had our own particular jobs to do in the trailer. The three flight control guys operated the controls and monitored the flight data beamed back from the RPV to the data recorders in the trailer. James Montgomery has a pilot's license, and was our main pilot. He had primary control of the flight control stick. He was like a kid with a new video game. He was a pro, but he really enjoyed what he was doing. James watched a huge 21-inch video monitor that showed a front view of what an imaginary person in the RPV cockpit would actually see. He used a joystick type of device to send commands by remote radio control to the on-board flight control system. He actually flew the plane just like a real pilot, but he did it from on the ground in front of a monitor instead of in the cockpit."

"Like the video game *Flight Simulator* all the kids play." interrupted Harvey.

"Exactly. But this is real, and it costs more than $50." Richard actually laughed for the first time in hours. Harvey joined in as the tension subsided a little more. Within a few minutes, reality checked back in— seriousness again prevailed as the two men went back to work.

"OK, I'll continue. Charley Wong watched his identical monitor to insure the pilot handled the controls correctly. Charley was also a pilot, but had less experience than James. He was a sort of co-pilot, like a second set of eyes with a second set of controls. Juan Gonzales monitored the flight data as it came in, looking for any abnormalities or problems. If some of the incoming data strayed outside of our pre-set parameters, he would alert Luis or myself. The four surveillance guys each had their own monitor."

Richard was on a roll. His confidence was returning, and his mind regained its usual sharpness. He momentarily forgot the trouble he faced.

He continued strongly and with a purpose. "There were two video cameras. The raw surveillance data was monitored on the fly. That means in real-time as it was actually happening. Tyron Johnson controlled and monitored the front view surveillance camera while Armand Fuentes controlled and monitored the view generally below or to the sides. Both men had a control lever that let them pan, tilt and zoom their respective views as they searched the scenery in almost a full hemispherical pattern. The raw data was recorded digitally, like a DVD movie, as it came into the trailer. The other two surveillance guys, Pierre and Damon, replayed specific segments of the video to get a better, more detailed re-look. They searched for things that might have been missed a few seconds before because events might have developed too quickly, or certain objects and activities were in view for too short a period of time. They had full slow-motion and freeze-frame capability on their DVD playback systems."

"Sort of like instant replay at a football game." Harvey was no slouch when it came to hi-tech electronic gadgets. His home and office boasted the newest, most hi-tech audio and video equipment available to an affluent amateur consumer. He was particularly fond of his new Digital Video Recorder from VideoCast, the TV Cable company.

"Exactly. You catch on fast." smiled Richard, finally realizing that Harvey might know what Richard was talking about.

"I'm into hi-tech toys." Harvey smiled back. Quickly changing the subject back to the RPV's, he continued, "What did Luis do?"

"During flight tests and demonstrations like the one this morning, Luis kept most of the statistics, such as time in the air, how far away from the trailer the RPV might be, its speed and altitude and other info we continually monitored. But, his major job was to coordinate the entire flight while the RPV was in the air. Each flight has a mission or reason to be in the air in the 1ˢᵗ place. He ensured we stayed focused on that mission. He acted like a director of a live concert that was being sent over the TV airwaves. He would sit behind everyone on a high stool that allowed him a view of every TV monitor. He'd point and direct particular pans and zooms. He was in a position to see all the monitors at once, giving him an overview of all the action that no other single surveillance man had. He might tell Tyrone or Armand to zoom in on this or that, look over here or over there. Or he would direct James to turn left, retrace a particular path, or whatever. It all depended on what was happening at the moment, and what particular concerns we had about what was going on as the mission unfolded."

"Okay. I think I understand the overall operation. And you? What did you do?"

"During this demonstration I was supposed to oversee everything. Luis was doing a great job, but he was actually still in training. So I stayed in the background and usually just observed. Occasionally I would make a comment to Luis who would then issue a command in response to whatever I was suggesting to him."

"OK. And all of them were in the trailer this morning?" quizzed Harvey as he pondered aloud and studied his scribbles.

Momentary hesitation. "Yes. This was our first major demonstration for the Secret Service. We wanted the demonstration to run perfectly. We needed everyone. We all had our jobs, and we all were at our respective stations doing them. Well, that is until I got sick and went back to my hotel. Yes. I'm sure of that. We were all locked in the trailer."

Harvey's head shot up from his yellow legal pad. "Richard. Only eight bodies were found in the trailer. You make the ninth person. Who is the tenth?"

Richard sank back in his chair, floored by this revelation. That was what was bothering him! The body count didn't add up. He smacked his forehead with the heel of his hand for emphasis.

"I'm absolutely positive all ten of us were in the trailer this morning until I left. We arrived at about eight o'clock together from the hotel. We had three cars. We then started to do preflight checks, equipment checks, and generally made damn sure we were prepared, and ensure that nothing would go wrong." Richard's blank stare at Harvey was genuine.

"Maybe one of them slipped out after I left." wondered Richard aloud trying to fathom the total impact.

"If one did leave, would he be noticed?"

"Someone would have to notice. The trailer is locked from the inside for security reasons. Secret Service people patrol every 15 minutes around the outside. No one goes in or out without the approval of Luis or myself. We have the only keys. I wonder if the Trailer was locked when the Police found the bodies inside."

"If someone could sneak out, could the demonstration continue?"

"Probably. It depends on who, since some job wouldn't get done."

"We don't know that all the jobs were being performed, do we? We also don't know when that person left the Trailer. Maybe he left after the attack, and not before." Harvey was throwing out fragments of a not yet fully formulated theory.

"Let's change course for a moment. Where was the Secret Service people during all of this?"

"Early in the project, Sterling & Associates and the Secret Service both agreed that they would have an almost duplicate monitoring room. The Trailer could not accommodate more than 10 people and all the equipment and support systems. It was a tight squeeze to get all 10 of us in there. The Secret Service would see everything we saw at exactly the same time. There was an open mike set up in the trailer and the Secret Service room so we all could speak to, and hear the other. There was video from the Control Trailer to the Secret Service room so they could observe our activities. There were two video cameras in the trailer that captured everything that went on inside and transmitted it to the Secret Service room. We had a switch inside the trailer to cut off the video for corporate trade secret reasons. The Secret Service knew about the switch and approved its use. The general idea was for the pilot or the surveillance guys to respond to Secret Service wishes or commands as they were given. The Secret Service agents could continuously hear what we were doing, but did not have any physical or visual control over the pilot. We knew what we wanted kept secret from the Fed's, and had planned to turn off the video immediately before the actual demonstration started. That was an actual written procedure suggested by Luis, I believe. The Secret Service guys have a copy of all our procedures, so I guess they knew what we would do. The audio was always on, though. The RPV is too delicate, and too incredibly expensive a flying machine to allow a loose-cannon Secret Service Agent free reign over a pilot to make a particular maneuver or set of maneuvers that might overstress the airframe. We could lose the plane with one wrong or stupid motion made in panic by an inexperienced operator, or by a startled operator being shouted at by the Secret Service guys. Luis and I always had veto authority over any of the Secret Service requests, but we would try to accommodate their general intent. That was part of the agreement." It took a long time to get all of this out. Richard stuttered and sputtered as he relayed these facts to Harvey, and the full impact sunk in.

Harvey was absorbing all of this and starting to solidify his theory and plot initial strategy.

"OK. Back to personnel. Who could have left the trailer after you?"

Richard stroked his chin, looked around the room for an imaginary, but illusive answer, and finally stated, "I honestly have no idea. If everyone was actually doing their job, no one could have left during the demonstration."

Harvey repeated his earlier thought. "Well, maybe not everyone was doing their job. Maybe he left after the attack occurred. Whoever it was is probably responsible for the attack on the President, for the deaths of the eight others and for the frame-up of you. I doubt that he acted alone!"

"So you believe me now?"

"Yes, Richard. I believe you. All we have to do now is find out who is behind all this and why. And I doubt the Federal Government will provide help any time soon, so we're on our own for now."

A small victory in a day full of defeats; but a very important victory for Richard none-the-less. Richard now had a comrade and confidant who might be able to help him stay alive. Maybe, just maybe he wouldn't be shot dead in the street like a mangy stray dog.

Richard exhaled a long sigh of relief, rolled his eyes upward and mouthed, "Thank you!"

CHAPTER EIGHT

Beth Shalom Synagogue
Washington, D.C.
Friday, Early March
5:08 p.m.

Harvey had filled his first legal pad with notes, and had started on the second. Most of the notes involved things Harvey needed to check out, items for his investigator to track down, and questions that he still had about this very strange case. Richard was again tense and now very tired.

"All right, Richard. I think we have enough to get started."

"Great, but what about me? What about my safety? Where can I go to be safe?"

"Simple. You're coming home with me," declared Harvey matter-of-factly.

"What? How can I be safe with you?"

"Look, my wife will be home for Shabbat by six. We'll have a nice meal and discuss what to do next. It'll be fine. You'll see."

"Wait a minute here. I understand about attorney-client privilege, but your wife? How can I be sure she won't say anything or turn me in to the Feds?"

"Good question. I forgot to tell you. Suzanne, my wife, is a reporter for the Washington Post. She writes under her maiden name of Suzanne

Westheim. She will gladly invoke her First Amendment Right not to divulge a source. She has been threatened with jail on more than one occasion. She won't rat on you. Besides, she's put up with my crazy stunts for years. Don't worry about Suzanne."

"Does Rabbi Teitelbaum know about this?" inquired Richard skeptically.

"I mentioned it to him an hour ago when you went to take a piss." lied Harvey, who immediately knew he couldn't take any chances, including even telling the trusted Rabbi what he was doing.

"And he approves?"

"Of course. Rabbi Teitelbaum is Suzanne's Uncle by marriage." That much was true. "Rabbi Teitelbaum is married to Suzanne's aunt on her mother's side. He trusts Suzanne completely, and so should you. Besides, what other real choice do you have? It's either the streets on your own, or home with Suzanne and me."

After a moment of obvious, but unnecessary contemplation, "OK, I'll go home with you if you're sure I'll be safe there."

"I'm sure. Let's get going." Harvey wasn't sure, but he wouldn't show it. In fact, he wasn't exactly sure what he should tell Suzanne.

Harvey also knew that as an attorney and officer of the court, that by hiding Richard he could get himself severely reprimanded by the Florida Bar Ethics Committee, even disbarred. The Attorney-Client privilege applied only to statements made between client and attorney, not physical evidence, and the privilege certainly did not apply to refusing to divulge the whereabouts of a person wanted in a nationwide manhunt. Harvey could even be charged with aiding and abetting a criminal by hiding Richard. Harvey needed time to think, to devise a plan. He wanted to protect Richard from the police and the public in general, while at the same time protecting himself from disciplinary problems.

Harvey gathered his suit coat, and carefully repacked and closed his briefcase. The solid sound of the twin clicks informed anyone listening that the case was expensive. Richard collected his windbreaker and Wizard's cap, returned the nearly empty pad of paper to the Rabbi and started reluctantly to leave. He was uneasy; still very skeptical and unsure about what to do.

Rabbi Teitelbaum sensed the uneasiness. "Richard. I know how frightened you must be. Believe me, you are in very good hands. Harvey is a fine lawyer," Rabbi Teitelbaum uttered sincerely with a gentle warm smile and an outstretched hand. Richard took the Rabbi's hand tightly in both of his.

"Thanks for your help and support, Rabbi. Especially your phone call to my wife. She must be as scared as I am. I do appreciate it. Some day when all this is cleared up, I'll find a way to repay you for your kindness." Richard was also sincere. Rabbi Teitelbaum appreciated the gesture, but expected nothing in return.

Shabbat Services started at 7:30 and Synagogue officers arrived at 7, sometimes earlier. "All right, all right already! We've got to be going before anyone else shows up here." Harvey was eager to leave. Turning directly towards Rabbi Teitelbaum, "Rabbi, I'll be in touch with you with whatever information I can divulge. Thanks for your help in keeping this quiet."

Harvey was surprising even himself. He was starting to like Richard. In fact, he really now pretty much believed Richard had been set up. He didn't know by whom, or why, but he was convinced Richard was innocent. He felt it in his gut. The same feelings he had many years ago in the early days of his criminal law practice before he hardened his heart to the true criminals and scumbags he usually represented. This case was different; a welcome change. He just hoped Suzanne understood, and would keep the secret—at least for now.

Once in the synagogue foyer, Harvey grabbed Richard by the arm to keep him from going through the main entrance door. "Richard, we have to be very careful. You wait here. I'll drive the car as close to the entrance as I can. I'll open the car door from the inside. When you see it open, you hurry outside and jump in."

"This is crazy. I'm running for my life by playing cops and robbers."

"Richard. You're forgetting that whoever set you up has already killed over twenty people. They purposefully spared you the first time, but they might not hesitate to kill you if it suits their purpose."

"I know. You're right. I know." repeated Richard, dejected again.

"Also, we don't know who *they* are. What *they* want. What *their* purpose is, or whether or not *they* intend to try another attack on the president— or on you. If you want to stay alive, you've got to be very careful. Your best hope to do that is to listen to me and do exactly as I say." Harvey hoped Richard believed him more than he believed himself.

"Got it! I know you're right. I'm just not used to all this cloak and dagger stuff."

"Neither am I!" whispered Harvey, too softly for Richard to hear.

"When you get in my car, which is a late model 4-door white Cadillac, slump down in the seat. Keep the brim of that ball cap pulled down over your face, and don't move a muscle until we get to my house."

"Is all this really necessary?"

"You were the one drugged and accused of attacking the president, with the whole world now looking for you. You decide."

"OK! OK! I get the point."

Harvey continued, "It isn't dark out yet, and my windows are only lightly tinted. Someone looking inside the car could still spot you. We must keep your whereabouts secret, so don't look around as we drive."

The ploy worked, and Richard got into the white Cadillac without being noticed. He did as he was told and slumped low into the white leather seat. A casual observer could easily mistake him for a young child being transported to a little league ball game.

Harvey drove Richard through the stop-and-go congested rush-hour traffic for 35 minutes—fifteen minutes longer than usual to get to the suburbs. Neither of them had much to say. Richard followed orders and kept his mouth shut and his head down. Both were lost in their own private thoughts.

The Weissman Neighborhood
Alexandria, VA
Friday, Early March
5:53 p.m.

"OK, we're here. My house is the third one on the left." was all Harvey said as the Cadillac eased smoothly around the corner. These were also the first words uttered by either man since they left the synagogue.

Richard sheepishly sat up and looked at the spacious homes that would be considered mansions in the Orlando neighborhood where he lived, and probably anywhere else. In Orlando, these huge homes were usually found only in the wealthier neighborhoods like Heathrow, Bay Hill, Windermere, Alaqua and similar upscale developments.

Richard was impressed. He had no idea what these homes cost, but they were obviously expensive. Harvey must really be a good lawyer to afford a home like this.

"That's my home," exclaimed Harvey again, pointing down the road, "I'll pull into the garage. Don't get out of the car until the garage door is closed behind us," he cautioned, breaking Richard's gaze at a beautiful two story colonial home with stark 20 foot tall white pillars in front. The majestic colonial-style house was next door to Harvey's.

Richard immediately stared at the home Harvey was pointing to; a rambling single story ranch style with a dramatic light brown colored brick exterior, trimmed elegantly in beige. Splashes of dark brown trimaccented the look perfectly. The house seemed to stretch for a whole block. Large windows and an etched glass double door entrance were striking. A long circular driveway was the centerpiece. The landscaping and lawn was immaculate. Beautiful trees with new spring leaves and early multi-colored blossoms gave the scene a very homey appearance.

Harvey pushed a button overhead inside the Cadillac, activating one of the three garage doors. After slowly entering the surprisingly uncluttered spacious garage, and waiting for the garage door to close behind them, Harvey opened his door, and Richard did the same. Silently Richard followed Harvey into a neat room that doubled as a passageway from the garage into the kitchen, and as a large laundry room. It too was uncluttered.

"Let me take your jacket," offered Harvey with an outstretched hand. Richard slipped off the jacket and ball cap, handing them to Harvey, who quickly hung them on one of several hooks conveniently placed just inside the doorway.

Richard mentally compared this spacious and beautiful home to his own in Orlando. He and Sherrie owned a small, but neat three-bedroom ranch home that could probably fit in Harvey's three-car garage. But,

Richard and Sherrie were content with their own home, which was no comparison to this.

On the drive to his house, Harvey formulated the first steps of his plan. First he would have to tell Richard the truth, and explain why he had lied to him about telling the Rabbi about where he was going. Second, he would solicit help from Suzanne in finding out some more of the details surrounding the attack on the President. Third, and the most difficult, he would discuss with Richard the details and problems associated with Richard turning himself in. Harvey decided to start implementing the first steps of his plan immediately.

"Let's sit here in the kitchen and discuss a few more details," declared Harvey as he motioned to the comfortable looking barrel chairs surrounding a large circular glass-top table. The kitchen was huge. It had a large island in the center, and seemingly endless cabinets and built-in spaces surrounded them on all 4 walls. The light gray ceramic floor tile was elegant. As Richard sat down, Harvey remembered his manners. "Can I get you a soda? Some juice perhaps? Whatever you want. I have some excellent bourbon, vodka and scotch if you need something stronger. I know I do."

"Maybe a screwdriver. A big glass with lots of ice and double vodka, please. I need something to calm my nerves. I only drink on special occasions. This qualifies, doesn't it?" he snickered.

"Sure, we have vodka, and orange juice is in the Fridge. If you get the juice, I'll get the vodka from the den." Both men rose and headed in opposite directions, each returning with their respective bottles. Harvey turned and retrieved two large glasses from a nearby cupboard, strode over to the refrigerator with both glasses in hand to load them with ice. The huge white double door refrigerator had an outside ice dispenser. It whirred and sputtered as the crushed ice filled one glass, than the next. Upon returning and sitting opposite Richard, he poured the clear vodka without measuring. Neither cared how much they would consume. A splash of orange juice from the glass bottle followed by a quick stir, and all was ready.

Handing the first glass to Richard, Harvey raised his and stated emphatically. "Here's to getting you out of this mess." And he meant it.

They clicked glasses and each drained over half before setting it carefully back on the table.

The cold vodka went down smoothly, easing the tension in both men. Harvey had no intention of having a second drink, and he hoped he could persuade Richard to stop at one as well. They had to keep their wits about themselves. But one soothing, calming drink before dinner, especially under these circumstances, would be OK.

Harvey was opening his mouth to explain to Richard why he lied about Rabbi Teitelbaum as the door from the laundry room flew open and a tall, elegantly dressed woman appeared in the doorway shouting for Harvey. "Harvey, I'm home. And have I got news for you."

Richard turned and could only gawk. She was also slender, under 110 pounds, and very pretty; nice figure, dark shoulder-length hair, dark eyes, pouty lips. Her long legs were perfectly proportioned to the rest of her body.

She strode quickly into the kitchen, turned the corner around the refrigerator and came face to face with Harvey and Richard. Harvey countered with a wide grin, "Hi, Hon. I've got a story for you too."

Suzanne's hand flew to her mouth to stifle her scream of surprise as she immediately recognized Richard. Her hand quivered uncontrollably at her lips. In the process, she dropped her pocketbook and keys. The contents of her bag spilled all over the kitchen floor and her keys scooted fifteen feet across the floor and banged against Richard's shoe.

"Suzanne, meet Richard Feinstein, my new client." Harvey motioned in the direction of Richard.

Suzanne could only look in amazement back and forth between Harvey and Richard. Words would not come to her. Her mouth was still open. Eyes wide with surprise.

Feeling faint, Suzanne shakily lowered herself into a chain next to Harvey, but as far from Richard as possible. She continued staring at one man, then the other, unable to speak. She grabbed the half-empty glass next to Harvey and downed the contents in one swallow.

Finally, she wheezed at her husband. "What is he doing here?"

"He's my new client. Look Suzanne, I can explain all of this. But first you must calm down and get a grip on yourself."

"OK. I'll try. Could you get me another cold drink? A Coke this time, please?" Harvey obliged.

Suzanne sipped the icy cold Coke, holding the glass with two trembling hands as she tried to calm her normally unshakable nerves. It took over twenty minutes and two full glasses of coke, but she finally could drink without fear of spilling her glass. Harvey and Richard waited patiently.

CHAPTER NINE

A Deserted Hanger
Tehran, Iran
Saturday, Early March
6:52 p.m. Local Time

The sleek silver corporate jet glided to the front of the run-down, but massive hanger. Heavily armed, bearded guards in colorful impressive Arab Robes with traditional Arab headpieces were conspicuous everywhere. As the plane slid gracefully to a stop and the door behind the pilot's seat fell open, a jet-black Mercedes screeched to a halt a few feet away. The lights on the Wings gave the car an eerie glow. The driver rushed around the rear and respectfully bowed stiffly from the waist as he open the door for his master. Abu'l Mahsin emerged from the limousine to await the arrival of his deplaning guest.

Years ago, before and during Desert Storm, Abu'l was the highest ranking General in the Iraqi Army, and the second most powerful figure in all of Iraq—until his unexpected and secret defection years ago.

The now executed Saddam Hussein had been skimming millions from the treasury of Iraq, and had entrusted Abu'l to stash the ill-gotten funds in various financially secure places around the world. While Abu'l was hiding 1.37 billion dollars for Saddam, he surreptitiously kept $283 million for himself. The paranoid Saddam eventually became suspicious, thinking that there was a crook, other than himself, in his regime. Saddam demanded an accounting and the immediate return of the money—even though he had no proof of any theft nor did he know any amounts that might be stolen. Abu'l was allowed to live temporarily because he was the only person who knew if there was a theft and if there was, the exact details and whereabouts of all of the hiding places, the exact amounts and the bank account numbers. Fortunately for Abu'l, he had gathered many loyal supporters around himself, and for a few measly millions was able to persuade his allies and not-so-loyal captors to help him escape from Saddam and his ruthless thugs.

Iran has been the bitter enemy of Iraq for generations. Its leaders welcomed Abu'l, because of the generous contribution to their own personal bank accounts of another mere 25 million dollars. Money and extreme religious ideology are formidable forces in many corrupt Middle Eastern countries.

Saddam reportedly was enraged, and summarily executed over fifty of his disloyal guards and troops. Not only did Saddam not get back the 283 million dollars Abu'l had liberated from him, but he also couldn't find another 350 million because Abu'l conveniently never got around to telling him the details of those accounts and their locations. Abu'l now had well over half a billion dollars in accounts of which only he knew the whereabouts. Saddam never really knew how much money he had stolen from his own people, and would never find out how much Abu'l had taken from him. Abu'l quickly liquidated the 350 million as well, and converted the money to secret accounts in his own name and various aliases in Europe, Hong Kong and the Caribbean. Abu'l was much smarter than Saddam. He trusted no one else with his money, and handled all of his assets, transactions and investing himself.

Now as a very wealthy Arab Sheik, Abu'l could devote his free time and energy to causes close to his heart—terrorist attacks and the embarrassment of the evil and decadent United States of America. "America is the enemy of Islam and all I believe in. They must be taught the error of their ways, and shown the glory and wisdom of Allah," he declared loudly and often to his followers.

Abu'l was well educated, extremely rich, and willing to spend his fortune to satisfy his passions. He made shrewd investments in Japan, China and Germany, carefully purchasing prime real estate and solid corporate securities, usually related to banking and finance. Abu'l tried to avoid investing in US owned companies, but was not always successful. Many multinational businesses have US ties, or originate in America. Abu'l was too obsessed with money and wealth to let minor ties to the US stop him from investing if he could turn a buck. In the years since his defection, Abu'l has almost doubled the value of his fortune. He too was now a billionaire. He lives in the penthouse of the most fashionable apartment building in Tehran. He wears $3,500 designer suits and $500 shoes when he closes business deals on foreign turf. He preferred the finer linen Robes from the best tailors in the Arab World when he is home in Iran. He owns seven luxury armored limousines, bought and refurbished two executive jets for his exclusive private use, employs a staff of almost two hundred, and in every way lives the life of a King. That actually is quite easy to do in most Arab countries if you have enough money and power for bribes, payoffs and corruption.

Before his being overthrown, Saddam had offered a fifty million dollar reward for Abu'l's "head-on-a-platter." Abu'l had successfully avoided all attempts on his life so far, but even with Saddam gone, his riches make him a target of other would-be Arab Tribal Leaders. To provide safety for himself, he has a 50 person security team that he pays very well—at least by Arabic standards; he installed state-of-the-art security protection devices in and around his penthouse, and makes elaborate security plans before he ventures out into the streets, which is not very often. The abandoned hanger in the middle of nowhere and the Uzi's are part of those precautions.

Luis Ramirez emerged from the passenger compartment of the plane squinting his eyes as they got used to the darkness that surrounded him. Nothing helped until his eyes adjusted. Sixteen hours in the air with a stopover in London for fuel was not as hard as Luis expected, especially in the luxury of Abu'l's private jet.

A man in a flowing white robe holding an Uzi pointed at the sky approached and bowed. "Welcome to my country. May I escort you to the car?" as he gestured broadly with the sweep of his free arm. Car headlights were visible fifty feet away.

Abu'l exited the luxury of his limo and extended his hand with a broad smile. The headlights and lights from inside the car were the only illumination. After a firm handshake, the two men embraced and kissed each other on one cheek then the other. Luis was a bit ill at ease with this traditional Arab greeting, but tried not to show it.

"Welcome. And I congratulate you on a job well done," beamed Abu'l while holding Luis's shoulders at arms length.

Abu'l spoke impeccable English, with only a trace of an Arabic accent. His western university education had paid off in many ways, even if it didn't change his hatred for democracy and religious tolerance. He never learned tolerance for anything or anyone he disliked. His dislikes usually turned to outright hatred. Israel and anything related to Judaism topped his list. America was a close second because of the American support for the State of Israel.

"Uh, thanks." Luis was confused.

"Unfortunately, the President did not die as planned. A minor setback. We will try another time. That was always a possibility. The most important thing is that we are not suspected, and that the people of the United States are in a panic. We have their attention. With Allah's blessing we will prevail." Abu'l tended to ramble when he was excited about something he was passionate about. Luis had no idea what he was talking about. There were only limited news reports on the fight from the States. All came from the pilot simply repeating what he was hearing from Air Traffic Control operators along the way. Luis did not yet know the true extent of the assassination attempt, the deaths or the injuries.

Luis continued on anyway. "The pilot said that the President was attacked and many innocent people were killed or injured."

"That is correct. Your initial assignment was completed."

"Initial assignment?" thought Luis to himself. "What the hell was going on here?"

Luis thought better of confronting Abu'l about the deception, and Luis never anticipated the terror and disaster that actually took place. Fearful of reprisal, Luis held his tongue.

"I know. I have my people monitoring the international TV and radio reports. I get hourly briefings. They tell me the entire country is looking for your boss, Richard Feinstein."

What? Richard? Luis was more confused than before. Luis could only gaze at the drab surroundings as he tried to avoid looking Abu'l in the eye.

"But enough of this shop-talk. We must celebrate. Come. You will join me for a late dinner and some pleasure." grinned Abu'l as he turned and bent to re-enter the limo. Luis and two bodyguards trailed behind. The driver closed the door and went around to his side.

This topic was a little less distressing. Luis knew from the only other time he met Abu'l personally that "pleasure" meant women. Abu'l had a harem of beautiful young Arab women that he personally trained to give extraordinary sexual pleasure. The better they performed, the better he treated them—and he actually paid them. The twelve or so women Abu'l kept were truly gifted, and their talents were exclusively for himself and his handpicked friends. Luis momentarily forgot the events in Washington. He was getting hard just thinking about the last time Abu'l offered him pleasure.

The plodding twenty-five minute drive back to the city was along a carefully chosen eight-mile set of back-roads; desolate stretches of pot-holed and crumbling asphalt little used and long forgotten by the masses. There were two cars in front of Abu'l's limo and two behind. The orders were very clear. The drivers were instructed to stop for nothing and no one. Shoot to kill anyone who tried to stop them; another security precaution. The only human they encountered was a peasant farmer carrying some baskets of fruits a few hundred feet from the roadway. The farmer didn't even look up from his backbreaking work. The guards watched him intently until he disappeared from view.

The entourage parked in a dark, obscure location in the underground garage beneath the exclusive apartment building. Large stone barricades kept unauthorized cars out of the garage. Four men were assigned to watch all of Abu'l's cars around the clock. Car bombs were a favorite assassination method of Saddam, and Abu'l took extreme precautions to prevent such a fate for himself. A push of an illuminated button and silent doors parted. The private elevator whisked Luis, Abu'l and three guards to the twelfth floor. Lavish highly polished dark mahogany double doors with intricate gold hardware greeted them as they stepped off the elevator. Even the hallway shouted *filthy rich*.

The penthouse suite could only be described as majestic. Luis's eyes darted everywhere as he tried to take in the beauty and splendor of the place. Marble and glass was prominent. Magnificent Persian rugs and exquisite artwork hung on every wall, and the expansive windows were draped with the finest, most beautiful and vibrantly colored tapestry Luis had ever seen. The view of the city and the surrounding areas from the expansive, but bulletproof glass windows was spectacular. Especially at night. To a casual observer, this could have been any luxury apartment in any modern city anywhere in the world. But this wasn't just anywhere. This was in a Country whose government was the enemy of all freedom loving people throughout the world. To them, freedom and democracy were evil; their kingdoms, wealth and power were threatened and were to be avoided at all cost.

Much of this Luis didn't totally remember from his last visit over two months earlier. At that time, Luis was extremely nervous, quite scared, and not fully aware of everything going on around him, or expected of him. Not to mention the distraction of the women Abu'l provided for him.

This time was different. Luis was in trouble—big trouble, and he could feel it in his bones. It didn't matter that his problems were not entirely of his own making. Luis had no choice but to stay. He was on the run, hiding secretly in this lavish penthouse. He had to settle his nerves. He might as well enjoy it.

"I could get used to this quite easily. I doubt I will ever see the US again," he muttered under his breath as he tried unsuccessfully to convince himself everything would be OK.

8:25 p.m.

Luis watched Abu'l carefully, marveling at how he was in total command of everything. Abu'l clapped his hands together twice—

servants hurried to bring huge trays of fruits, cut up vegetables, eggs cooked in a variety of ways, cheeses of different color and taste, and an assortment of other delicious American style finger foods. All this was for Luis and Abu'l. The guards and servants never ate with Abu'l. They were not invited into his private world; a world of rich, self-indulgent Arab Sheiks. It never even occurred to Abu'l to mingle with, or share anything with lowly commoners and hired servants.

Abu'l pressed a secret button under the table and wine was immediately brought, then the silver pitcher of coffee, and finally an entire golden brown cooked turkey with all the trimmings. This could feed a small village for a week marveled Luis as he surveyed the vast offering.

"I hope you enjoy this meal, my friend. I know you were not entirely delighted with the more traditional Arab meal we shared the last time you honored my house." Abu'l was nothing if not sincere in trying to please his guests.

Luis couldn't believe the quality and quantity of food before him. "This is great, but there is so much…"

Abu'l cut him off in mid-sentence with a wave. "My friend, we fight and die for worthy causes, but what else is worth living for besides good food?"

Luis could think of at least one other thing to live for as he waited with growing anticipation of the girls. He had no desire to fight or die for any cause Abu'l extolled—but he would take Abu'l's money and generous hospitality to help achieve it.

They ate for over an hour, barely making a dent in the mounds of food. Luis was unaccustomed to eating this much, and was getting bored with it. Abu'l immediately recognized the carnal look in Luis's eyes. "Even a beautiful women giving a man wonderful satisfaction is only momentary. As a man grows older, his needs change, the desire diminishes, he can no longer perform the way he could in his youth. He slows down; he doesn't need the sexual pleasure of women as much. But," he continued with flair, "he still has to eat at any age. Good food is a luxury I will not deny myself or my friends."

Luis was still young—at least 25 years younger than Abu'l, and still needed the companionship of a woman that would do the things to him that he desperately needed, but infrequently got. Luis was thirty-one years old, and never married. There were a few serious romances in his life, but they never lasted more than a year. The last ended tragically almost two years ago, and Luis never really got over it, even though he won't admit it.

Catherine Maloney was not a raving beauty, but she was reasonably attractive in her own sort of way. Her long flaming red hair was always full and fluffy. It swirled and billowed around her head like a halo. Her face was long and narrow, and didn't seem to belong on her short neck and slightly overweight body. Her steel blue eyes pierced into your soul. Her pale freckled skin was attractive in a cutesy way, and her ample full-figured breasts were obvious to anyone who looked. Her Irish accent was delightful. Henry Callahan, one of Luis's college buddies who felt sorry for him, fixed up the two on a blind date. The first date to a movie and a snack bar for a bite was slow and ponderous. Neither felt entirely comfortable with the other, and the conversation lagged. The evening ended after only three hours on Catherine's front door step with an insincere good-bye, a limp handshake and no kiss.

In spite of the slow beginning, Luis liked Catherine. He couldn't exactly put his finger on why though. Luis didn't call Catherine, but felt bad about not asking her for another date. He didn't call because he expected to be politely, but firmly turned down if he did. He'd had enough rejection in his life already from an absent father and an alcoholic mother. The previous two relationships ended when the girls dumped him unexpectedly with no explanation. He didn't need or want any more rejection.

Catherine was also in a quandary. She hoped Luis would call, but was not holding her breath because of how badly the first date had gone. Both confided their feelings separately to Henry over about a three-week period. Henry finally realized what the problem was—both were too shy and lacked the self-confidence to take another stab at building a relationship. Both had readily admitted to Henry that they liked the other, but both were reluctant to pursue what each mistakenly felt would be a one-sided romance.

They only needed a gentle push—another opportunity. This time Henry was sneakier. He invited them both over to his apartment for dinner, but didn't let on that the other was going to be there. An old trick, but it usually works. They both showed up, and with a little coaxing, went out for coffee together later that evening. This time, the hours they spent together was priceless. They each admitted their hidden anxieties and fears about romance, hopes for future relationships, their own past failed affairs, each other. They talked until the little shop closed at 1:30 in the morning, and then continued pouring their hearts out to each other until 5am in Luis's car.

They both were relieved to discover that they each were terribly lonely. Both had disastrous relationships in the recent past that hurt them deeply. Instinctively they both knew they needed, and could help each other to get over those fears and move on with their lives.

For the next two months they saw each other at least four times a week. Long passionate kisses and soothing caresses was as far as either was willing to go. Neither had even tried to sexually arouse the other even though each was aroused themself. Their relationship was physical, but not intimate. Catherine was the first to take a bold step toward a more serious relationship as they petted in Luis's car after a weekend movie date.

Luis was holding Catherine close, arms snug around her back, rhythmically rubbing her neck and shoulders as they took turns exploring the inside of each other's mouth with their tongues. Without warning, Catherine calmly and casually slid her hand down between Luis's legs and rubbed his crotch through his slacks.

Luis was glad one of them finally made a move, but was still cautious. "Are you sure you want to do this?" Luis questioned as he pulled away slightly, unsure how to respond, wanting her desperately, but fearing he might drive her away if he moved too fast.

"Yes. No, I don't know what I want, but I do know that I can't just keep kissing and pretending that I don't have other desires."

"All right. Let's take this slowly and see what happens." offered Luis, still very concerned about how fast or slow to move.

"I love you." was her response.

"Look, we don't really have any privacy in my car. Let's go to my place, and just let nature take its course."

Catherine was quite perky by now, and she didn't remove her hand from Luis's crotch. "We're here in front of my apartment. It's only 11:15. My roommate won't be home for hours. Her boyfriend took her to a 10 o'clock movie, then they'll go to his place to screw and G-d knows what else until about 3 in the morning. They do the same thing every Saturday night. We've got hours of privacy right here, right now."

"Luis was now hard as a rock. A pleasant condition he has not really experienced recently unless he brought it on himself with a strong right hand and XXX videos. Catherine could easily feel him through his slacks.

They got out of Luis's car quickly. Catherine excitedly turned the key and opened the door to a small but neat apartment. Giggling softly, she tried hard to control herself by offering Luis a beer. She moved seductively to the wall stereo and turned on the radio to a late night mood music station. "Let's dance," she whispered in a soft voice more husky than Luis had heard from her before.

They held each other close and swayed to the beautiful music of an old Johnny Mathis love song. Catherine sang the words softly in Luis's ear as her arms engulfed his neck. She pressed her body tightly against his, rubbing his groin with her swaying pelvis. Luis felt like he was about to explode. The searing heat between his legs was intense. His heart raced, his mouth was dry. He held her tighter.

The passion raced in both of them. Neither could stand it any longer. They gave in to their enormous unspoken needs as they frantically ripped off each other's clothes, tossing them with abandon. Luis was eager, but Catherine wanted the moment to last. She pushed herself away gently from his clutches and dropped to her knees in front of him. She stroked his throbbing penis with both hands before taking it fully into her mouth.

Luis felt as if he was floating ten feet off the ground. She obviously had done this before. His past partners enjoyed sex, but none of the three other women he had been intimate with liked oral sex, and two refused to even try. This was a real treat as Catherine worked her magical lips and tongue up and down, back and forth. Small guttural sounds erupted from her throat as she pumped her head faster and faster.

Luis grabbed her hair and pulled her away. "I want to cum inside you," he moaned.

"You will the next time." she retorted returning to her work on his erection.

Within 30 seconds Luis erupted in a massive orgasm and crumpled to the floor. Catherine fell on top of him and they held each other tightly until the spasms subsided. They made love three times before 1:30, something else Luis's previous lovers refused to do. Once a night was always enough for them.

For the next eight months, they were inseparable. They made love two, three even four times after every date, trying all sorts of positions and locations. They were quite imaginative and adventuresome. They had sex in the front and back seat of Luis's car, the back seat of Catherine's, every room in his apartment, on the kitchen counter and table, every room in her apartment, on the floor, with and without undressing fully, even on a running vibrating washing machine. They even explored ways to use food in their lovemaking—whipped cream, cake icing, Jell-O, pudding; anything to be different and creative. In public, they held hands, kissed, caressed each other, and in general displayed the obvious deep affection they each felt for the other. Luis talked about getting married. Catherine uncharacteristically was reluctant to discuss the subject, but agreed to make plans to visit her family in Ireland in four months, over the Christmas holidays. They never made the trip.

Unexpectedly, Luis began noticing small changes in Catherine. When confronted, she laughed and denied them. He noticed the difficulty she was having during their extended love making, and she rationalized it as aging and of their getting used to each other. Her minor pain and inability to bend and contort into the familiar sexual positions they used in the past were sloughed off as meaningless. The dark bruises to her arms and thighs were likewise attributed to Luis being a little too aggressive. Catherine's inability to climb a flight of stairs without wheezing was from lack of real exercise. And on and on. She flatly refused to discuss the matter, or to see a doctor.

Luis will never forget that rainy Thursday night in late November. They were leaving a movie theater near Fashion Square Mall in East

Orlando and walking across the parking lot to his car when she just collapsed in a heap on the wet asphalt. Luis dropped to her side in a panic. "Please help me. Call 911. Someone get an ambulance," he screamed in the direction of the emerging crowd.

Catherine was rushed to the closest hospital. The doctors in the emergency room at Florida Hospital tried to calm Luis, and explain what had happened. Catherine had been in this very hospital before. She was extensively tested and diagnosed over a year ago, and at that time she was given only one year to live. She was told she was dying, and that the inoperable ovarian cancer had spread unchecked and untreated to most of her vital organs. She demanded that the doctors tell no one. She refused possible lifesaving radiation and Chemotherapy treatments because she had watched her beloved father suffer the sever side effects of that treatment protocol, just to die anyway. She only wanted to live out the rest of her life as normally and pain-free as possible, and experience whatever happiness she could in the few short months she had left. Luis was a G-d-send. She never could have survived this long without his love and support.

Catherine was admitted to the cancer unit and heavily sedated. She was conscious enough to speak a few words to Luis, who was beside himself after learning she was dying.

"This past year has been the happiest I have ever had. You gave that to me, and I can never thank you enough for that." Her lungs were very weak, and her voice was barely audible.

"I love you Catherine. Why didn't you tell me?" Luis was crying now.

"I know you do, and I love you more than anyone in the world. I was afraid you would leave me if you knew that I was sick. I couldn't risk losing you. Please don't hate me."

Luis was holding his ear an inch from her mouth so he could hear her. His tears stained her sterile gown.

"I could never hate you. I love you." He kissed her tenderly on the lips.

Catherine smiled, squeezed his hand and pulled his head to her chest. She closed her eyes and never opened them again. Catherine was gone.

Luis was a wreck for over a month. He barely ate, hardly slept, he quit his job and didn't go to work, and he rarely even got dressed. Showering and shaving was almost forgotten. He didn't grieve and feel this horrible when his own mother died nine years ago.

Finally, Luis pulled himself together with the generous help of Henry, and swore he would never have a serious relationship with another woman ever again. It was too painful. He would masturbate if he felt like it, screw whenever a woman was willing, but never ever get romantically involved again. He swore to himself he would never fall in love again.

Luis's entire personality also changed. He became unemotional and indifferent. He didn't care about anybody else's feelings. He cared only about himself and his own personal satisfaction. He took advantage of old friendships until the friendships crumbled, and in general became a self-centered, self-absorbed obnoxious jerk: a pain in the ass that few were willing to be around.

That was exactly the kind of person Abu'l needed for his "Secret War" plan.

CHAPTER TEN

Luxury Penthouse
Tehran, Iran
Saturday, Early March
8:25 p.m. Local Time

Abu'l and Luis lounged on richly covered velvet cushions surrounded by mountains of food, attentive servants and the opulence extraordinary wealth provides. They made light conversation usually guided in whatever direction Abu'l wanted to take. The reason Luis was summoned there, the assassination attempt, the deception or Abu'l's Secret War plan had not been mentioned. The time was not yet ready for such conversation.

"And now my friend, let's have some enjoyment." grinned Abu'l as he pushed another button on his concealed panel. Massive curtains closed silently on mechanical tracks shutting out the light of the city. The already subdued lights in the room dimmed to near darkness. High energy, but somewhat erotic music erupted from hidden speakers. Rhythmic drum beats, a mix of several types of horns and a few other indistinguishable instruments created a stirring mood. A series of yellow and orange floodlights illuminated at the far end of the expansive room. Luis watched with anxious anticipation and marveled at this production. Abu'l made quite a big deal about getting laid. He did it in style. The rush-up to screwing was quite important to Abu'l.

The girls danced and twirled into the room from a far entrance. They proceeded to spin and frolic in front of the spotlights as the music intensified. The backlighting effect was dramatic. Luis could see the outline of each girl's superb figure through the thin softly colored fabric draped loosely over each girl's shoulders and looped around their waists. They wore nothing else except for a few dangling bracelets and colored necklaces. They danced in their bare feet. Some had bright jeweled necklaces, others sparkling wrist or ankle bracelets. Luis was glad he wasn't a judge in this beauty contest. Nobody could pick one girl over the rest—they were all magnificently fine creatures. Each had obvious good looks, perfect athletic bodies, sensual skills and a captivating desire to perform and please.

Luis had visited his share of topless bars and recalled the pure animal instincts he felt watching American girls dance and gyrate. They would bump and grind to offbeat music, using poles and other props, even special effect lighting. American girls were big busted and sexual, but that was no comparison to this spectacle. These girls were incredibly sensual. These girls took erotic dancing to unparalleled new heights.

Abu'l watched his girls with justified satisfaction and immense personal pride. He knew what each was capable of, and meticulously rotated his personal choice whenever the mood struck him. More often than not, Abu'l would select two or three different girls at the same time for a few hours of group sexual play. He would simply lay back and let them work their magic on him. Sometimes he would retreat to the privacy of his personal quarters, while on other occasions he would just stay here and allow anyone around to watch. Few ever did, because no one was allowed to participate unless personally invited by Abu'l. But today, Abu'l had a respected guest. His concern for Luis's need for privacy was admirable, and a sign of a civilized gentleman. Concern for anyone other than himself was not a trait usually attributed to Abu'l.

"These are all the same girls as the last time. I believe you selected Mahara when you were here before. She pleased you?"

"Uh, yes." responded Luis impishly from his sexual stupor as he continued staring.

"She's the third from the left in the light orange," offered Abu'l as he pointed in her general direction with a pudgy finger.

Luis had already spotted her, and was lost in his memories of their last extraordinary encounter. Not since Catherine's death had anyone stirred such passion and pure animal desire deep within himself. He had momentarily lapsed back into the loving caring person he used to be, and struggled for weeks afterwards to forget Mahara. He couldn't.

* * *

Luis drifted back to early January, only two short months ago. Mahara was the only name she used, and Luis hadn't inquired further. Names didn't really matter. Only hard driving sex held any interest for Luis at that time. Last time, when Abu'l gave Mahara to Luis, he stated in a sexist way that she would please him like no other woman ever had. Luis hadn't even noticed her yet. All the girls were so exquisite, and each made personal appeals to be chosen with winks, head nods, shoulder shimmies, and other sensual arm and hip motions. Luis didn't really care. Any of these girls would be a fantastic sex partner. He only wanted to get a great blowjob and screw his brains out.

To Luis's surprise and delight, Abu'l was right about Mahara.

Mahara al-Zaharri was tiny by American standards. She stood only 4'-11" tall, and weighed in at just less than 100 pounds. She was strikingly beautiful. Her curvaceous body was perfectly proportioned. Her large dark eyes glistened in reflected light, and were a central feature of her small round face. Flowing shinny jet-black hair stretched to below her waist. She carried herself and moved with the confidence and grace of a ballerina. In public Luis imagined she would turn heads.

At first Luis was reluctant to accept Mahara. How could this tiny woman with small boobs give him all that he wanted? Luis's view of sexual pleasure was limited and immature. He just wanted to smother his face between huge breasts and suck on plump nipples; have his cock swallowed whole by soft expert lips; ram himself into a wet, experienced woman; and slap their bodies together in frantic hard sex. But, he didn't want to insult his host, Abu'l. So he relented; Mahara would have to do.

GERARD RELDAN

Still skeptical, Luis had politely requested privacy and his wishes were immediately and graciously granted. Abu'l muttered something in a strange language Luis couldn't hope to understand. Mahara nodded, and then led him gently by the hand through a doorway. She carefully closed and locked the door behind them.

The room was huge—35 feet by 24 feet. Luis could see parts of other connecting rooms through open archways. The furnishings were as tasteful and beautiful as in the rest of the penthouse. But by now Luis had expected nothing less.

Mahara spoke no English, so she led him by the hand to the center of the room. A gorgeous Persian rug adorned the shinny wooden parquet floor. Its perfectly formed patterns of radiant colored tiny flowers was stunning. They reached the center of this masterpiece when she motioned for him to stop and just stand there. Slowly and delicately she undressed him. Her deft fingers carefully unbuttoned his shirt and eased it off his arms behind him. Next, she attacked his shoes, socks, slacks and Jockey shorts, sliding them down his legs slowly and deliberately. Her touch was delicate. She treated each piece of clothing with dignity and respect, carefully folding them before placing them neatly on a nearby chair. Now completely naked, Luis just stood motionless, thoroughly enjoying every movement—his penis saluted the ceiling

All the while, Luis was staring at her body through the flimsy orange netting. She ignored his stares and continued her work. Her small firm breasts and dark erect nipples became visible when she moved in a way that allowed the gathering material to flatten against her skin. Occasionally Luis caught a glimpse of her perfectly triangular shaped patch of jet-black pubic hair. When she was finished with his clothes, Mahara moved back slightly and spread her arms wide. Luis correctly interpreted this as a signal to unwrap the revealing fabric. Luis obliged by mimicking her slow deliberate actions.

Undressing a woman, or being undressed by one, was nothing new to Luis. But this was definitely a new experience. He didn't expect it and he couldn't explain it, but he really liked it.

Now both were completely naked. Without touching any other part of his body, Mahara took his hand and led him through an archway into a huge bathing area. A very large bay window rested on the outside edge of an immense black marble Roman-style sunken bathtub. Light gray and white streaks swirled in a dramatic array of color. Intricately carved gold faucets adorned one end. The bay window effect made the entire room seem bright, open and airy even in the dark Iranian night.

Mahara daintily knelt near the faucets and started the water flow. Her free hand tested for the proper mix of hot and cold. With a few swift adjustments, she was satisfied. Next she poured in a vial of a pink thick liquid. The fluid immediately created a mass of tiny bubbles that emitted a pleasant flowery fragrance. Luis closed his eyes and imagined he was in a spacious mountain field somewhere in Colorado. The entire effect and mood was intoxicating.

Mahara gracefully rose and stepped smoothly and effortlessly down the marble steps into the tub. She turned and offered her hand to help Luis down the now bubble covered steps. Together holding hands they knelt and immersed themselves up to their waists in the warm water and soothing suds. Mahara turned the knobs to stop the water.

Mahara then took a soft washcloth hanging near the tub and ever so gently began washing Luis all over. She started with his back. Luis was sitting in the tub with Mahara kneeling behind him. She used exactly the right amount of hand pressure as she slowly and meticulously swished the cloth around his back. His neck and shoulder muscles relaxed as never before. The tension drifted away. First one arm, then the other. Luis was in heaven. He even blinked and looked around to make sure he was still alive and this ecstasy was real.

Mahara reached around Luis to wash his chest. In doing so she intentionally lightly grazed his back with her hard nipples. Luis just sat there, smiling to himself and praying this was not a dream. The chest wash took at least five minutes, but seemed like only seconds. Luis had lost all track of time in this private world of pleasure.

Mahara helped Luis slide to one end of the tub and indicated he should rest his back against the far end. He willingly obliged. Her forearms and hands submerged to find his right leg which she proceeded to stroke and wash, gently raising it a few inches to get underneath and do the calf and foot. Then on to the left thigh.

GERARD RELDAN

Luis did not know what to do, so he simply laid there and waited for Mahara to lead. That was also a new experience for him. Except for Catherine, all his past lovers were unsatisfying passive. Some would submit to two or three minutes of foreplay and agree to a few sexual positions beyond the Missionary one. One sex partner grudgingly acquiesced to occasional oral sex, but only when he sternly requested it or angrily demanded it. Screwing from behind was usually out of the question. None took any initiative in giving or receiving sexual pleasure. If there was to be any meaningful foreplay or sexual activity, he had to initiate it or do without.

Without a sound, Mahara leaned over and kissed him lightly on the lips then rocked back to her kneeling position beside him. Her upper torso was erect and above the mound of bubbles. Her olive skin was shiny from the wetness. Little patches of bubbles clinging here and there. She looked magnificent. They stared deep into each other's eyes for several moments, and then she bent forward again to give him a longer more passionate kiss.

Luis wrapped his arms around her slender body and pulled her tightly to him. Mahara eased away holding her hand up in a "Stop" motion. Luis stopped as commanded. Mahara then immersed her hands into the water, quickly finding his erect penis. She stroked and rubbed him until he squirmed to keep up with her pace. As she sensed he was about to climax, she straddled his hips and lowered herself down onto him, guiding him into her gently with her hands. The oily water helped him easily slide deep inside her. Luis moaned with pleasure. Mahara began slowly and began gyrating her hips. She braced herself on the side of the tub and started pumping up and down on him, each time with more force and a tighter squeeze. Luis cupped her silken breasts with both hands. He wanted this feeling to last forever, but couldn't hold himself any longer and convulsed in a massive orgasm that seemed to never end. Mahara eased herself down and rested against his chest. He was still hard and pulsating inside her. She tenderly kissed his exhausted face repeatedly with little short pecks until the spasms subsided and his erection went limp.

They rested in their embrace for a long time enjoying the warm water and each other's embrace.

After a long lazy time, Mahara opened the drain to let the water out.

She quickly got a very large towel from a compartment next to the tub and they wrapped it around both of their bodies. They stepped out of the tub together, snugly wrapped in the soft towel. While still wrapped in the massive towel, Mahara began the soothing rubdown to dry off Luis. He did the same to her.

Now dry, Mahara took his hand again and led him to the oversized bed. They sat down together on the side, kissed and embraced. She gently pulled his head down her chest and pushed his face into her lap, spreading her legs wide. He did not resist. Luis instinctively knew what she meant and what she wanted. His tongue was well trained if not often used. He called on all his past, but limited experiences. To his surprise she quickly climaxed, moaning and groaning softly as she writhed in ecstasy from his tender touch. She firmly held his head there demanding more. He willingly gave it to her.

They spent three and a half hours together, each taking turns bringing the other to climax. Luis lost count after five orgasms for himself and eleven for her. It was amazing—fantastic.

This experience with Mahara was really unique. He had forgotten that sex could be soft, sensual and beautiful when freely and honestly shared between two gifted people willing and able to please the other. He thought he had lost interest in love and romance, but he knew that this time together with Mahara was special—one he would never forget.

* * *

Luis jerked himself back to reality. He acknowledged Abu'l's gesture of hospitality and gladly requested Mahara again. She genuinely smiled when he held out his hand to her. To his surprise she spoke. "Welcome, Luis."

Abu'l chuckled. "She has been taking English lessons for two months. She hopes you are pleased." Her accent was unmistakably Arabic, and it was obvious she was trying hard to please him.

Luis didn't know what to say. "That's great," was the best he could do at the moment.

"Take your time. Enjoy yourself. We can get to our business in the morning. My servants will come and get you from the guest room at 9:30 tomorrow," instructed Abu'l, meaning every word.

Mahara and Luis took their leave from Abu'l with a slight bow and left the room hand-in-hand. Luis was eager to repeat the experience of last time, and the spring in his step confirmed it.

He was not disappointed. Mahara was as wonderful as before. They experimented with countless positions, all of which her agile body and acrobatic skills made even more thrilling and enjoyable. She could bend and contort into unimaginable positions. But each time, she was careful to make sure Luis could get into her or otherwise receive sexual pleasure.

Mahara proudly displayed her newfound, but limited language skills. "We kiss now," "Touch me here," "You like this?" were among other simple words and phrases. Luis quickly noticed that she didn't use any crude four-letter words, disgusting body part names, or anything else that might seem vulgar and trampy. This girl had class.

As Mahara helped Luis leisurely get dressed, she said in her now familiar clipped English, "Mahara yours now."

Luis looked at her with surprise and skepticism, but didn't respond.

"I go with you." She tried to repeat her thought.

"Uh, sure. That's great." He smiled with an apprehensive grin, still not exactly sure what she was trying to tell him.

Mahara returned the smile showing perfect white teeth and twinkling eyes.

As promised, promptly at 9:30 a servant appeared and escorted Luis and Mahara back to Abu'l who was now perched on a massive chair at the end of a long table. Another expanse of food, wine, gleaming silver and gorgeous flowers adorned the table before him.

"Ah, I see you are well rested." extolled Abu'l with a wink.

"Yes, thank you. I am."

Abu'l made a shooing motion with his hand in the direction of the waiting Mahara, who immediately bowed and backed out of the room.

"Mahara likes to please you. Has she done well?" inquired Abu'l with genuine interest.

Luis was always uncomfortable talking about his sexual encounters. "Uh, sure." He tried to limit his response.

"Good. She is yours to keep." said Abu'l matter-of-factly as he reached for his large wine goblet.

"What do you mean, she is mine?"

"She is yours to keep and do with as you choose. She is my gift to you." Luis stared at Abu'l. The dumbfounded look on his face was obvious.

"It is simple. Here in my country when a friend is pleased with something, the owner gives it to him in honor of that friendship. Besides, Mahara asked me to do it."

"You mean that if I admired one of your paintings you would give it to me?"

"Yes, of course," responded Abu'l without looking up from his fork-full of salad.

Luis slumped back in his seat, stunned. He liked what Mahara and he had together—but to own her.

CHAPTER ELEVEN

The Weissman Home
Alexandria, VA
Friday, Early March
6:22 p.m.

Harvey tried to explain the events of the day that Suzanne might not yet know about. He wasn't sure if he was getting through. She sat bolt upright, primly at the table, hands folded neatly in her lap. Ankles crossed, knees together. Staring straight at her husband with saucer eyes. No blinking. Occasionally, she would nod or glance at Richard. Otherwise she seemed like she was in another world.

As she listened as attentively as she could, the shock and fear of having an accused assassin sitting in her own kitchen slowly subsided. She was calmer now. At least as calm as anyone could be sitting across the table from a man wanted for attacking the President—someone the entire country was looking for. Her first impulse was to call the Police or the FBI, but she resisted the temptation not knowing exactly why. Perhaps it was her investigative reporter instincts. Maybe Harvey was getting through. There may be a story here—possibly an exclusive. She had to find out more. Then she would consider turning him in.

Suzanne tried desperately to make sense of all Harvey was telling her. She knew what she had to do. She would listen to Harvey, digest what he was saying and then make up her own mind. She alone would try to make sense of how, if in fact Richard was set up. How the body count discrepancy fit into this mess. What did Richard's steadfast proclamation of innocence mean, if anything? Guilty people shout their innocence to the rafters. Could she, or even should she believe Richard? She believed nothing as fact until she was absolutely certain. Lots of questions flashed through her mind—few answers readily developed.

Should she be taking notes? Would Harvey let her tape-record any of this? Why is Harvey even confiding in her about this? A dozen more unanswered questions screamed from her overloaded brain. She still had no answers, only a deep inner sense that Harvey wanted something from her. She was right.

"Suzanne, what do you think about all of this?" inquired Harvey after a pause in his dizzying dissertation.

Suzanne was startled from her confusing and muddled thoughts. Harvey never confided in her about his other cases, or asked for advice. And he had represented some real kooks in the past. They never had intimate pillow talk about secret details of what the other was doing. She maintained her strict journalist-source confidentiality and he did the same with his attorney-client privilege. It wasn't that they distrusted each other, but rather a compelling inner need to be true to their own professional ethics. They were comfortable with that arrangement even after seven happy years of marriage. Even though the confidentiality issue arose several times before, both respected the other's position and quickly put any hurt feelings behind them. It never came between them in the privacy of their bedroom, or even over casual conversation at the dinner table.

"I don't know," she stammered blankly after a long hesitation. Her head was still spinning with her million unanswered questions.

Harvey is now excited and animated. He is caught up in the thrill of a desperate client that he can really help, and at the same time thrust his name into the public spotlight. Any lawyer worth his salt would feel this way if they were in Harvey's shoes. Harvey talks with his hands when he gets this way. Suzanne generally ignores his dramatic gesturing.

With eyes wide and arms flailing, Harvey bursts forward. "Suzanne, Richard is in serious personal danger. He needs our help. He has a wife who's expecting"; a rehearsed pause for dramatic effect. "But most of all, I believe he is innocent."

Richard rolled his eyes and looked at the ceiling. This from a man who only a few hours before was ready to feed him to the street thugs. *This guy is either a really good actor, or he did change his mind.*

"What can we do?" Suzanne queried bewilderedly.

"We can find out who framed Richard," said Harvey as he sat back in his chair exasperated at his wife's lack of shared excitement.

"How? How can we help him? The best criminal minds in the government have already started their investigation. Do they think he was framed?" she snapped.

"Nooo…" she mocked, drawing out the simple word. Now standing with hands on hips, tilting menacingly toward her husband.

Suzanne was back in control of all her faculties and thinking clearly for the first time in an hour.

"Look, Suzanne. The FBI does not have the information we have. They don't have Richard," shot back Harvey, up to the challenge of his wife's arguments.

Harvey and Suzanne often picked little fights with each other. They enjoyed challenging the strength of each other's character and will. They teased and pushed each other to extreme limits, verbally jabbing and jousting as they tried to change the others point of view, to draw out more details, to clarify reasoning or just to make a point. Neither ever argued just to be mean or vindictive. And all was forgiven and forgotten when the arguing ended.

They actually made a good team. This verbal combat made them both think about, and more importantly, justify their own position. They had argued about buying, and then furnishing this house, about when to buy a new car, and other issues facing every married couple. The facts and issues were always placed squarely before them. The pros and cons thoroughly discussed and dissected. It did not matter if one of them actually won any of these little skirmishes. Both were star debaters on their respective college teams. What mattered to both Harvey and Suzanne was that each respected the other, and they complimented each other when eventually coming to a mutual agreement. After a few minutes of this bantering and posturing, they usually found some common ground they both could live with. Neither ever kept score. Neither expected to win one time because they lost last time. Each verbal battle was decided on its own merits.

"They will soon enough." Suzanne was playing the fatalist.

"Why? Are you going to turn him in?" jibed Harvey only half seriously.

Richard was becoming tense and uncomfortable. He didn't understand what was going on. He had no way of knowing that both Harvey and Suzanne were in a familiar dance that should eventually benefit him once they finally agreed on an acceptable position—the best possible one for him.

The questions, accusations and counter attacks were coming in rapid succession from both sides. Neither Harvey nor Suzanne seemed willing to see the other's point of view. This time there was no middle ground. This time it wasn't working, and both reluctantly sensed it. Richard just watched and listened without a clue about what was happening.

Finally Harvey had enough. He seemingly cracked, and slammed his fist on the table. Glasses jiggled, ice cubes sloshed around and coke spilled. Suzanne sat down quickly. Richard immediately jerked around from blankly staring at the far wall to glare intently at Harvey.

"Suzanne. Will you do one little thing for me? For Richard?" he appealed in a surprisingly calm tone. Suzanne busied herself with wiping up the mess.

"I can't promise anything. Tell me what it is you want me to do, and then I'll let you know." Suzanne's nose was in the air as she looked away and defied Harvey to convince her. They both knew he hadn't done so thus far.

"OK. Fair enough." Harvey had no other choice.

Harvey jumped from his chair and bolted across the kitchen to his briefcase. Quickly opening it, he rummaged around until he found his yellow legal pad filled with almost indecipherable scribbling.

Harvey returned to his seat and began flipping pages, scanning each before moving on to the next. Harvey abruptly stopped turning pages and carefully reread the one he was currently staring at. Suzanne and Richard just watched and waited.

"Richard, correct me if I got this wrong," he muttered without looking up or even expecting a response. "There were ten of you in the trailer early this morning. You got sick, probably drugged, and left before the President spoke. That leaves nine people. Only eight bodies were found in the trailer. Right so far?"

"Yes, that's correct."

"OK. Suzanne, can you find out the names of the victims in the trailer?"

"I don't know. I do have a few sources that might know before the families are notified, and then released to the press." She was curious, but not yet convinced.

"Good, will you please try to get them?"

"Why? What difference does it make who died in the trailer? Maybe the police count was wrong. Maybe the information already provided by the cops was intentionally wrong. You know misinformation—it's done all the time." Suzanne did not fully grasp the significance of this fact and was now playing devil's advocate. She was not yet convinced it was even a fact. She had not taken the logical next step as Harvey already leaped over.

Being careful not to sound condescending, Harvey continued to explain his theory in soft measured tones. "It is very likely that if there were nine people still in the trailer when Richard left to go back to his hotel, and only eight bodies were found, that the ninth person may have had something to do with the assassination attempt. At worst, he may know something about the killings of the Sterling guys. Most likely, he may have even killed the other eight and framed Richard. At the very least he had some involvement in the assassination attempt, the eight deaths and the framing of Richard."

Richard was frantically bobbing his head up and down as he looked from Harvey to Suzanne then back at Harvey.

Suzanne sat silently for a long moment and pondered all of this. Her mind raced again as she mentally pieced the puzzle together.

Her investigative reporter instinct kicked in. She turned and talked rapidly to Richard. "Are you sure about all of this? The number of co-workers present when you left the trailer?"

"Absolutely positive. We couldn't have conducted the demonstration with less than nine people. All nine stations were manned as they should be when I left."

"How can you be sure? You said yourself that you were drugged."

"Each man was given specific instructions by me to proceed. They each knew their particular jobs, and had trained for months to perform them well. I was the supervisor of the entire operation. My assistant, Luis, actually manned the overseeing position. I did not. Had I stayed, I would have been only an observer. I was the only one that was unnecessary. Don't misunderstand, I played an important Management role, but I was not involved in the hands-on operation of the RPV. I'm positive all nine were in the trailer when I left."

Turning quickly in her seat. "Harvey, don't you think the FBI will figure this out?" Suzanne was now in complete control. Harvey learned long ago not to interfere when she started her head-on charge. The signals were obvious to him.

"The FBI will barrel along the path of least resistance. If they think Richard is guilty, they will search for evidence to prove it. They will not, I repeat, will not give much credence to any evidence that points to someone else until that evidence is either so overwhelming or they are forced under extreme high level pressure to do so. Legally, that is called exculpatory evidence, and prosecutors hate it. They do not like to be embarrassed. Once they get their teeth into a suspect, they never let go. Biases established under extreme circumstances are hard to overcome. And, careers are at stake in high-profile cases, so they hold on even tighter."

"Sure. Like the Oklahoma City bombing by Timothy McVay. Theodore Kaczynski, the Unabomber. OJ. How many Americans don't trust Arabs or Muslims after the attack on the Twin Towers." Suzanne paused to contemplate her next query. "Then it is fair to assume that the Feds might ignore the body count discrepancy or somehow explain it away."

"Probably." Harvey quickly responded, relieved Suzanne was now finally on the same wavelength.

Harvey interjected, "Maybe they don't even know there is a discrepancy."

"Let me make a few calls. If this pans out, I may be able to help."

"Thanks Hon," Harvey wheezed, exhausted, and felt he won this one. Richard too was relieved.

* * *

"Jim, hello. This is Suzanne from the Post. How are you? ... I'm fine. Thanks for asking." Suzanne and Jim Spartan engaged in idle chitchat for a few minutes. They each apologized for not keeping in touch and made a lunch date for next Thursday, agreeing on Luigi's in Arlington. They both liked Italian.

"Listen, Jim, I'm thinking about doing an in-depth story about the tragedy this morning. I might focus on the poor guys slaughtered in the trailer. They were just innocent victims of some crazy man's fantasy. I don't think they should be forgotten? Don't you agree?"

Suzanne winked seductively at Harvey. He smiled back. They both knew that little white lies and half-truths go a long way in investigative reporting circles. Suzanne had expertly cast out the bait and was patiently waiting to hook her fish and reel in her catch. It didn't work as easily this time.

"Uh, Suzanne, I don't know about that." Jim was skeptical, and he covered himself deftly. "Those names aren't available to the public just yet."

"Now Jim, I am not the public, am I? What if I promise not to publish anything until you guys officially release the names to the Press?"

"Why don't I promise to FAX you the names the moment they are released?" Jim countered, mimicking her tone.

Suzanne was coy, and anticipated just such a response. She cooed back in her sweetest voice, "I want to beat the other reporters to the story. I need some time to put together a biography of each of these poor souls. I want to memorialize the tragedy their families are facing."

Silence on Jim's end of the phone. He wasn't moved.

"Jim." Suzanne was now more stern. "You owe me. Who was it that fed you the information about a certain US Senator, who will remain unnamed, that allowed your boss at Justice to take all the credit for busting the un-named Senator for soliciting sex from his male pages? Who, Jim? Who?"

Suzanne was tough. She knew how the game was played, and she was very good at it. When one tactic didn't work, go to plan "B."

More silence.

"Jim? Hello. Are you there?" Suzanne looked at the receiver, and then returned it to her ear.

"I'm here, Suzanne." Jim finally replied knowing he owed her big-time, but was still torn by his own ethics.

"Look, we've been ordered to keep this very quiet. I shouldn't even be talking to you about this. No leaks of any kind. I just can't do it."

Suzanne was quick on her feet. She snatched the papers from Harvey and returned to Jim on the other end of the phone.

"If I read a name to you and tell you that he died in the trailer, will you answer "yes" or "no" to each name?"

More hesitation and silence as Jim pondered this turn of events. Jim knew he owed Suzanne a big favor. He desperately wanted to repay her, if only to avoid future encounters like this one. He began to rationalize. If she already knows the names, what harm is there in telling her if that person died in the trailer or not? Besides, those names will be released in a day or so anyway—maybe even in a few hours.

"OK, Suzanne. But only if you promise not to publish the names or anything about them or their families until Justice officially releases the list. Promise? And by the way, how did you get the names anyway?"

Suzanne ignored the question.

"Certainly, Jim. I promise." Suzanne fully intended to keep her promise.

Jim knew Suzanne would rather go to jail than reveal a source. She'd done it before—once over night, and once for two days.

"And, Suzanne, you can never reveal where you got this information." Jim queried just to be sure, and to reinforce his point.

"Of course not. You know me better than that." Suzanne was defiant about the threat to her reputation. Her ethics were impeccable.

Harvey and Richard sat in silence, staring at her across the kitchen as Suzanne worked her magic. Suzanne started reading the names in a clipped cadence, pausing only long enough for Jim to respond. She placed a check mark next to each name that Jim answered "yes" to. She purposely read Richard's name fourth so as to not draw any suspicion to him. When she read his name Jim did not respond immediately.

"Jim. Richard Feinstein. Dead?" she repeated.

"We don't know. He is the only suspect, and we are looking for him now? Every police officer in the country probably has a copy of his picture by now. We will find him sooner or later if he is alive. Then if I have my way, we will hang the bastard by his government-hating balls from the top of the Washington Monument." Jim could be intense and quite descriptive when his passions moved him.

Suzanne turned to the other two men and winked, even though this time they had no clue as to why.

"OK. Next name." She continued methodically through the entire list.

"Thanks Jim. I guess we're even now. See you on Thursday, and don't be late." she cajoled him.

Suzanne hung up the phone and slowly returned to her seat at the table. She stared at the check marks on Harvey's list and was deep in thought. Harvey was familiar with this look. Suzanne was on the brink of a major revelation. Both men waited anxiously for her to speak.

"Jim stated emphatically that Richard is the only suspect. They do not know if he is alive or dead. They are conducting an intensive search for him as we speak." She mercifully did not repeat what Jim would do to a private part of Richard's anatomy when they found him.

Continuing without looking up from her papers. "Jim also confirmed that these men are dead." Then she slowly read the names of the eight men she had checked off.

"Luis's name is not on the list of the dead?" Richard blurted out in shocked disbelief. He immediately knew what that implied. Suzanne nodded affirmatively.

These three people were thrust together in a most unlikely and unnerving set of events. They looked cautiously at each other, now united in the belief that Richard was telling the truth.

All three knew what this information meant. They also knew that they were the only ones who knew this at the moment. But what to do about it? How long will it take the FBI or Secret Service to figure this out—if ever? How should this trio proceed? Could Suzanne and Harvey help Richard? Both were unsure.

CHAPTER TWELVE

Luxury Penthouse
Tehran, Iran
Sunday, Early March
9:17 a.m. Local Time

The ample feast was finished. The servants had cleared the dishes. Coffee and light finger foods were placed before them. Abu'l was pleasant and full of conversation about a variety of subjects. Luis was churning inside, but he held his tongue and politely listened, occasionally offered a comment. He was reluctant to confront Abu'l. Luis was justifiably afraid.

Abu'l finally broached the subject.

"Luis, we must alter our schedule. The imperialist US Government is near chaos. If we act swiftly, Allah and the teachings of Islam will prevail. I will then control the American soul."

Luis looked up from his dainty china cup of rich dark coffee. He hoped this was coming. Here was his opportunity to speak his mind and not be immediately decapitated by Abu'l's henchmen.

"Abu'l, I did my part. In fact, I did more than you asked, and I now am in serious trouble myself with the American authorities."

"My friend, don't get so angry. Your food will not digest." Abu'l was evasive about the deception. Luis persisted.

"I was supposed to put a sleeping drug in the coffee. A drug your men gave me. Now eight of my friends are dead. Why, Abu'l? Why did they have to die? Why did you set me up?"

Luis hoped for an answer, but got none. Abu'l went back to his cakes.

Luis decided to take another tact. "You paid me well. I did my job. It is over. There is nothing more I can do. I can't show my face anywhere in the United States. Doing so would raise too much suspicion and I might get arrested. If the Police figure out my role, they will probably uncover your involvement. So by protecting me, you protect yourself. Surely, you now realize that."

"Certainly I do. But, you work for me now. Your job is over when I say it is over," glared Abu'l, unaccustomed to being confronted or questioned.

"Besides," he continued in a calmer tone, "You are not going to the United States. You are going to London."

"London? London, England? What do you expect me to do there?" Luis was both annoyed and surprised. He wanted out. If he could leave right now with Mahara, he would.

Abu'l was not quite so accommodating. He went on to explain exactly what he expected of Luis; who to meet, where, when. And finally, what Luis was to do in London. Luis expressed his hesitancy. Abu'l ignored him. "One of my men will accompany you and Mahara until your job is finished." And the conversation was finalized.

This was more cloak and dagger stuff. Luis didn't trust Abu'l, but at least Mahara was not being held hostage to force him into following orders. Luis was not relishing his newly acquired role as an international terrorist. He never expected to get this involved, or for the stakes to be so high. In fact, he hated himself for what he had done. He was such a fool. His lack of family ties, his lost friendships, and his self-indulgence after Catherine's death were all a factor. He lost his focus and even his will to be himself—at least what he was before. Being with Mahara again had yanked him back. Something inside snapped him back to reality. His entire attitude towards life was now different. He had almost instantly returned to the sensitive and caring man of days and years long ago. He felt better with this persona. But, he had done some terrible things.

Even though he never imagined it would happen, he could never forget that he was, at least indirectly, responsible for the deaths and injuries of many US officials, dozens of people he never met, and eight of his co-workers. He was personally responsible. It was as if he had lined them up and shot them in the head himself. It didn't matter that he was lied to, deceived, manipulated, tricked. He had done nothing to stop it from happening. He was guilty and he knew it, and he couldn't take it back or turn back the clock.

His reward for all the death and injury was Mahara and $500,000 stashed safely in a Caribbean Bank, neither of which he was willing to relinquish. Abu'l was right. He was bought and paid for. No better than a common hooker, and this time he was the one to get screwed—royally.

Luis knew his options were very limited. He could do as Abu'l demanded, or leave the penthouse headless in an unmarked plain cloth coffin.

He decided to try and reason with Abu'l. "How do you know the President will travel to London so soon after this tragedy?"

"It's simple, my friend. The trip has been planned for weeks. The President must show the American people he is not being held hostage by terrorists. Remember Jimmy Carter and Iran? He stayed in Washington and lost the election. Your President will not make the same mistake. Bush returned immediately to Washington after the successful attacks on 3,000 Americans, but this is different. Mr. Chandler is a man of honor. He will abide by his commitment to his friends." Abu'l went back to his snacks as Luis slumped back into the gold flowered cushions.

* * *

Earlier That Night

Mahara was a little surprised when Luis kept losing interest in their love play. He went suddenly limp right in the middle of an otherwise fabulous blowjob. Try as she might she could not re-arouse him until many minutes of inactivity had passed. Or he would unexplainably become absolutely motionless even as Mahara tried to maintain the frantic rhythm and gyrations that sent him into a frenzy only a few short seconds earlier. Luis was in another world. At times, she didn't exist. He wasn't there.

Her English was not very good, but she tried to converse with him. "Luis. I not please you?" she would sadly inquire with pouting lips and fluttering round eyes.

"No. No, it's not you. I've got other things on my mind."

Mahara only stared, her cute head tilted provocatively. The language barrier was still a problem between them. She did not fully comprehend, especially when Luis spoke quickly.

Luis sensed she didn't understand. To his own surprise, he felt a great need to console her. Her wrapped his arms around her and held her tight. Their bodies damp with the perspiration of their earlier exertion. They cuddled. She nuzzled even closer. He stroked her long straight hair. Mahara lay quietly in his embrace for a long peaceful time. She was totally unaware of the beasts snarling and tearing through his thoughts.

Mahara was soothed. She understood only that he still wanted only her. She knew of nothing else, nor did she care.

Luis was still deep in thought. The monsters roared. His mind flashed back. He quickly and sickeningly relived the vivid events of the past 24 hours. He gasped and gagged. He wanted to puke. Mahara held him tight, trying to calm whatever it was that provoked this terror. She feared for the worst, not knowing what to think.

* * *

Luis knew he must do as Abu'l demanded. To do otherwise would be suicide for him, and probably death for Mahara as well.

Choking back his disgust, and clearing his head of the images of death and destruction, Luis formulated a plan of his own.

First he must try to get Abu'l to disclose more of his "Secret War Plan." Perhaps Luis could somehow sabotage it and try to make things right, knowing he could never undo what was already done.

Second, he must try to keep himself, and especially Mahara, as safe as possible. She is guilty of only doing what her culture expects of her—

nothing more. She should not be harmed. His personal safety was secondary. He was a murderer, at least an unwitting co-conspirator to murder. Eventually, he would be tracked down and either killed on the spot, or executed after a showy trial back in a US Federal Court.

Third, he must convince Abu'l that his services were worth more than Abu'l had already paid. Maybe with enough money he could buy their safety and try to find some place to hide.

Satisfied with himself, he put his plan in motion in reverse order.

"Abu'l, you of all people know that nothing worth having comes cheap."

"But, of course," not immediately picking up on Luis's meaning.

"Than you will certainly realize that I am indispensable to your operation." Luis refused to call it a Secret War.

Abu'l was now listening intently. "Yes, go on."

"My services are worth ten times what you paid me." Luis had no idea how much an assassin's services were worth to a wealthy motivated Arab Sheik, but what the hell—shoot for the moon.

"Then why did you agree to work for less?" Abu'l called his bluff.

Luis swallowed hard. He knew Abu'l could order him killed on the spot. "I agreed to put sleeping drugs in the coffee. I agreed to get you copies of the RPV schematics. I agreed to leave your little note implicating Richard. Nothing more. That is not the role of an assassin, and that was all I was paid to do."

"So you did." Abu'l admired a man with guts, even if the man was challenging his authority, his honor. A sinister smirk crossed his lips.

"I now am responsible for the deaths of eight of my friends, the death and injury of countless others, and the framing of my boss. I never expected any of that to happen, and you never told me the full extent of what I was doing. Now you want me to go to London, meet one of your men there, exchange G-d knows what, complete your mission, and then simply disappear. I am, or soon will be, a wanted international terrorist. More Americans will recognize my face and know my name than Bin Laden's. My life won't be worth a plug nickel unless I can buy my own safety." Luis eased back in his chair hoping and praying that he was convincing.

Abu'l rubbed his thin immaculately trimmed beard pensively. "You are right, my friend. I did not tell you everything, but I did not lie. Tell you what. I will deposit another $2,000,000 into your account. When the job in England is accomplished I will deposit another $2,500,000. That will be the 10 times more value you seek. Correct?"

Abu'l needed Luis, and he needed an incentive for Luis to complete his mission in this Secret War. Abu'l knew money was a great motivator.

Luis didn't expect Abu'l to be so generous. "Agreed, but there is one more thing, and it won't cost you anything extra." Luis was pushing, trying to catch Abu'l in a talkative mood.

Abu'l grinned. He was willing to do small things that didn't cost money. "What is it my friend? What else do you want?"

"I am unclear about your dreams and aspirations. Why are you so dead set about taking over America? How can you do that anyway? Their form of government prevents outsiders from gaining any control." Luis chose his words carefully. He had to make Abu'l think he was really interested, and not hint at his real motive for asking.

Abu'l was quite forthcoming. He saw no harm in sharing his grand scheme with his ally, especially since Luis was now such an integral part of his overall Secret War.

"It is quite simple. The real power in America comes from money. The Jews have all the money, and they control the government. Hitler knew this, and so does the contemporary Germans, Bin Laden, Castro, the Japanese and now also the Chinese."

Luis sat dumbfounded. He was sure Abu'l had no idea what he was talking about. Abu'l was living in a fantasy world filled with hatred and distrust of anyone different than himself. Luis had thought Abu'l hated western ideas and ideology. He was sadly mistaken. Abu'l was an anti-Semite, a middle-eastern religious fanatic—a full-blown bigot; pure and simple. Intolerance was a way of life in his polluted and distorted world.

But Abu'l was also immensely wealthy, and with his fortunes he could force his personal demagoguery and hatred on others. Impoverished idealistic young Arab men and women were eager to take up the battle cries, strap bombs on their backs and kill as many non-believers as they could. To them, their cause was just, and you fight your enemies any way you can.

Abu'l continued with his diatribe while Luis tried desperately to mask his disgust. "The President and the people around him are controlled by big business. The banks own the big businesses, and the Jews own the banks and the newspapers. The President is a puppet of the Jews."

Luis forced his way through the illogical gibberish, failing to comprehend anything Abu'l said. Not knowing what else to say, Luis just pressed farther. "The government is automatically changed every four years when we elect a new president. All senators and congressmen regularly stand for re-election. How can you control that?"

Luis was really confused. How could the assassination of a current sitting president benefit Abu'l? He asked exactly that question. Abu'l by now was up to the challenge. He never missed an opportunity to convert a non-believer.

"It is precisely the normal change of presidential command that I will use to my advantage."

Luis stared blankly. His mind raced, trying to comprehend the incomprehensible. How do you hold a rational conversation with an irrational person? Abu'l surged forward with his blurry illogical arguments founded on untruths and blind hatred.

"If the President dies, then the Vice President automatically takes over. Succession, you Americans call it. If the Vice President dies, then the Speaker of the House succeeds him."

"So what?" Luis shrugged and flung his arms in the air, totally unaware of the Constitutional laws of Presidential succession.

"Because of William Tyler Post?"

"Who?"

"The Speaker of the House. William Tyler Post. Don't you know who the Speaker of the House is? You should study your own government, my friend."

"OK." Luis said with a touch of trepidation, playing along, hoping Abu'l would explain the significance of this fact—a fact of which Luis was not entirely certain.

"The Secret Service assigns men to guard the President, Vice President and members of their family. The Speaker of the House is not assigned any Secret Service Protection unless he travels overseas or is actually threatened, of course."

"Uh huh." Luis nodded, thoroughly confused, unable to even guess where Abu'l's seemingly tortured logic would take them.

"Mrs. William Tyler Post is a guest of mine at one my villas."

"What? You kidnapped his wife?" Luis was shocked, but not surprised.

"Kidnapped is such a harsh word. I prefer to say we persuaded her to stay with us while her husband forever changes the American Government and abolishes the imperialistic Jews from power," pooh-poohed Abu'l as if this was of no importance.

Luis's mind did a back-flip. Did Abu'l really have Mrs. Post? Was Mr. Post willing to co-operate? "G-d, what have I gotten myself into?" he thought to himself. He tried to make sense of all the wild crap he had just heard, and hoped Abu'l would continue with more specifics, and not just the gross generalities like his past remarks.

Luis knew he had to get control of himself, and not let on that he was planning to double-cross Abu'l. He had to be extra-careful. He took a deep breath, exhaled slowly and proceeded cautiously.

Luis was slowly putting the pieces together. "So, after you assassinate the President and Vice President, Mr. Post automatically becomes President. Right? You then force Mr. Post into passing legislation that will eliminate the Jews just like Hitler tried to do?"

Abu'l was impressed. Luis could have won an Oscar for this performance.

"Again with the harsh words. I will strongly suggest that Mr. Post cooperate. You know, for the good of his wife."

Luis doubted that one man could actually control the entire United States. He was terrified that one man could scare the hell out of an entire country. Luis probed further.

"So you intend to try to kill the President again?"

"But of course. And I must do it before he appoints another Vice President. We have a few weeks. America moves so slowly in these matters. Doing away with both the President and the Vice President at the same time is quite difficult. We failed at our last attempt. I prefer the simplest approach."

Luis was really getting peeved that Abu'l kept including him in his Secret War.

"Will you use an RPV again?" asked Luis, seriously interested in his response.

"Certainly. They have proved to be ineffective in the way we originally planned. But they can still serve my purposes. I have men who can strike at any time and at any place. They will use an RPV remotely guided by you."

"Me? How can I do that? I've never piloted an RPV before." Luis was stunned.

Abu'l ignored Luis's comments. "The RPV will be loaded with much more explosive power than the last time. You only have to fly it into Air Force One when the President arrives in London for his European Summit in a few days. A 747 is a large target. Surely even you can fly an RPV into something that big."

More hired hit-men. More RPV's. More explosives. More involvement. More death. Luis felt sick, but he gathered himself and pushed on. He wanted—no, he needed more information. His own plan was taking shape, but he still needed a few details cleared up.

"What about Sterling and Associates? Certainly the FED's will investigate and connect you to them?"

"How can they? I own Sterling and Associates through private international holding companies. It would take a team of investigators years to discover my relationship." Abu'l was confident of this. His few trusted business advisors and high paid international lawyers had assured him that the international corporate maze they set up was nearly impenetrable. Iranian companies owned Japanese companies. Japanese companies owned German companies. German companies owned Chinese and Caribbean companies, and they owned pieces of Sterling and Associates through a series of phony non-existent stockholders. There was literally no easy-to-follow paper trail to tie Abu'l to Sterling and Associates.

Luis reflected on his first encounter with officials at Sterling and Associates. He was looking for a job after he got over the depression caused by losing Catherine. He saw an ad in the Orlando Sentinel Employment Section. Luis had saved the ad. It read:

"Great opportunity for a young man with experience designing and testing RPV's. Some travel required, possibly for extended periods. For National Security reasons, no family members are allowed to travel with you. Engineering degree required. Send resume with salary history to Orlando Sentinel Box Number 3425."

Luis immediately responded to the ad. He had no family. Traveling sounded exciting. Besides, his experience four years ago at Cape Kennedy with RPV's was just getting stale. Here he could dust off all his old notes, and at the same time get his life back in order again. He didn't care about anyone or anything. He just wanted to get back to work somewhere, doing something. He didn't really care what it was he would be doing. His personal life didn't matter anymore. This job would be perfect.

Luis related this to Abu'l. To Luis's surprise, Abu'l was intimately familiar with the details of his being hired. "When The Orlando Sentinel forwarded eighteen resumes to our people, I began having the three most promising candidates checked out. Two of the three were you and the Jew, Richard Feinstein."

"So that's why it took about six weeks for Sterling and Associates to call me in for an interview?"

"Yes. We had trouble finding out what you were doing for about a three-month period. Finally, we discovered the tragedy you suffered and we stopped searching. That is when we talked to you. We had already hired the Jew."

"We hired the Jew for two reasons. First, he did have admirable experience with RPV's. We couldn't find anyone else. We needed that type of expertise. So we settled and adjusted our 'Secret War Plan'. Which leads to the second, and most important reason: a Jew would be implicated in the killings. I had planned for that from the outset. The Jew, Feinstein, offered me the opportunity to show the world that Jews are criminals." Abu'l was pleased with himself.

Luis believed him. "Then you know about Catherine?"

"Of course. We know everything about you and your lover. That is why we selected you. You had no family, no girl friend after Catherine died. Your attitude toward life showed that you didn't care if you got involved in, let's say, something others might call unsavory. In fact, that was the major criteria for hiring all of you, except the Jew, of course. No real family ties, and a willingness or lack of concern about being involved in secret activity."

"Than why were the others killed?"

"They were expendable. They had no families. They did their jobs, and no one misses them now."

Luis could only stare at Abu'l as he choked back the desperate need to vomit.

CHAPTER THIRTEEN

The Oval Office
Washington, D.C.
Friday, Early March
4:54 p.m.

The mood in the Oval Office was somber. This task is something no President looks forward to. Doc was putting the finishing touches on his address to the Nation about the horrific events of this day. He was reluctant to put any political spin into his heartfelt anger. He knew he had to be as truthful as possible, while at the same time not impede the just-started investigation. He must also reassure the country and the world that the United States is strong, its borders secure and could withstand any attack on it. That includes an attack on its leaders and elected officials, or on our fundamental ideals of life, liberty and the pursuit of happiness as granted to all Americans over two centuries ago by our founding fathers. The fundamental rights and liberties guaranteed to all citizens by the Constitution are safe and well protected by this government of the people.

The President was working alone. He had no new information from the Secret Service, the FBI or Homeland Security. Richard Feinstein was still the prime suspect, and he was still at large. On the bright side, if there was one, the death count had not increased, and some of the injured have left the hospital after treatment.

But by now, Doc's initial anger had given way to his "Prosecutor Instincts." He was becoming skeptical, and knew that new evidence could fall either way. There might be some very rational reasons for Richard Feinstein's actions—or he can be guilty as hell. Cooler heads and much more evidence were needed. Nothing less would satisfy the American public or the Courts.

In the end, Doc decided to not even mention Richard by name. The Press could do that all they wanted, but he saw no reason to condemn a man not yet found guilty by the very system Feinstein might be trying to overthrow—or might not. More time was needed for the investigation to run its course.

The President summoned Sarge to bat around the last few points before calling in the Video Crew to set up for the live telecast. The Networks and other media outlets had been notified that a Presidential Address to the Nation would occur at 9pm Eastern Standard Time, allowing for live broadcasts on the West Coast at a reasonable time in the late afternoon.

"Read this over" he said to Sarge as he handed the stack of papers across the desk.

"You going to implicate Feinstein?"

"Not by name. Let the Press run with that. If he is caught and charged with this, I don't see how he can ever get a fair trial with the intense Press coverage already. I don't see any reason to make that chore any worse."

"Don't get soft in your old age, Doc" Sarge chided as he turned his attention and his focus on the neatly typed papers. It was immediately obvious that Doc had made only a few changes; there were just a few scrawls here and there on each page.

"Your tribute to the men and women that were killed looks really good." smiled Sarge as he looked up after about 2 minutes of reading. There were still 3 more pages, and Sarge went back to work as Doc nodded his appreciation for the compliment but said nothing.

The two old friends were quiet as Sarge continued his reading and the President rocked rhythmically, looked at the ceiling, lost in his own thoughts.

Doc broke the silence. "Should I announce the selection of a panel to pick the next VP, or just say that I am in the process of doing so?"

Sarge dropped his arms with the papers to his lap and sucked in air. He knew this was coming and was prepared with an answer—as he always was. "It is important for the American People, and for that matter the whole World, to know that you are still in command and the head of Government, and the leader of the Free World. The American Government is functioning as it should, and that we, meaning this Administration elected by the American People will go on. Yes, we are temporarily disrupted by Henry's death, we mourn his loss and praise his service, but our Government has, can and will deal with this tragedy, and will do so within the Constitutional guidelines."

A pause for a response. When none came, Sarge continued "I suggest that you say that you are beginning the selection process, looking at and talking to several very well qualified individuals. I know you have only started thinking about some names, but we can't say that. Once you have made the final choice the Senate will use their Advice and Consent authority granted by the Constitution when that person goes before them. I also suggest that you make it very clear that you, and you alone make the final choice. We can't let our friends from across the Isle turn this into something they can use against us politically."

Doc was taking notes. "You're right. We just started making headway in mending fences. Whomever I choose, that person was not elected as VP, as President Ford was under Nixon. I will appoint him— or her. The only way the public will have a say is through their elected Senators."

Sarge's eyebrows rose dramatically at the hint of a woman VP. Several names flashed through his mind, but he said nothing.

A pause as each stared at the other. "Sarge, how long will this process take? We have Constitutional Succession, but I need a VP, and so do the American people."

"We can get a Short List together by tomorrow evening; start the vetting process in a day or so. We can begin inviting them to the White House within a few days, but I doubt you will be able to announce a selection before we leave for London. Remember, whomever you choose, that person will have to think it over, talk to their family, make arrangements to change jobs—all that takes time also."

"OK. Sounds like a plan. Get me a Short List by 4:00 tomorrow afternoon. After I review and approve it I'll decide what order we want them to come in."

"My staff is already working on it. Five or less names by 4 it is. Should I notify the Press Secretary?"

"Not yet. Any more comments on the speech?"

Sarge waved the papers dramatically. "Seems to capture how we all are feeling. You will come across as human, caring and in charge."

"Thanks. I'll buzz you in a few minutes."

"See ya." And Sarge stood, turned on his heel and left the way he came in.

* * *

The Oval Office
Washington, D.C.
Friday, Early March
8:27 p.m.

The 3-person video crew was finishing setting up the lights, the 2 tripods and the cameras. Two cameras were standard practice for a major Presidential address. If one failed, the other was ready and waiting. The lady who acted like the Crew Chief was busy lining up the viewfinder of each camera, careful to make sure the upper torso and head of the stand-in person sitting in the President's chair was properly centered. Once satisfied, she tightened down all the knobs locking each camera in position.

It is strictly understood that no exaggerated video movements were allowed during a Presidential address from the Oval Office. The cameraman was allowed to slowly zoom in or out, but not allowed to tilt or pan the camera. Any zooming was usually noted on the typed script given to the cameramen just before an address.

As the video crew collected their tools and prepared to leave the

Oval Office, Ms. Brenda Bennett watched with amused satisfaction. She was the Assistant to the President's personal Secretary, and as such got little notice. Performing seemingly mundane assignments like watching the Video Crew set up for an address from the Oval Office gave her personal satisfaction even if no one else noticed. Ms. Bennett had carefully observed all the activity, and mentally noted that all was as it should be. She'd done this before and knew what was expected.

After a quick look around to make sure, for a second time, that everything was in place, Ms. Bennett followed the 2 women and one man out of the Oval Office and closed the door behind her.

In her normal efficient manner, she neatly wrote out a note on a yellow Post-it that the Oval Office was set for the address. After carefully placing it on her boss's desk where it would be obviously seen, she turned smartly and went back to her own desk in a nearby small office.

* * *

Sarge followed Doc into the Oval Office seven minutes before the address was scheduled to begin. Since all three Networks, Fox, CNN and other Cable News Stations were broadcasting live, timing was critical. The two cameras in the Oval Office were hooked up to a complex Video system that fed the signals to the TV Stations while recording the entire production on high speed, high definition digital Video Recorders. The Networks did not have cameras of their own in the Oval Office. Rather, they relied in this cooperative method.

A woman Video Producer, the person who was in charge of the set-up earlier, and two Cameramen, one male and the other female, were busy with their preparations. Ms Bennett was primly seated on a far wall observing the activities. Sarge greeted her by name and Doc nodded in her direction as they entered. Ms. Bennett smiled back, sat up straighter and felt all warm and fuzzy inside—these very important men noticed her.

* * *

The Producer was also the Floor Manager. She stood directly behind the Video Prompter where the Presidential Address was loaded and ready to roll. Her headphones were covering her ears as she listened to another more senior Producer in the Control Room set up nearby. Both cameras were turned on and operating perfectly. The Floor Manager counted down in a strong clear voice; "10, 9, 8, 7, 6" then held up five fingers and silently curled each in turn as the seconds ticked off. At 1, the Presidential Seal flashed proudly on the screen and remained there for five seconds. Then she dramatically pointed directly to the President indicating he was cleared to speak soon.

The Presidents face appeared on the screen for two seconds as he waited for his cue. The Floor Manager nodded and mouthed "Go." Looking straight at the cameras, but reading confidently from the smoothly scrolling teleprompter, Doc started immediately. "My fellow Americans, it is with great sorrow that I must address you this evening. As most of you know from the ongoing news reports, our Government was attacked this morning. Our dedicated Vice President, several Cabinet Members and members of Law Enforcement from four States were also killed. Two heroic Secret Service Agents died doing their job of protecting others. Dozens more were injured. The thoughts and prayers of a strong, but saddened nation are with their families. The Press has been provided with their names and other personal information, all of which will be published over the next 24 hours or so. We as a nation mourn their loss, acknowledge their sacrifice and praise their service to our country. They will not be forgotten."

Changing his expression from compassionate to stern, Doc continued, "We do not know if this was a terrorist attack, or just an anti-American group trying to get our attention. The FBI, Secret Service and Homeland Security are working closely together on this most important Investigation. I am told that there is no, I repeat, no indication that another attack on American soil is imminent or even likely. It is too early to be absolutely certain, but from what we do know, there is no evidence that a foreign government has any involvement. I caution all Americans to be patient and not rush to any unfounded conclusions about this attack or who might be behind it, and I pledge to you that my Administration will disclose whatever we know as verifiable information becomes available."

Pausing again to collect his thoughts and take a breath, Doc proceeded, "This intense Investigation has just begun, and all the facts are not yet known or fully understood. I promise you, the American people, that whoever is behind this will be identified, hunted down and prosecuted to the fullest extent of the law. It is imperative that we all remain calm, and let the Law Enforcement Officers complete their investigation."

Doc took in a noticeable deep breath before continuing. "I can confidently assure the American People, and the entire World, that our Government is as strong as ever, functioning within the boundaries of the Constitution, and will continue to do so. We will remain a World Leader promoting democracy to all Freedom-seeking people throughout the World. As new information comes to light, we will share it with the Press. I trust they will in turn, share that information with the Public."

Smiling broadly into the camera, "We all have others in our lives that love us, and whom we love in return. Don't hesitate to give them a big Bear Hug. Life can be good, even great much of the time, but sometimes it tosses us a curve ball, shocks our senses and drains us of the desire to go on. We must remain strong, as a people and as a nation. Together, we can overcome this time of tragedy, senseless death and carnage. We are a proud, strong and resourceful nation. We should never forget the events of today, but we must move forward. Thank you for your time and attention. Good night to all, and G-d bless America."

The Floor Manager made a slicing motion across her throat, and the cameramen clicked off their equipment. Doc collected the papers he never looked down at while Sarge rushed over and shook hands with both Cameramen and the Floor Manager, thanking them for a job well done. Ms. Bennett rose and headed for the door as Doc called out to her. "Ms. Bennett. Thank you for your hard work. I know that pulling all of this together on short notice is very hard to do."

Ms. Bennett turned primly and smiled at the President. "Thank you, Mr. President. Just doing my job, Sir."

"Don't be so modest, Ms. Bennett. You earned the right to be proud of yourself. You did a good job, and I'm grateful."

"Yes, Sir. Thank you, Mr. President."

Once outside the Oval Office, and behind the closed door, Brenda stifled a scream and pumped her fist into the air. All was fine in her world.

CHAPTER FOURTEEN

Secret Service Headquarters
Washington, D.C.
Friday, Early March
4:35 p.m.

Carl Worthington convened the meeting of his dozen top aides and investigators. Several of them were summarily pulled from other assignments without notice.

"You all have a briefing file, and are aware of the urgency of this investigation."

Some of the men opened their files and flipped pages. Others, who already had a chance to glance at the papers, just kept staring at Carl.

"We have information suggesting that Richard Feinstein contacted a Rabbi here in DC. There also seems to be a lawyer involved. We need to identify and find the Rabbi and the lawyer."

Todd Levinston, a 12-year veteran of the Secret Service, interrupted Carl.

"Are we sure the Rabbi is from just DC proper and not the entire DC area?"

"No we are not sure. We do know that Feinstein could not have gotten very far, even by car or cab. We've already been to his hotel room, the Holiday Inn Crown Plaza. The bed was rumpled, but the maid thinks she had made it up around 10:30, give or take a 15 minutes. They don't keep accurate records of when the maids make up beds. We also have accounted for all the cars rented by Sterling. Feinstein didn't take any of them."

"OK. So what are we talking about here? How many synagogues?"

"Well, the phone book of an area surrounding DC, covering a 50 mile radius shows 18 synagogues. A further computer search lists 42 Rabbis."

"That shouldn't take very long. There are 12 of us here."

"The problem is the Jewish Sabbath, which starts in a few hours at sunset. The Orthodox Jewish Rabbis won't even answer the phones on the Sabbath. Neither will most of the Conservative Rabbis."

"Also, the pulpit Rabbis and their assistant Rabbis are preparing for Sabbath dinner and services, usually at their own homes. We will have a hard time getting a hold of them any time this evening." Jerry Schwartz, the lone Jewish investigator, was quick to add to the cumulative knowledge.

"Right. So, we have our work cut out for us."

A pause to gather his thoughts. "Jerry. Is there any way to narrow the search? What do we know about Feinstein anyway? Who would be the most likely for him to contact?"

"Generally speaking, the number of Reform Jews outnumbers Conservative Jews, who outnumber Orthodox Jews."

Carl looked at his computer printout again. "There are only two Orthodox synagogues on the list."

Using his finger to point as he counted, "Ten Reform, and six Conservative."

Jerry offered, "The odds are that most likely he is Reform, but possibly Conservative. It is unlikely that he is Orthodox—because of his chosen profession, but still possible. Also, he isn't wearing a Keepah, or head covering in his Security Badge photo, so it's likely he's not ultra religious. But Senator Joe Lieberman, an Orthodox Jew doesn't wear one in public—so who knows."

Carl surveyed the room, mentally assigning partners. "Jerry, you and Herb take the Conservative Synagogues and their Rabbis. Being Jewish may help you here." No one snickered at Carl's poor attempt at humor.

Carl proceeded to assign two teams to the Reform synagogues, one to the Orthodox, and the remaining two to the Rabbis not directly associated with a synagogue.

Then, a few more words from Carl about the urgency of their task. Several team members shook hands and made small talk about being assigned as partners with each other. Within minutes the papers were picked up and the room deserted.

Jerry and Herb had worked on several cases in the past, and got along well. Both were experienced investigators with impressive credentials. Jerry graduated third in his class from Columbia School of Law. Herb was a top investigator in the Navy before moving to the Secret Service seven years ago. Neither had ever interrogated a Rabbi in an official investigation before.

Herb was still not fully at ease with talking to a Rabbi on their Sabbath. He didn't understand their rituals and traditions, nor how an observant Jew behaves. Other than Jerry, Herb had little close contact with other Jewish people. He held no particular feelings toward them one-way or the other. Long ago as a boy of fifteen, he stopped going to Mass. He returned to church only once in the past 30 years to see his niece married. He was the epitome of religious tolerance. More accurately, he could care less what religion a person followed. He also never bothered to learn anything about any religion. To him, religion was a crutch, something believers used to make themselves feel better when they were in the dumps. As he saw it, hee just didn't need such phoniness.

"Look, Herb. Rabbis are just like everyone else. They are really just learned men who graduated from a Rabbinical School. Often, and because of their studies, some of them are more observant. That means they will not drive, light a fire, or turn on a light switch during the Sabbath. The Sabbath is a day of rest and a time to pray and study Torah. They are forbidden to do any work on the Sabbath. The Jewish Sabbath runs from Friday at sundown to Saturday at sundown. In fact, every Jewish day is sundown to sundown. During the Sabbath time, the more observant Jews only study and pray."

"So what do we do when their Sabbath starts? Do we stop the investigation because they are praying?"

"No. We can try to contact as many as we can in the next half hour by phone. After that, we can go to the synagogues and talk to the Rabbis after Friday night services. There is no prohibition against talking. We can only get to one, possibly two synagogues tonight. Then finish up after Saturday morning services tomorrow."

"There are Saturday Services too? OK! OK, but I don't know if this will work."

Neither did Jerry. Both men had experience with Preachers and Ministers refusing to talk about their congregants. Why would a Rabbi be any different?

Jerry divided the list in the easiest manner possible. He started at the top, and Herb at the bottom. Jerry would work his way down the list, Herb would work up from the bottom. They would call as many as they could in the next few minutes.

The first three phone calls by each man took fifteen minutes, mostly because the Rabbi's wives were very good at running interference for their husbands, especially just before Sabbath dinner.

"Hello. My name is Jerry Schwartz. I'm a Special Agent from the Secret Service. May I speak with Rabbi Moshe Stein, please?"

"I'm sorry. Rabbi Stein is unavailable. You can contact him at the Synagogue on Monday Morning after 9:00am. I can give you the phone number if you need it." Mrs. Stein was polite, but stern.

"Mrs. Stein. I must speak with your husband as soon as possible. It's very important."

"May I inquire what this is about? Perhaps I can relay a message."

"I'm afraid that I can't tell you the exact nature of why I am calling. But, I assure you it is very important that I speak to your husband personally, and as soon as possible."

Mrs. Stein was not convinced. She was getting annoyed. "This is a very awkward time, Mr. Schwartz. We are about to have our Shabbat dinner. It's almost sundown. The Shabbat prayers and candles cannot wait."

"I understand how late it is, and I apologize for the intrusion. But, please let me talk to Rabbi Stein?"

More hesitation. More time wasted.

"All right. I'll see if my husband will talk to you at this late hour."

Another shot as she unwillingly gave in. Two more precious minutes passed.

"Hello. This is Rabbi Moshe Stein. What can I do for you, young man?"

Jerry quickly introduces himself again. More time lost.

"Rabbi Stein. I'm sure you are aware of the tragedy that occurred at the White House this morning."

"Yes. I've been following the news broadcasts. There are some real kooks out there."

"We are looking for a Mr. Richard Feinstein. Do you know him, or has he tried to contact you today?"

"No. No, I don't believe I ever met him. At least the name is not familiar, except for hearing it on the news of course."

Hesitation. "No. I'm sure of it. No one by that name has tried to contact me. Perhaps he called the synagogue and talked to my secretary."

"We believe that he contacted a Rabbi directly."

"No. I'm sorry. He didn't contact me."

"You're sure? You understand how important it is that we find this man?"

"Of course I understand. But I can't help you. He did not contact me."

"OK. Thank you for your time. Sorry to have intruded on your Sabbath meal. If Richard Feinstein does try to contact you, please notify us immediately." Jerry read the phone number of the Secret Service special lines as Rabbi Stein copied it down.

"That's all right. You have a tough job. I understand."

"Thank you. Please call our office if Mr. Feinstein does contact you," Jerry repeated.

"I will do that."

"Good Shabbas, Rabbi. Please give my regards and apologies for the intrusion to Mrs. Stein."

"Shalom, Mr. Schwartz. I will. And good luck with your investigation."

The line went dead. Jerry hung up his receiver and turned to his list. He carefully drew a neat line though the name of Rabbi Moshe Stein. The next name was Rabbi Meyer Teitelbaum. Jerry dialed the number just three minutes before sundown, and crossed his fingers.

The phone rang four times before a very winded voice gasped, "Hello. This is Rabbi Teitelbaum. Can I help you?"

Jerry was immediately apologetic. "I'm sorry to disturb you this late Rabbi Teitelbaum, but it is very important that I talk to you."

"What is this about? Who are you?"

"Forgive me, Rabbi. My name is Jerry Schwartz. I'm a Special Agent for the Secret Service."

Rabbi's heart skipped a beat. His hands began to shake. How could they have found out so quickly? He tried to remain calm.

"My family and I were just sitting down to Sabbath dinner. Rifka, my wife, just finished the candle blessings."

"I am really very sorry about calling at this hour. I never would have unless it was really urgent."

Rabbi dreaded the next question. "Go on. Ask your questions."

"OK. I'm one of many investigators involved in gathering evidence in the attack on the President this morning. We need to talk to anyone who may have some information concerning that attack. Specifically, we are looking for a Mr. Richard Feinstein. We have reason to believe that Mr. Feinstein may have some important information we need to question him about. We need to talk to him, and we believe he contacted a Rabbi in the DC area this afternoon. Do you know Mr. Feinstein?"

Rabbi Teitelbaum knew he had to be careful. He also knew he couldn't lie. He never had, and he never would. He had to watch what he says and how he says it. He never appreciated his rabbinical training more than at that moment. He won't lie, but he won't volunteer anything either.

"Yes. I know Richard. He came by Beth Shalom synagogue a week or so ago for Sabbath Morning services."

Pay dirt. Jerry motioned to Herb, and pointed dramatically at the phone, then on to the name on the list. Herb stopped his note taking, read the name on the list and listened attentively—pen poised over paper. He was ready for action.

"Did you talk to Mr. Feinstein?"

"Yes, a very nice young man. We spoke for a few minutes after

134

services. He told me he came to the synagogue to say Kaddish for his father's Yartzeit. Do you know what a Yartzeit is?"

"Yes I do Rabbi. It is the anniversary of a death and when Jews recite the traditional Kaddish prayer for the deceased." Changing the conversation back to the investigation, he continued "Have you seen or heard from Mr. Feinstein since then?"

Hesitation. Rabbi Teitelbaum just couldn't bring himself to implicate Richard. Doing so would surely jeopardize Richard's safety and certainly his freedom.

"I'm not sure. I see a lot of people every day. Remembering them all is not something I'm very good at."

Jerry sensed he was stalling, and tried to appeal to the Rabbi's sense of duty and integrity. "Rabbi, this is very important. I sympathize with your predicament. But if you know anything else and don't tell us, then the consequences for Mr. Feinstein could be quite severe."

More silence as Rabbi Teitelbaum debated his choices in his mind. After a few moments, Rabbi Teitelbaum mustered the courage he needed.

"I'm sorry. I cannot tell you anything else."

"You don't know anything else, or you won't tell us anything else?"

"I can't say anything else. I'm sorry. Good bye."

The phone went dead. Jerry and Herb looked at each other, then grabbed the list and bolted for the door snatching their coats as they rushed out.

* * *

Rifka Teitelbaum could only stare at her husband as he almost stumbled into the dining room. He was ashen. His hands shook. His eyes glazed over, focused far in the distance.

"Meyer. What is it? What has happened?"

Rabbi Teitelbaum eased himself into his chair at the head of the table. He looked twenty years older than when he left the room. He didn't respond.

Rifka became frightened. "Meyer. Tell me what has happened." She was almost frantic—fearing something terrible had happened to their son or his family.

With great effort, Rabbi Teitelbaum tried to calm his wife. "Nothing has happened. Do not concern yourself."

Rifka wasn't buying that. She knew her husband too well. She feared the worst; this time for her husband. Her fears ran wild; his doctor had called and told him he had some horrible terminal disease. After all, he hadn't been taking very good care of himself lately. He was overweight. He didn't watch his diet, nor would he cut down on red meat as she repeatedly had begged him to do. He never exercised. It had to be cancer or heart disease—she was sure of that.

Rifka had a knack for believing everything seemed worse than it really was. She was a strong woman, but a worrier.

"Meyer. Don't keep whatever this is from me. I will help you. I'll take care of you. Whatever it is, we will get through it together, just like we always have." She was pleading with him now. She was frantic and scaring herself half to death in the process.

"Rifka. I told you there is nothing to be concerned about."

"Something is bothering you. Something terrible has happened. When you are this troubled, what do you expect me to think?"

"Please. Don't do this to yourself. There is nothing you can do to help."

Rifka was getting more frightened. She stared directly into his blank eyes. He looked back, but saw nothing.

Abruptly Rabbi Teitelbaum leaped from his chair and dashed into the den. Rifka was only two steps behind, tears starting to flow. He snatched the phone and punched the numbers with trembling fingers, Rifka could only watch, terrified.

"Harvey. This is Meyer. I've got to talk to you… Yes it's important… Now. As soon as possible… Yes. It is very private… OK, I'll meet you at the Shul in 30 minutes… Yes, bring your guest. It concerns him. … Yes, come in the back entrance directly into my study. … No, I won't let anyone else in."

Rifka returned to the dinning room and plopped herself down at the table as Rabbi Teitelbaum grabbed his coat from the closet.

"I've got to get to the Shul. Please don't be frightened. There is nothing wrong with me. I'm not sick. I'm fine. Davey and his family are also fine." Rabbi Teitelbaum covered all the bases trying to sooth her inconsolable fears.

"What about Shabbat Dinner?" she pleaded vainly.

"We'll eat after services. You drive yourself. I'll see you there later."

He kissed her on the forehead and was gone.

Rifka's tears splashed onto the Shabbat china as she buried her head in her hands. She could not understand what was going on. Now she feared for her husband's life without knowing why.

CHAPTER FIFTEEN

Heathrow Airport
London, England
Monday, Early March
4:20 p.m. Local Time

The EuropeanAir flight from Tehran made a scheduled stopover in Berlin. Luis and Mahara stayed in their seats, ignoring Rafiq al-Zayyat, the bodyguard Abu'l ordered along for "protection." Abu'l did not fool Luis. He knew the real reason Rafiq was sent—to make sure Luis did as he was told.

In spite of the underlying circumstances of the trip, Luis was very pleased with himself. Any man would be proud to have a woman as stunning as Mahara clinging to his arm. She wore a smart looking light blue pantsuit with a white collared shirt. Her hair was combed back, completely straight, swishing provocatively across her back to her waist as she walked. Her hips swayed gently, like the elegant super models on a fashion runway. Men turned and stared, but Mahara seemed not to notice. Luis did.

Mahara had never flown before. She gripped Luis's hand so hard during the take-off that his fingers fell asleep. Mahara giggled as Luis shook his numb hand, trying to regain his circulation. That seemed to loosen Mahara up, and she was calmer from then on.

Once the plane was at cruising altitude and the pilot turned off the "Fasten Seat Belt" sign, Luis and Mahara cuddled and tried to sleep. The plane took off from Tehran at 12:45pm Tehran time, about 7 hours earlier. Luis knew that the only sleep either of them might get would be on the plane ride from Tehran to Berlin, then again from Berlin to London. Ninety-minute catnaps were the best they could hope for.

The party of three was to be picked up at Heathrow and driven to their hotel. Luis did not know which hotel they would stay at. Abu'l refused to tell him any more about his "Secret War Plan" until Luis had to know. Besides, what difference does it make where they stayed?

Rafiq spotted the white Lincoln Town Car—a stretch-limo—as they waited at the Arriving Flights level. They each had one small suitcase. The driver pulled smoothly to a stop and released the trunk latch from inside. Rafiq carefully picked up his bag and laid inside and stood back patiently watching Luis. Luis correctly realized that Rafiq was not a servant, and reluctantly snatched the two other bags from the pavement. He tossed them into the trunk and slammed the lid shut.

Rafiq was a big man. Six foot four, at least 265 pounds, solidly built. Thick neck, strong arms, big thighs. In America, he could have been a professional football player; perhaps a running-back. He was immaculately dressed in a conservative dark gray suit, light blue shirt and tasteful tie. He appeared to be well educated and knowledgeable about the ways of the Western world. His presence was quite imposing. He did not arouse any scrutiny by the local Customs officials or police.

The driver had opened the passenger door and all three climbed in. Rafiq positioned himself facing the rear where he could constantly observe the other two. They ignored him as they watched the British scenery fly by outside their dark tinted car window. Luis had never been to London. Mahara had never been more than 100 miles from downtown Tehran. This trip, the plane ride, the London scenery, was fascinating to both of them. Luis momentarily forgot why he was there. Mahara never suspected.

It took 35 minutes to get to the hotel, a fairly modern Hilton. Luis expected an old British stone monstrosity. He was surprised to see the modern steel and glass 12-story structure somewhere near downtown.

Luis could just barely make out the tall buildings through the famous London fog. He guessed they were three or four miles away from downtown London.

The lobby was a huge atrium. A striking stone waterfall surrounded by a massive array of foliage stood in the center. The U-shaped second, third, fourth and fifth floor balconies curved around behind the waterfall. The atrium's glass enclosure went up to the base of the sixth floor. Very dramatic.

The trio marched to the check-in counter. Rafiq spoke first. "Good Morning. I am Rafiq al-Zayyat. There are two rooms reserved for us."

A middle-aged gentleman with a very proper mustache and British accent greeted him warmly. His hotel name badge read "Arthur Foley, Assistant Manager."

"Why yes, nice to see you Mr. al-Zayyat. We have been anticipating your arrival. Your rooms are ready. We have you prepaid and scheduled for four nights. Is that correct?"

"Yes." Rafiq used only as many words as were necessary.

"The porter will help you with your bags. You have adjoining rooms 1214 and 1216. I'm sure they will meet with your satisfaction." Mr. Foley held the collection of papers and plastic Card-keys in one hand and was poised to ring for the Bell Captain.

"Thank you, but we can manage our own bags." Rafiq held out his hand for the keys and papers.

"Certainly. As you wish sir…" Mr. Foley handed Rafiq the papers and keys, then continued, "The elevators are behind the waterfall."

Rafiq looked over his shoulder towards the waterfall, and then bent to retrieve his own bag. Luis picked up his and Mahara's. Rafiq walked very fast across the spacious lobby. Luis managed to keep up, but Mahara's legs were too short. She had to almost run.

The elevator was designed into the waterfall. The Plexiglas shaft actually went through the water rushing over boulders near the top. It was quite impressive. You can see the inside of the atrium from either side of the glass enclosed elevator car. When you look out the back, you see the underside of the cascading water for the first three floors. For the next three floors you see the entire inside of the atrium. From the sixth to the twelfth, the elevator is outside the hotel. You get a panoramic view of London. There are few elevator rides that are even memorable. This is one takes your breath away. What a rush.

Rafiq reached room 1214 first. Luis and Mahara were several steps behind. "This is your room. The phone has been disconnected. I am in constant contact with Abu'l. If you need to contact him, just knock on my door. Do not leave the hotel for any reason without asking me first. Here is your key."

Rafiq didn't wait for a response. He didn't need one. He was ordering, not discussing. Luis and Mahara watched as Rafiq swiftly unlocked the door right next to theirs, opened it with a jerk and slammed it shut behind him.

Luis inserted his card key and opened the door to room 1214. Inside they surveyed the expansive three-room suite. Hand in hand, they walked slowly through each room looking at the paintings, the sculptured artwork, and the elegant furniture. Neither of them had ever seen a hotel suite like this. They each imagined a royal castle in their minds eye.

After about ten minutes of gawking at the interior furnishings and the spectacular view of London, Luis came back down to earth.

He left Mahara lounging on the sofa and checked to make sure the locks on the front door were secure. He didn't trust Rafiq, and wasn't taking any unnecessary chances. They were. Next he checked the door connecting the adjoining rooms. There were actually two doors, back to back. He opened the one on his side to make sure that it could not be unlocked from the other side. It couldn't. There was no handle or keyhole on the other side. The door could be secured and opened only from inside their room. The rooms could only be connected if both doors were unlocked from their respective sides. If he kept the door on his side locked, Rafiq could not intrude. He closed the door quietly and locked it from inside his suite. Then he rechecked the lock. Next, he went to the phone in the living room and picked up the receiver. No dial tone. The phone was dead. So was the one in the bedroom and the bathroom.

Luis sat down across from Mahara who, though motionless, was intently watching all this strange activity. She had no idea what Luis was doing. She didn't know why he was acting this way. Finally, as Luis was deep in thought, she simply asked him. "Luis. What is wrong? Why you act funny?"

Luis was yanked abruptly from his concentration. He looked up with a start, stared at her blankly, and then tried to smile. "Oh. I'm sorry. Don't be concerned. Everything is all right. I just wanted to check on the locks. You can never be too careful."

Mahara caught a few words, and was satisfied. She still had no idea why they were here or what they were supposed to do. She was not worldly enough to suspect anything sinister. All she knew was to be obedient to the man who took care of her.

Luis started pacing nervously. He looked out the expansive window at the skyline of London. He flipped pages in the hotel magazine. He rearranged the bags, moving them from one room to the other, then to the closet. He went to the bathroom to take a long, loud piss.

Mahara remained motionless on the couch. She contemplated getting undressed and coaxing him into another round of sexual ecstasy, but decided against it. Mahara didn't know what to do, so she did nothing.

All the while Luis was thinking. Pondering his fate. Their fate. What should he do? He hated himself for the death and destruction he already caused. He knew Rafiq would force him to attack the President again, probably within the next 3 days because the rooms were booked for only 4 nights. If there was only some way to warn the President, maybe the attack could be prevented. Then it struck him like a bolt of lightning.

If he could somehow contact Richard, then together they could prevent another attack and clear Richard's name. Good idea, but how could he find a person the entire United States Law enforcement community couldn't find?

More pacing. "Maybe I could contact Sherrie? She might know where Richard is. Bad idea. The FED's have certainly already done that, and they probably have her phone taped to boot." Luis thought silently to himself. Luis was not ready for the FED's to be listening in just yet.

Luis went to the john again—a short piss this time. He always peed when he was nervous and tense.

Then he remembered. Richard installed a FAX machine in his home about two months ago with a dedicated phone line. That way he could transfer messages that needed immediate attention back and forth between Washington and Orlando at any time of the day or night and not interfere with Sherrie's phone calls.

Luis grabbed his wallet from his right hip pocket and began rummaging through it. He always carried a list of phone numbers that he might need. The writing was neat, but small. Some of the printing was smudged, but he found the number of Richard's home FAX machine.

It was the only chance he had. He would somehow get a FAX to Sherrie and hope that the FED's either didn't know about the FAX machine, or couldn't technologically tap into that line.

Luis yanked open the desk drawer and snatched a piece of hotel stationary. He looked around for a pen. "Damn it. At these prices, why can't hotels provide at least 10 cent pens?"

Mahara understood the word "pen." She glanced around the suite, spotting one next to the phone in the bedroom. She bounced off the couch and quickly retrieved it, and with a broad smile presented it to Luis. He took it graciously and smiled back. She bent to give him a peck on the cheek. He swatted her lovingly on her perfect rear end.

Mahara was rightfully very proud of herself. Satisfied that she had made Luis happy, she retreated silently back to her position on the couch. Luis began to compose his FAX. After a few false starts and crossed out sentences, he settled on:

"Sherrie,

This will sound very strange, but please read this letter completely. First, let me apologize for the nightmare you are probably going through. I am suffering my own horror, and know how you must feel. My next point is the most important.

Second, all of what I am telling you in this message is true. I have undeniable proof. I personally have information that will completely clear Richard of any involvement in the attack on the President. Richard had nothing to do with the assassination attempt. He was falsely implicated. I also know that there will be another attack on the President when he arrives in London for the European Summit in a few days. There will most likely be an attempt to shoot down Air Force One as it approaches Heathrow Airport. He must not make that trip.

I cannot go to the authorities myself, but you can and must. Get in touch with Lindsay Hawthorn at the Secret Service office. She is a friend. Lindsay has the power to stop the President's trip. The terrorism and killings must stop now.

You must do this for Richard, and for our country.

Regards, Luis Ramirez."

Luis was satisfied after re-reading the message twice. He then carefully folded the sheet of paper and put it into his shirt pocket. Luis checked the mirror to see if it would be noticed. It wasn't. Now the only problem was to get to the front desk to send the FAX.

Over an hour had passed since Luis and Mahara parted with Rafiq and went to their respective rooms. No sound from Rafiq. Could Luis just saunter down to the front desk and send the FAX? Was Rafiq watching the door?

Luis knew he had to keep his real intentions secret from Rafiq, while at the same time appear to be doing exactly as ordered. Under the circumstances, the prudent course of action seemed to be to simply tell a little white lie.

Luis went to Mahara and held out his hand. "Are you hungry? I am. Let's go down stairs and get something to eat at the hotel restaurant."

"Good. I hungry, too," she chirped, uncurling her legs from under her bottom.

Mahara stopped by the bathroom. She instinctively went to the mirror to freshen her still perfect face, comb her gorgeous hair even though not a single strand was out of place, and smooth non-existent wrinkles from her pantsuit. Abu'l taught her the ways of modern Western Women well—she took enormous pride in her modern appearance.

Luis could only watch and marvel. He still wasn't completely at ease knowing that she was "his." He, of course thought of her as a live-in girl friend, not as a bought-and-paid-for whore.

Mahara admired herself in the mirror, and then turned to Luis. "You like."

"You're beautiful. Let's go."

Luis knocked lightly on the door to room 1216 from the empty hallway. "Who is it?" came the now familiar voice of Rafiq, as he peeked through the peep-hole. Luis smiled back at him through the fish-eye lens.

"It's me. Luis." Locks clicked and the door opened a fraction.

"What is it?"

"We're hungry. Mahara and I are going to the hotel restaurant to get some dinner."

"Order room service."

"We don't want room service. We're just getting something to eat. Promise." as Luis held up his hand in a fake pledge of honor.

Rafiq looked at Mahara, then back at Luis. "Don't set foot outside the hotel."

"We won't. I swear."

"Let me know when you get back to your room."

"Sure. We'll be back in an hour or so. Can we bring something up for you?" Luis was laying it on thick.

"No. I'll order room service."

The door closed silently and the locks clicked shut. Luis had made it this far. They strolled hand-in-hand to the elevator like two kids on their honeymoon. Luis struggled to contain his tremors of fright.

The fog had lifted a little and the view of London was even more spectacular as they whisked silently down the side of the hotel. There were a few people wondering around the lobby, but mostly it was quiet. One elderly German couple was checking in. Luis waited patiently, but couldn't help overhearing their conversation. The German couple spoke fluent English, but with an unmistakable heavy thick German accent. His was stronger than hers.

"It's terrible what this world is coming to. Terrorists everywhere. Remember last year when a bomb in the subway killed all those people, not two miles from here."

The wife interrupted. "And the bombing in Oklahoma City. The attack in New York. Even in Saudi Arabia where all those poor American young men were murdered. Good people aren't safe from these terrorists anywhere anymore."

Mr. Foley was only half listening. Instead he was concentrating on his paperwork to get Ralf and Bertha Rubinstein checked in. "Uh. Yes, there is tragedy everywhere. But I assure you nothing like that will happen here at this Hotel. We're very careful about who we let stay here, and the Bobbies patrol every hour."

Mr. Foley handed them their room key and papers. "I'll ring for the bell captain."

Luis watched Ralf and Bertha in amazement as they followed the porter who was pushing an overloaded gold cart full of their suitcases and garment bags. They were staying for two weeks.

Luis was next in line. "Good Morning, Mr. Foley. I'd like to send a FAX."

"Certainly, sir. I can have it sent within the next ten minutes. Is that satisfactory?"

"That will be fine. Thank you." Luis unfolded the one page letter, but didn't hand it to Mr. Foley.

"Do you have a FAX Cover sheet that I can use?"

Mr. Foley searched quickly through some nearby files and answered: "Will this do?"

Luis scanned the hotel standard FAX cover sheet form. "That's fine. Let me fill it out."

As Luis wrote the name and FAX number in the appropriate blanks, Mr. Foley continued. "Shall I put the charges onto your room bill?"

"Uh, no. I'll pay cash. How much will it be?"

"To where are you sending the FAX, sir?"

"Orlando, Florida...in the United States."

Mr. Foley was a little miffed at Luis's assumption that he didn't know Orlando was in the United States. Mr. Foley snatched up a small stack of papers and began searching for the area code of Orlando, FL. "Here it is. United States, Area Code 407. In American money, the long distance phone charges are $14.50 per minute, and we charge $2.50 per page. One page plus the cover page should be less than one minute. The total comes to $19.50 American."

Luis fished into his pocket and retrieved his money clip. He handed Mr. Foley a twenty-dollar bill.

"Do you want American coins in change?"

"Whatever is easiest for you. I haven't had time to exchange my

American money for British." Luis was trying to look like an embarrassed first-time traveler.

Luis handed Mr. Foley the FAX with the filled out FAX cover sheet on top, hoping Mr. Foley wouldn't read the second sheet. Mr. Foley took the papers without even glancing at them and handed Luis back two quarters. Luis was relieved—another hurdle crossed without incident.

Luis went to collect Mahara as she watched the waterfall and people-watched. A few men turned to watch her. Silently Luis prayed for the first time since his childhood. "Please G-d help Sherrie Feinstein to understand, and to know what to do to stop all this madness."

CHAPTER SIXTEEN

Beth Shalom Synagogue
Near Washington, D.C.
Friday, Early March
10:25 p.m.

Some of the 150 congregants celebrating the B'nia Mitzvah of Josh and Jeremy Steinmetz were still milling around congratulating the twin boys and their parents on the fine job the youngsters did that evening. Most of the guests were from out of town. As such, they were reluctant to leave each other's company. They had a lot of family chit-chat and catching up to do. It didn't matter that Dr. Steven Steinmetz, a world renowned heart specialist, father of the identical twins had spared no expense at the Hotel where he put most of them up, the Sabbath Lunch scheduled for tomorrow, and the fancy party planned for Saturday evening. The decorations and balloons for the upcoming events were rumored to be extravagant. There was even a Sunday Brunch planned for everyone to attend. Ruth Goldfarb-Steinmetz was Josh and Jeremy's mother. Her family was actually larger than the Steinmetz family, but many of them are older and were afraid to make the trip from Chicago and Detroit. They were snowed in and fearful of traveling under these conditions. The two plane crashes in the last five months swayed them to reluctantly miss this joyous occasion—they would settle for sending lavish gifts and phoning in their congratulations over the next three or so days. To Jews who survived the death camps of Germany and Poland, they felt they should wait and make it to the next simchah, the next joyous occasion. Two Aunts, an Uncle and five older cousins didn't show up.

Those that could attend included dozens of children, some still in diapers. Most of the kids were in their pre or early teens. The young ladies were dressed in cute little outfits that showed off their newly developing figures. They giggled and teased the boys, also nicely dressed in long sleeve white shirts and ties. Several boys had on sport coats—most did not. What a wonderful sight; the youth of today learning and practicing the traditions of the ancient Jewish heritage to carry on for the future.

Jerry and Herb waited patiently for over a half hour while the well-wishers huddled in groups schmoozing about old times. Rabbi Teitelbaum was easy to spot. He was first corralled by one group, then another, then a third. Heaps of praise was shoveled upon him for the way he taught the boys to actually lead the service.

In reality, Josh and Jeremy were good students; both very bright with IQ's over 130. They worked hard to learn their traditional Bar Mitzvah parts, and practiced their deliveries together. Rabbi Teitelbaum just kept giving them another prayer to learn as soon as they mastered the last one. The boys could have been poster children for what is right about the young people in America today. They were nice looking—they took after their mother's side. Most of all, they were well mannered and respectful of others. Everyone marveled at how cute they looked in their new suits. They insisted that they not be dressed alike. Mom relented and allowed them to each pick out their own wardrobes for this festive occasion. Today they began their journey into manhood in the eyes of the Jewish people. Tomorrow they would complete the trip when they each read from the sacred Torah.

It was getting late. The crowd began to thin. Rabbi Teitelbaum finally excused himself from the last small group. Jerry and Herb approached him as he was hurrying towards his study. He had not noticed them.

"Excuse us. Are you Rabbi Meyer Teitelbaum?"

Rabbi Teitelbaum stopped and looked both men up and down. He did not recognize either one of them. "Yes. What can I do for you?"

Both men displayed their Secret Service Badges while trying to conceal their actions from anyone else that might be watching. They respected how delicate such a situation might be to the respected Rabbi.

"I am Jerry Schwartz. My partner is Herb Frost." Jerry thrust out his hand. Rabbi Teitelbaum shook it tentatively. "I spoke to you earlier this evening."

"Yes. I remember. What do you want now? I already told you what I know."

"It's just procedure," lied Herb. Jerry glared at Herb to shut him up.

"May we go somewhere more private?" Jerry was more diplomatic.

"It's late. I really must be getting home. My wife isn't feeling very well."

"This should only take a few minutes. Besides, it is very important. Every minute we delay could cost someone else their life."

"But I already told you what I know." The Rabbi repeated himself because he couldn't think of any other excuse. He knew that they suspected that he knew more than he was telling.

"OK. I can give you five minutes. No longer. We can talk in my study."

Jerry and Herb followed Rabbi Teitelbaum to his study. His hands quivered as he struggled to unlock the door. Once inside, he flipped the light switch and offered the men a chair. They declined. Rabbi Teitelbaum did not strictly observe all the traditional demands on more Orthodox Jews.

"OK. Ask your questions."

"We're a little unclear about what you told me about Richard Feinstein." Jerry flipped pages in his little notebook. "You said he was here a week or two ago to say Kaddish for his father."

"That's right. He was."

"Which was it? One or two weeks ago?"

"I'm not sure. I don't keep track of who comes to Shul to pray." Sarcasm was unusual for Rabbi Teitelbaum.

"All right. Have you seen or heard from him since then?" asked Jerry as he scribbled more notes.

"I can't remember." Rabbi Teitelbaum was not a very good liar—he had very little prior practice. He broke out in a sweat. His hands trembled more now than a few moments earlier. He could not look either of the men in the eye. This did not go unnoticed by the trained Agents.

"Rabbi Teitelbaum. This is serious business. I'm sure you know that."

"Yes. I know it is."

"It will be much better for everyone involved if you cooperate with us."

Rabbi Teitelbaum looked up from staring at his shoes to see Jerry genuinely concerned. Their eyes met. Rabbi Teitelbaum knew he should tell the truth—but he just couldn't. Jerry was the first to sense the quandary the Rabbi was in.

"Rabbi, I realize that this may create a difficult situation for you. The courts recognize the clergy-parishioner privilege. This is not a court of law. We are only trying to find Richard Feinstein so we can question him. Maybe even protect him from harm. If he is guilty of the attacks this morning, then we must stop him before he tries again. If he is not guilty, then evidence to that effect will acquit him. Every minute he is on the run increases the likelihood that he may be injured or even killed by some angry fanatic who spots him on the street and takes the law into his own hands. Do you understand what I am telling you?"

Rabbi Teitelbaum nodded twice, but was still torn. He didn't know if he should say any more or not. He just stared at Jerry with a blank expression. All the while he was thinking. What should he do? What does the Torah teach about such matters? He couldn't think of any lesson that touched on this subject. Rabbinical School dealt briefly with the Rabbi-Congregant legal issue, but the material was dry and presented with a much less dramatic set of circumstances. The Rabbinical Instructors used simple situations as examples; a drug dealer or a petty criminal might tell of his exploits to the Rabbi during counseling sessions perhaps. In those cases, the only human being that the Rabbi had to consider was the person sitting across from him. Even then, the course of action was not always clear.

This was very different. Lives, perhaps many lives were at stake. The safety of the President of the United States was in jeopardy. Dozens of people, maybe hundreds would be affected.

Finally, long after the five minutes ticked past, Rabbi Teitelbaum asked in desperation, "May I make a call to one of my congregants? He is a lawyer. I need his advice before I say anything else. Please."

"OK. Sure. That's fair. We'll wait outside your door."

The two Secret Service Agents left and gently closed the door behind them. Rabbi Teitelbaum collapsed into his chair. He was drained. He wiped his forehead with his handkerchief, and rubbed his temples. His palms were moist, his head ached, his heart pounded. He squinted to read the home phone number of Harvey Weissman from the synagogue directory. Rabbi Teitelbaum must call Harvey for the second time in a few hours to get his professional advice—again. He misdialed the first time, apologized profusely to the drowsy voice on the other end, then tried again.

The phone rang four times before Suzanne answered. She was on the phone asking questions, getting answers. Thank goodness for call waiting.

Rabbi Teitelbaum spoke rapidly. Suzanne didn't recognize his voice at first. "Uncle Meyer? Is that you? What's wrong?"

He was almost panting. Obviously very excited, probably scared. "Suzanne, I must speak to Harvey. Is he there?"

"Yes. He's here. What's wrong? Are you sick? Is Aunty Rifka OK?"

"I'm OK. Everyone is fine. Please. Just put Harvey on." He was more emphatic than she had ever seen or heard him.

"I'll get him right away." Suzanne was very concerned, but did as she was asked.

Rabbi heard footsteps through the phone as Harvey marched across the ceramic floor. "Hello. Meyer, what's wrong? Suzanne said you were upset and had to speak with me immediately."

"Those men you warned me about this evening when you came by; they're here There are two men from the Secret Service here. Right here in my synagogue. They want me to tell them if I saw Richard Feinstein recently."

"Did you tell them?"

"No. I followed your advice and told them nothing. But they are very suspicious. I asked them to wait outside while I called you for advice."

"How did they find you? Did they say anything else?"

"I don't know how they found me. They aren't very talkative, except

152

to rattle off questions. What should I do now?" Rabbi Teitelbaum was near panic and Harvey sensed it.

Harvey had not expected them to show up in person so quickly.

"Tell them to wait. I'll be there in half an hour. Don't tell them anything else. And for G-d sakes don't mention anything about Richard." Harvey hung up. Rabbi Teitelbaum looked at the phone as if it were haunted. He replaced it gingerly and fell back into his chair.

A few more minutes passed before Rabbi Teitelbaum could muster the strength and courage to get up and open the door. Jerry and Herb were waiting patiently a few paces from his Study. Herb was leaning on a nearby wall staring into space. Jerry was admiring a display of old Jewish sculptures and art in the lobby.

The Synagogue was now deserted except for the three men. The congregants had all left. Even the Rabbi's wife left without him. By now she was used to his interminable delays. It was always something important. Years ago she stopped quizzing him about his habit of staying long after everyone else. On this evening she caught a ride home with some friends. Rifka left her car in the parking lot, preferring not to drive home alone that late. Her friends didn't ask questions either; they just gladly obliged.

"Gentlemen." Rabbi Teitelbaum motioned for the men to come back into his study. They entered without a word and took the same places they vacated ten minutes earlier.

Once settled and apparently comfortable, Herb started first, which annoyed Jerry. "Did you contact your attorney?"

"Yes." Short, honest, concise, giving out no additional information, no elaboration.

"And... What did he say?" Herb's voice showed his annoyance at the lack of cooperation.

"He told me not to say anything until he gets here."

"He's coming here? And when will that be?"

"Less than a half an hour."

Jerry finally took over to try to ease the tension. "Can you please tell us his name?"

This condescending tone didn't go over very well. Now Rabbi

Teitelbaum was also annoyed. "What makes you think it's a he? Women are very capable attorneys as well."

Herb and Jerry looked at each other, then back at the Rabbi. "Uh, a slip of the tongue. Sorry. We don't mean to offend," Jerry replied somewhat sheepishly.

"Well, he is a man. His name is Harvey Weissman." Herb and Jerry again looked at each other. The Rabbi was playing games with them.

Herb and Jerry fumed while the Rabbi pretended to busy himself with paperwork. Only Rabbi Teitelbaum sat. No one spoke. The air was so thick with anxiety you could almost reach out and grab it. Precious time was being wasted, but there was nothing they could do about it. So Herb and Jerry just shuffled back and forth while they waited.

Ten minutes crept by. Then fifteen. Another six minutes that seemed like six hours slowly ticked off before they heard sounds in the foyer. Herb and Jerry turned to watch the door. Rabbi Teitelbaum looked up, and then rose to lumber forward to greet the entering Harvey Weissman.

The agents turned and displayed their badges. Harvey took Jerry's first. Examined it closely and compared the color picture to the face of the man standing before him. Satisfied, he returned the leather wallet. The same process was repeated with Herb's ID.

"All right, gentlemen. My name is Harvey Weissman." He handed each agent a tastefully, but obviously expensive printed business card. They took it, barely glancing at the raised embossed lettering. "I understand from Rabbi Teitelbaum that there is a problem here."

Jerry jumped in before Herb could open his mouth. "There is, Mr. Weissman. We have reason to believe that Rabbi Teitelbaum has some information about a Mr. Richard Feinstein, but he is refusing to tell us anything."

Harvey played dumb. "What has Mr. Feinstein done? Why are you looking for him?"

"I don't mean to be rude, but don't you pay attention to what is going on? The President was attacked this morning. We need to question Mr. Feinstein about those events."

"Oh, that Mr. Feinstein." Harvey was playing it cool.

"Yes, Mr. Richard Feinstein. Rabbi Teitelbaum will not talk to us about him."

"And why is that?"

"Rabbi Teitelbaum is claiming a Clergy-Congregant privilege."

"A well recognized legal concept. Rabbi Teitelbaum is within his rights to not discuss Mr. Feinstein with you or anyone else in authority."

Jerry was really irritated now. "Look, Mr. Weissman. We're dealing with a very serious incident here. Twenty or so people died. Dozens injured—some very seriously. What about their rights? What about the rights of G-d knows how many others Feinstein might kill next?" Harvey accomplished his initial mission. Get the Secret Service agents riled up and confused, unable to really think straight. He now had the advantage—and intended to keep it

"A few more questions, gentlemen. First. How did you connect Rabbi Teitelbaum with Mr. Feinstein?"

"We don't have to reveal that information to you." The hair on the back of Herb's neck was standing straight up as he sneered through clinched teeth.

"OK. Then how do you know that Mr. Feinstein is the one responsible for the attack?"

Daggers flew from Herb's eyes straight at Harvey. "I repeat. We don't have to reveal anything to you. We are conducting an official investigation of a crime that carries a possible death sentence. We ask the questions. Your client answers them. Got that?"

Harvey flew out of his chair and pushed his nose to within inches of Herb's. "Now you get this, Mr. Secret Service agent. This is the United States of America. Everybody has rights, and you can't just barge into a house of worship and threaten the clergy. You got that?"

Harvey was an experienced trial lawyer who respected, but had no fear of the Government. The Secret Service agents were no match for Harvey's expertise. Harvey knew how to control his temper, his emotions. Herb and Jerry really didn't. They had little practice doing so. Score another for Harvey—Secret Service was still Zip.

Jerry regained his composure first, and jumped between Herb and Harvey. "Look, this isn't getting us anywhere. All we want to do is talk to

Richard Feinstein. Eventually, we will find him. Perhaps a police officer will spot him. There might be a chase. Maybe gunfire. Where would we be if Richard is gunned down trying to avoid arrest?"

Harvey stood up and stared at the agents, then at Rabbi Teitelbaum. "Give me a few moments alone with Rabbi Teitelbaum, please?"

"Sure, but don't take too long." Both Agents turned on their heels in unison and were gone. The door closed behind them.

Harvey immediately turned to Rabbi Teitelbaum. "I'm going to try to negotiate a safe way to turn Richard in to the authorities. I can't hide him forever. And he's not safe on the streets."

"I know, Harvey. But please do whatever you can to protect him. He is innocent."

"I know. I'll do my best."

Harvey opened the door and motioned the two men back into the study. "All right. Here's the deal."

"We don't make deals." More hostility.

"Hear me out first. OK?"

Herb and Jerry looked at each other. They knew they had no other choice.

"Go on," declared Jerry dejectedly.

"First, there will be no mention of any connection between Rabbi Teitelbaum and Mr. Feinstein. No leaks to the press, no further questioning of the Rabbi by you or anyone else about this matter. Rabbi Teitelbaum will not be called as a witness at any trial if there is one, nor will he be charged or prosecuted."

"What the hell do you think this is? We are not part of *Let's Make a Deal.* You haven't offered anything—you've only make demands."

"What would you say if I could deliver Richard Feinstein himself?"

Herb and Jerry's eyes flew open. Their mouths dropped. Herb dropped his pen.

"You know where Richard Feinstein is?"

"I will not answer that question until you agree to my terms." Harvey stood his ground.

Jerry leaned over and whispered into Herb's ear, his hand covering his mouth. Herb whispered back the same way.

"OK. We will forget about Rabbi Teitelbaum. Where is Richard?"

"Not so fast. Rabbi, hand me a sheet of paper, please." Rabbi obliged. Harvey tried to write slowly so his words would be legible. He handed the paper to Jerry, who read it slowly and carefully. Indeed, it said exactly what Harvey had demanded earlier.

"I can't sign this," was Jerry's reaction.

"Why not? You agree to it, don't you?"

"Well, yes. But I can't agree in writing." Harvey knew he had to get the agreement in writing or the agents could later deny ever doing so.

"Fine. Have it your way." Harvey reached for the paper.

He rose and turned to the Rabbi, ignoring Jerry and Herb. "We're done here. I'll escort these men out. You lock up. I'll call you in the morning."

"Wait a minute. You can't just leave. We agree to your demands. Where is Richard?"

"If you don't sign the paper, there is no agreement."

The agents were backed into a corner with only one way out. "Give me the damn paper." Jerry snatched it from Harvey, scribbled his name, and thrust it back.

Harvey examined the signature. "Please write your official title and badge number under your signature. Then write today's date."

"Damn you lawyers." Jerry muttered loud enough for everyone to hear as he did as he was instructed.

"OK. Here. Now where is Richard?"

"He's in a safe place. I must ensure his continued safety before he turns himself in."

"Fair enough. But we pride ourselves in protecting those in our custody."

"I'm sure you do. Tell you what. I'll give you some important information about the incident this morning. You set up a meeting with the head of the Secret Service. After I get his assurances, then I'll personally guarantee that Richard will turn himself in."

"What do you know that we don't?"

"I know that there were nine men in the trailer when the incident occurred, but only eight men were found inside. I also know who that ninth man is. He is your killer. Not Richard Feinstein."

Again the two Secret Service men were stunned by this revelation. Could they even believe him? They had no choice, and they knew it. Neither spoke.

"I'll tell the head man his name when we meet. I'll call your boss to make an appointment early next week when I'm ready. We do this on my terms or not at all. And that's not negotiable." Harvey was all smiles. Herb and Jerry were a wreck.

Harvey needed time to work out his plan to protect Richard's best interests.

CHAPTER SEVENTEEN

The Feinstein Home
The Northern Suburbs of Orlando, FL
Monday, Early March
7:30 a.m.

Almost three full days had come and gone since Sherrie first learned of the assassination attempt on the President. Sherrie awoke from a fitful sleep. She didn't feel rested. She strained to push her swollen body to a sitting position on the side of the bed. Her head was spinning. Her eyes were red and puffy. She wondered if the nightmare of last Friday was only a dream, and hoped against hope that today she would wake up to the bright future she and Richard often talked and laughed about.

She leaned over to retrieve the TV remote from the nightstand. The pain in her belly shot through her entire body like a sword. Grabbing her stomach with one hand and lowering herself back to a prone position, she waited for the muscle strain to subside. Within a few moments, the searing jolt diminished. This had happened before, and Sherrie dutifully reported it to her doctor immediately. She assured Sherrie it was just a pulled muscle or tender nerve endings; nothing to get concerned about. Lots of women have this problem during pregnancy. The baby was fine, and so was she. There was absolutely no danger to either one of them. The doctor was kind and upbeat—Sherrie would know if labor pains started. They would be much more intense than these.

To calm her own anxiety, Sherrie asked her mother and other girlfriends who had experienced childbirth about their experiences. Most cheerfully reported that minor pain and discomfort were to be expected; just another part of being pregnant. That made Sherrie feel a little better, but she was still concerned about the upcoming labor pains. How would she know the difference? When she quizzed her friends about that, to a woman they informed her that every expectant mother knows when labor pains start. None would elaborate further except to say that the pain felt during labor is unlike anything she had ever felt before. Sherrie could only cringe at the thought of pain greater than this.

At least this pain was not the onset of labor. Soon it was gone completely—just as predicted. Sherrie rubbed her huge belly and wished Richard was here to do it for her. He had such a soothing and gentle touch. She longed for those times they spent together—not worrying about anything except each other.

Slowly and carefully this time, Sherrie sat up. She waited a few seconds to see if the pain would return. It didn't. She straightened up cautiously, and this time walked gingerly over to the nightstand to get the remote.

Sherrie pointed the remote at the TV and pressed the On button. The picture flickered and faded in and out for about five seconds as the TV warmed up. As she waited, she punched in channel 6, CBS. Perhaps the morning news show would provide some more information.

The tail-end of a report about the attack was wrapping up. She only caught a few words of the report. Just as before, Richard's ID photo flashed across the screen at the conclusion. This was not a dream. She was still living her own private nightmare. Sherrie's reaction was the same as before. She buried her face in her hands and sobbed.

Half listening, not really paying attention, Sherrie just sat there in her own little world. Frightened, scared, afraid for her yet unborn child. What was she going to do? How could she raise a child by herself? How would she explain to her child what Richard, the baby's father had done? The sobbing started all over again. The tears fell on her nightgown creating little wet blotches.

Mercifully, there were no further reports about the attack. Eventually, daytime programming started, and Sherrie clicked off the TV. She tried to compose herself. She instinctively knew she had to be strong. Strong for herself, for Richard, and for their baby. Richard couldn't have done what everyone was accusing him of. She just knew it. Sherrie pulled herself together, sat up straight, took a deep breath, and walked, actually waddled into the master bath. She splashed water on her face, brushed her hair and teeth, and tried to smile at her own reflection in the mirror, with some success.

"I can do this." She told herself, and at least for a few moments, even she believed that she could.

She walked leisurely into the kitchen to get some cereal and juice. She had to eat; if for no other reason other than to keep the baby healthy. As she opened the refrigerator to get the milk carton and juice pitcher, she noticed the papers in the FAX machine.

Curious, she set the milk and juice down and gingerly picked up the two pages. Richard was sending and receiving FAXes almost daily when he was home. But no one had ever sent a FAX to the house when he was out of town.

She carefully looked at the first page. It was very stylish. Bold letters identifying it as a FAX Cover Sheet. The letterhead declared that it was sent from a Hotel in London. In the middle of the page was the information about for whom it was intended—Sherrie Feinstein. The receiver's location and FAX number were there as well. Finally she read the name of the sender—Luis Ramirez. Then she reread it. "How can this be? The news reports said everyone in the trailer was dead. Luis should be dead, not alive sending FAXes from London"

Sherrie shuffled to the second page, holding them like they were contaminated with a lethal virus. She couldn't be sure of what she was reading. After reading the entire letter the third time, the words had not changed.

"My G-d. I don't believe this? This has to be some kind of trick. A sick joke."

Angrily, Sherrie wadded up the papers and threw them across the room in the direction of the trashcan. She missed.

Sherrie was petrified and desperate. "I've got to call Jenn." She dialed the number with trembling hands, and spoke in a soft whisper when a voice on the other end answered.

No greeting or introduction. "Oh, Jenn. I'm so miserable. People are playing sick jokes on me. I can't stand it."

"What happened?"

"Some sicko sent me a mean FAX. I was trying to make myself feel better. Then whammo."

Sherrie wasn't making much sense. "Look, you're still in shock over this whole mess. Tell you what. I'll come right over and fix us both some breakfast. What do you say about that?"

"Thanks, Jenn. I don't know what I'd do without you."

Jenn arrived by 8:30. She forced herself to be cheerful. It was hard, but she managed it anyway. Jennifer quickly immersed Sherrie in the cooking and preparation duties hoping to get her mind off Richard, the press, everything. It was working. Sherrie wasn't crying, nor did she seem as depressed as she sounded over the phone.

Soon the scrambled eggs, toasted bagels, cream cheese, lox, cold orange juice and hot coffee were ready. Amazingly, all at the same time. Jenn ushered Sherrie to a chair at the kitchen table, which had already been set for two. Jenn placed everything in the center of the table and slipped into a chair next to Sherrie. Like mothers always do, she began to fill Sherrie's plate with a huge helping of eggs. Next she placed a perfectly cut bagel on her plate and offered Sherrie the serving dish piled with mounds of cream cheese and several strips of lox. Sherrie politely took a big chunk of cream cheese and began smearing it on her bagel. Next she pierced a few strips of lox and plopped them on top. Jenn poured juice for both of them, then coffee. All was ready for a lovely quiet breakfast to be shared by two best friends. The worries of the world could be shut out for an hour or so.

After the filling breakfast, Jenn shooed Sherrie back into her chair. "I'll clean up. You just sit there and relax. This is your day off."

Sherrie shrugged and obliged. Soon the dishes were rinsed and put in the dishwasher. The pans washed, rinsed and left in the kitchen drainer to dry. Finally, Jenn began accumulating the trash. Napkins, the cream

SECRET WARS

cheese wrapper, the box the lox came in, bagel crumbs. The paper was picked up, and the crumbs swept from the counter top into Jenn's hand. Jenn carried all the trash to the trashcan across the room. Closing the lid and wiping her hands, she spied the wadded up papers on the floor and bent to pick them up intending to throw them away as well.

Sherrie was watching all of the housecleaning, and offered. "That is the joke someone played on me."

Jenn was curious, and unfolded the papers. She flattened the creases and scanned them, then read them again, slowly this time—absorbing every word.

"Sherrie. What if this is not a joke?" Jenn was dead serious. Sherrie didn't immediately respond.

Finally, "What else could it be?"

"Let's try to figure this out." Jenn was staring intently at both sheets of wrinkled-up paper, one page in each hand.

"How? I don't even understand what that guy, if it is a guy, is saying."

"This is an international phone number from England. Do you know anyone in London, or someone on a trip to London?"

"No. I don't think so." Sherrie was thinking hard about that.

"Well, then let's start with the person who sent it. Do you know a Luis Ramirez?"

"Yes. He works with Richard at Sterling."

"OK. How about Lindsay Hawthorn. Do you know her? At least I think it's a her."

"Maybe. I think she's with the government. Yes. I remember her now. She came over for dinner a few months ago." Sherrie was getting excited. So was Jennifer.

"Now, remember the strange phone call on Friday from a Rabbi claiming that Richard was set up. This says the same thing. That is too much of a coincidence, don't you think?"

The two friends looked at each other, then back to the FAX. "Sherrie. You have no choice here. You've got to call this Lindsay person. If this is a sick joke, it won't matter. The worst that could happen is she laughs in your face and hangs up on you. But, if this is for real, then there will be another attack on the president soon. Can you risk that?"

163

Sherrie thought about that logic for a few seconds. "Do you really think I should call her? I'll feel like such a fool if this is a joke."

"No you won't. Especially if this FAX is legit."

Sherrie thought about her choices some more. She could ignore the note or make a simple phone call. Jenn watched her intently, patiently waiting for Sherrie to make the decision she knew she would.

"You're right. Just like always. You can always figure out what to do. I usually get confused."

"Don't concern yourself with that nonsense—just make the call."

"OK. I will." Sherrie rose and marched into the bedroom. She was now on her own mission. She knew what she had to do. She rummaged quickly through some papers on Richard's dresser until she found the phone list he kept at home. He was always calling somebody about that damned RPV project. She scanned the list with her finger until she found the name of Lindsay Hawthorn. Luckily, there was an office phone number next to the address of her office at Secret Service headquarters.

Jenn watched all this while leaning on the bedroom door jam, arms folded across her ample chest. A satisfied smile peeked from her face. She really enjoyed watching how once Sherrie set her mind on something, she bulled her way through to the conclusion. She just had to get a push sometimes before her head of steam built up.

"I knew it was here." Sherrie declared triumphantly waving the phone list. "I'll call from the den."

Jennifer scurried behind Sherrie to the den, and sat opposite her as Sherrie carefully poked out the numbers.

Jenn kept rhythmically rocking, watching and listening.

* * *

In a van filled with electronic equipment a few blocks away, the three FBI agents looked at each other in disgust. Ain't technology great?

"G-d damn it. Why didn't we know about the fucking FAX machine?

"I don't know how we missed it. But, it's not on the computer printout."

"Well, shit. Now we'll miss the second transmission of that same damn fucking FAX."

"Someone's ass is going to get kicked from here to China for this, and it ain't gonna be mine. I guarantee that."

The agent in charge threw his headset across the van. The other two agents dodged it just in time.

CHAPTER EIGHTEEN

Luis's Suite at the Hilton Hotel
London, England
Tuesday, Early March
12:19 p.m. Local Time

Luis had finished showering and shaving. Mahara was sitting naked by the vanity combing her hair. They looked at each other questioningly as the knocks on the door reverberated through the suite. Luis grabbed the fluffy white embroidered robe from the foot of the bed as he went to peek though the peephole in the door. It was Rafiq standing tall and looking grim-faced. Luis opened the door as he tied the sash around his waist. Mahara quietly pushed the door to the bathroom shut just as Luis bid Rafiq a fake "Good Morning" through the crack in the door unaware of the actual time. The safety chain was still attached.

"Good. You are getting ready. We have work to do."

No pleasantries; nothing except commands from Rafiq. Luis was immediately reluctant. He sensed the time for another attack on the President was nearing. He was right. He tried to stall.

"I'm not dressed, and we haven't eaten breakfast yet." Luis pleaded.

Rafiq didn't care about their stomachs. He had his orders, and he was going to do as he was commanded. "Get dressed. I'll be back for you in fifteen minutes."

"What about breakfast?"

"I've eaten already. You can eat when your work is over," was all he said. Then he was gone as he disappeared from the crack in the door.

Luis closed the door very deliberately. He had to think. He had to protect Mahara. He didn't care about himself. Then it hit him. There was only one way.

Forcing himself to be calm, he strode back to the bathroom and slowly pushed the door open. His beautiful Mahara was still sitting naked on the vanity stool. Her gorgeous body glimmering in the soft light; her beautiful small round face looking up at him. Her eyes questioning. He knew he must do this terrible thing—he must send her away before Rafiq returned. But, he couldn't bring himself to hurt her feelings, so he lied. Lying was coming much easier to him now.

"Mahara, try to understand what I am trying to tell you."

"Luis. What wrong?" She sensed his uneasiness immediately.

"Rafiq and I have work to do. You cannot come with us. We will be back soon though. I promise," he said as soothingly as he could. For good measure, he pulled her up and held her close—savoring what he felt deep in his soul. This could be the last time their naked bodies touched. He continued with hidden tears in his eyes.

"You must get dressed as fast as you can and leave this hotel. Go shopping, do some sightseeing."

"I want to stay with you." She pleaded.

"We'll be together again real soon." Luis knew he had to be firm. He raised his voice for the first time in front of Mahara. "You must leave this hotel right now!"

Mahara was startled, but finally nodded her agreement as she was trained to do. She didn't understand what was happening, but she knew she must obey Luis. She rose quickly, snatched her underwear and outfit from the foot of the bed and slipped into them quickly.

"Hurry, you must get out of here before Rafiq returns."

Luis handed Mahara her purse and $500-American as he opened the door. Before she could walk through it, he grabbed her and pulled her close. "I love you. See you soon." Letting her go was unbearable.

A quick kiss on the lips, and she was down the hall, around the corner and out of sight. She would be safe. Luis was miserable as he wiped the tears from his cheeks with the sleeve of his robe.

Regaining his strength, Luis closed the door behind him, and proceeded to get dressed himself. Three minutes later, the dreaded knock on the door. Luis opened it calmly and greeted Rafiq with a smile. Rafiq did not return the gesture. Responding, "Let's go."

Luis stepped into the hall and started to close the door. Rafiq jammed it open with a strong right arm and demanded, "Where is Mahara? She is coming with us."

"You never said she was coming with us. This is only between you and me and Abu'l."

"Where is she?" he shouted, glancing around to see if anyone overheard him. The halls were disserted.

Luis stalled. "She went downstairs shopping about an hour ago."

"Let's go get her." Ordered Rafiq as he pulled Luis aside and slammed the door shut behind them. Grabbing Luis by the arm, Rafiq swiftly moved toward the elevators at the far end of the winding hallway. Rafiq was impatient waiting for the elevator to ascend the twelve floors, and fidgeted as he looked around searching for any sign of Mahara. The Elevator arrived with a pleasant chime.

Neither spoke as the bright elevator plummeted through the waterfall towards the lobby. Rafiq resumed his frantic search for Mahara as soon as the shops were in view. Relief. She was nowhere to be found.

Rafiq grumbled as he shoved Luis towards the row of elegant shops. Rafiq went into each one and made a complete visual sweep looking for her. Luis was thankful that she was actually safely out of the hotel.

"This is not good for you." Rafiq snarled.

"Why? You still have me. I will do as you and Abu'l expect. Mahara has nothing to do with any of this."

Luis's reasoning did not dissuade Rafiq, who had his orders: Mahara was to remain with them at all times. She was the insurance Abu'l demanded for Luis's cooperation. Abu'l would not be pleased that Rafiq allowed Mahara to slip away. Now, there was no time to argue with Luis. There was no time to determine if Luis was involved in Mahara's disappearance. And now there certainly was no time to try and find her.

Preparations for the next attack had to be made in the next few hours or that opportunity would be lost forever.

"You come with me now. I'll find Mahara later." Rafiq had no other options.

Luis let out a silent sigh of relief. He instinctively knew the rules of this game were simple. Do exactly as he was told or both he and Mahara would be hurt or killed.

The two men left the hotel in the same white limo, and drove for about 45 minutes towards the general direction of Heathrow. As the airport got closer, Rafiq watched to see the direction of the inbound and outgoing airplanes. When he determined that they were landing from the north, and taking off to the south, he switched on a device that looked like a police radio scanner. He fiddled with some dials until the voices of the Air-Traffic-Controllers could be heard clearly.

Their brief, but calm dialogue with various pilots confirmed that the landing pattern would remain constant for at least twelve more hours, because the weather conditions were predicted to remain constant for at least that long. Rafiq immediately instructed the driver to head for location "C."

Luis correctly assumed that several potential sites had previously been scouted, and that location "C" was near the north end of the runway. Every plane landing from the north had to fly within one mile of location "C." The RPV's could easily attack a 747 from a concealed location a mile away.

Luis watched the outskirts of the city flash by. He had only a vague idea where he was and where the limo was headed. He did correctly guess they were headed north somewhere near Heathrow. He could only wait and see what might happen next.

The limo stopped at what looked like an abandoned warehouse. Luis could see the planes on their final approach patterns gliding majestically towards Heathrow to the south. Luis judged that they were about a mile from the end of the parallel runways. Luis estimated that the shiny planes were no more than 1,000 feet up as they passed a few hundred yards to the east. Luis could easily make out the markings and colored logos on each plane. United. American. Delta. British Airways. Japan Air. He could hear the roar of the powerful jet engines as they whined to maintain landing speeds of over 150 miles an hour as they descended in smooth gliding straight lines. Easy targets.

Luis knew that Air Force One, the President's private 747 would be just as easy to spot. He also knew that an RPV loaded with powerful explosives could bring it down, killing all on board as it crashed into a pile of expensive twisted burning metal parts.

He once again offered a silent prayer that Sherrie received the FAX and had taken action. He also prayed for Mahara's safety. He instinctively knew that if he didn't succeed in killing the President this time, Abu'l would not stop until both he and Mahara were hunted down, caught, tortured and eventually killed in some agonizing manner—possibly beheaded while they screamed for their lives.

He had no idea what Rafiq expected of him—but he had his suspicions. He had to play along with Rafiq. To do otherwise would mean instant death to him and a horrible ending to Mahara's short life after she was hunted down like a mangy dog.

Rafiq fiddled with the dials of the scanner again. This time he picked up conversations between pilots and the Air-Traffic-Controllers that monitor the high-altitude corridors in the skies between cities and continents.

Rafiq just sat and listened. After a few minutes he would switch to other frequencies and listen some more. He said nothing. Neither did the motionless driver or Luis.

"He must not be nearby yet," was the first sound anyone heard in almost an hour, except for the constant roar of the landing jet planes and the squawking of a nearby flock of birds.

Just as suddenly, Rafiq ordered the driver to open the trunk using the inside switch as Rafiq got out of the limo. The driver silently, but quickly obliged. Luis could not see what Rafiq was doing because the open trunk lid blocked his view. Luis watched the trunk lid from inside the limo anyway. The driver stared straight ahead.

Rafiq returned without closing the trunk. He gently set down another device that also looked like a radio, but was bigger and seemingly much heavier. Rafiq immediately began hooking up wires and adjusting antennas, while barking orders to Luis.

"The RPV is in the trunk. The explosives are already loaded into the fuselage. All you have to do is attach the wings and check out the controls."

Luis tried to delay the inevitable. "I don't have any tools."

"They are in a brown pouch next to the wing section." Rafiq had anticipated and planned for everything. Luis was not surprised.

Luis had no choice. He slowly got out of the limo and went around to the trunk. Just as Rafiq had said, there was the fuselage, wing section and brown leather pouch.

"Work over there," said Rafiq as he pointed to the warehouse. "Take everything inside. Assemble the RPV. Check it out. Do whatever you have to do, but do not come out unless everything is ready."

"You know that this may take a while?" inquired Luis.

"We have a few hours. I'll tell you when to put the RPV into the air, and it had better be ready," glared Rafiq. His annoyance about losing Mahara had not abated.

Luis did as he was ordered. He just took his time, triing to make it look like he was busy. Luis took 15 minutes to connect the wing section; normally a five to seven minute operation. All the flight control circuitry came from inside the fuselage and made electrical contact through tiny plugs and connectors as the wing was joined to the fuselage. Luis toyed with the idea of sabotaging the connections making the RPV uncontrollable, but quickly discarded that notion as being too obvious and too dangerous for his own safety. Luis reasoned that Rafiq could probably assemble the RPV and make a serious attempt at attacking Air Force One all by himself.

Luis's only real hope was that Sherrie had contacted Lindsay and Lindsay had informed the White House of the pending threat. Hopefully, the White House believed Lindsay and altered or canceled the flight. Of course, Luis had no idea what Rafiq would do if the President's plane never showed up.

"Are you ready yet? Air Force One is about 20 minutes outside of Heathrow Ground Control."

Luis momentarily froze as Rafiq's words cut through him like a knife. "Almost ready." Luis lied, trying to stall for more time.

Rafiq called his bluff. "No more lies! No more stalling. Get out here now with the RPV or I will kill you where you stand."

Luis had no choice—he complied. He hefted the 80-pound contraption and slowly made his way out of the warehouse. Rafiq and the driver were waiting. Rafiq pointed to a nearby concrete pathway and instructed Luis to get the RPV into the air.

Chapter Nineteen

Lindsey Hawthorn's Office
Washington, D.C.
Tuesday, Early March
9:26 a.m.

Things around the office were quiet, and very little work was getting done. Lindsay was not involved in the investigation, and had nothing else to do. She dutifully read reports, and seriously considered if she should seek a transfer. The RPV program was history and it was time to move on.

Lindsey was in her office engrossed in the details of a spreadsheet lying in front of her. Thick files surrounded the perimeter of the small desk, but each was neat and orderly. That was the way Lindsey liked to work—neat and orderly with minimal interruptions. She was still stewing over her skirmish last week with that idiot Carl Worthington and was in no mood for any more interruptions. Unfortunately, in Lindsey's experience, many high-level government appointees were really not up to the job—some were real jerks. Political patronage, even of incompetent assholes and sneaky micromanagers was still prevalent here.

The phone rang. Lindsey glanced over at it and initially tried to ignore the incessant noise. She snatched up the receiver on the fourth ring with an abrupt "Yes, who is this?"

A barely audible voice whispered, "Is this Lindsey Hawthorn?"

Distracted with her own thoughts, Lindsey couldn't completely hear the soft-spoken words, and continued antagonistically. "What do you want, and speak up. I can't hear you."

Sherrie was startled and felt like hanging up, but instead she screwed up her courage and tried again. "This is Sherrie Feinstein. I don't know if you remember me or not."

Lindsey was stopped short. She sucked in air. The line went silent.

"Hello. Hello. Are you there?" a little louder this time.

Regaining her composure, "Yes, I'm here. I'm just having a bad day. I'm sorry Mrs. Feinstein. I apologize for my rudeness."

Sherrie didn't pick up on Lindsay's self-absorption.

"Can we talk? Do you have a few minutes?"

Lindsey hesitated. She was sure her office was not bugged, but didn't want anyone barging in while she talked to Sherrie in private.

"Can I call you back in three or four minutes?"

"I guess so, but it is very important that I speak with you."

"I know it is, that's why I have to call you back. I have to be very careful. I'm sure you understand."

"Yes. I think so. But please hurry. I do have something very important to tell you." Sherrie was repeating herself.

"Don't say anything else until I call you back on your cell phone. OK? I've got your number."

They both hung up. Lindsey snatched her purse from the floor next to her chair and bolted for the door. She pulled it shut behind her and made a mad dash for the pay phones in the lobby. They were the old style with folding doors that shut the caller in and everyone else out. Only in DC would you find such relics—cell phones were everywhere now. Her cell phone battery was dead—she forgot to charge it overnight. She was sure the FBI or the Secret Service did not bug the pay phones, and hoped the Feinstein Cell phone wasn't bugged either.

Fortunately, Lindsay had bought a Long Distance Phone Card a few months ago when she went camping in Colorado but was informed that cell phones didn't work out there in the woods. She hoped she still had minutes left on the card. She had the calling card out before she found an open booth, stepped inside and shut the door. It seemed like an eternity as she punched in the dizzying string of numbers. Finally, a phone was ringing on the other end. After two short rings, the same soft voice answered, "Hello."

"Mrs. Feinstein, this is Lindsey Hawthorn. We can talk privately now."

Feeling the need to get everything out immediately, Sherrie began rapidly. "OK. Please call me Sherrie."

"Certainly, Sherrie. Please continue."

"I don't know where to begin. I'm so confused. I just got this FAX and it said to call you."

"What? Slow down, Sherrie. What FAX? Who sent you a FAX?"

"The FAX cover page says it is from Luis Ramirez. He works with Richard on the RPV project."

"OK" Lindsey uttered skeptically. She knew Luis, and she knew all the co-workers were killed. So how could one of them send Sherrie a FAX?

"Are you sure it said Luis Ramirez?"

"Yes. He even signed it."

"Can you tell where he sent it from?"

"The cover sheet says the London Hilton Hotel. Do you need the address?"

"No, not yet. What does the FAX say?" Lindsay's mind was racing. Was this a ruse by Richard; some way of contacting Sherrie in secret from some hiding place in London?

Sherrie read the message carefully and slowly. She then reread it when Lindsay asked her to.

Lindsay was still uncertain. Could she believe this FAX and take this information to the higher-ups at Secret Service? Some of the folks at Secret Service already hated and distrusted her, and probably wouldn't even return her phone calls, so why even try. On the other hand, if this was really true and the President was in jeopardy again, she had an obligation to do her best to inform the proper authorities. She made an instant decision. She knew the President was taking a trip to Europe, but she wasn't sure when he was scheduled to go or exactly where he was going. She did know she couldn't take any chances and delay doing something.

"Sherrie, write down my FAX number, and FAX me a copy of what was sent to you. Include the Cover Sheet."

Sherrie diligently wrote down the number and repeated it to make sure she had it right. She did. "I'll do it right now. Thanks. Bye." Sherrie was relived as she hung up her phone. She even felt better.

The line went silent as Lindsay let out a long low sigh. The pressure was building and Lindsay didn't feel "warm and fuzzy" about what she was about to do. She suddenly had a huge burden and a grave responsibility. Lindsay slumped on the seat as she contemplated her next move after collecting the FAX from Sherrie.

After several deep breaths, Lindsay gathered her purse and headed for the FAX machine a few yards from her office. It was humming as she approached. She snatched up the pile of papers before the last page was finished, and began scanning them. The first FAX was for Larry, another agent, and the second was for her, but not from Sherrie. She thumbed through to the last page. It was from Sherrie. She grabbed the last page from the FAX Tray, and dropped the rest on the table where the proper addressees could find them.

Lindsay read the FAX as she walked quickly to her office and closed the door behind her. Her heart was pounding as she dreaded making the phone call she knew she couldn't avoid. Taking deep breaths and exhaling slowly, she calmed herself enough to search her phone directory for the number. It jumped out at her menacingly.

Still procrastinating, she reached for the coffee cup; a cute pink one with "You're the best!" printed in fancy lettering—a gift from her old college roommate. She took a sip of the now cold liquid, then another. She couldn't avoid the call any longer. Time was at a premium, and her personal feelings must be held in check. She punched in the number and braced herself by sitting stiffly in her chair.

A pleasant female voice answered, "Mr. Worthington's Office. Kelly speaking. May I help you?"

"My name in Lindsay Hawthorn. I am a lawyer working for the Military on assignment with the Secret Service. May I speak to Mr. Worthington, please?"

"Mr. Worthington isn't taking any calls right now. He is very busy with the investigation."

"This involves the investigation, and is very important. I'm sure Mr. Worthington would agree if you told him I am calling."

"Please hold. I'll check with Mr. Worthington." Elevator music switched in. Lindsay waited impatiently. After two minutes, Kelly returned. "Mr. Worthington instructed me to tell you he is busy, and not to call again until he contacts you first."

"What? I work for Mr. Worthington. What is wrong with him?"

"I'm sorry, but Mr. Worthington was quite emphatic."

"Fine. Please relay another message to Mr. Worthington."

"I'll try, but I can't promise he'll even talk to me."

"Please, just try. Tell Mr. Worthington that I have information about another immanent attack on the President. This time while he is in Air Force One. Will you give him that message?"

"What? Uh, sure. I'll try, Ms. Hawthorn." The line went dead. Ten minutes passed, then twenty. Lindsay paced around her meager office, she drank more cold coffee, sat down, stood up, paced some more. She dared not go beyond earshot of her phone.

The phone rang. She stretched across her desk to snatch it up before the second ring. "Hello. Hello, this is Lindsay Hawthorn."

"Carl Worthington here. You just scared the crap out of my secretary, young lady. What's all this garbage about another attack on the President? No one is dumb enough to try again this soon."

"Well, Mr. Worthington, I can't comment on that, but I do have some information I'm sure you will be interested in."

"Come on, Lindsay. We have a couple of hundred very skilled agents working on this around the clock from the FBI, Homeland Security and Secret Service. What can you possibly know that we don't?"

"Will you give me a chance to show you?"

Ignoring her, "What kind of information?"

"A FAX from Luis Ramirez in London"

Exasperated, he continued. "Bull shit. Luis Ramirez is dead. His body is in the morgue with all the others from Sterling."

"Are you sure about that?"

Carl hesitated. "I haven't seen the confirmed list of Sterling fatalities, but he was one of the crew in the trailer, and all the people in the trailer, except for Feinstein were killed. We've known that from the outset. What else do you know?"

Ignoring his crassness and sarcasm, Lindsay injecting her own. "Were they? I don't think so."

"Lindsay, what the hell are you trying to say?"

"I'm not sure, but shouldn't we be safe, rather than sorry?"

A flicker of caution. "OK. No more double talk. Get over to my office as soon as you can. I'll clear you with Kelly."

"Thank you, sir. I'll be there in ten minutes."

No good-bye's, just simultaneous hang-ups. Lindsay grabbed her purse, shoved the FAX into a large brown envelope, and locked her office, and then she walked quickly towards Carl Worthington's office in the next building.

As Lindsay passed the copy center, she realized she should make a copy of the FAX—just in case. She detoured, ran the copy, folded it in quarters and stuffed it in her purse. Turning, she continued her trek, confidant in her mission.

Upon arriving at the reception area, Lindsay introduced herself to Kelly, and was greeted cordially, but the iciness in Kelly's voice was unmistakable. Kelly was annoyed that she failed to prevent an outsider into the Worthington inner sanctum. Kelly buzzed her boss, and Lindsay was immediately ushered into a small conference room. Several men and women were already present. Lindsay never saw any of them before. Gradually a few more stragglers arrived, some she knew. Carl Worthington followed the last person in.

Carl surveyed the gathering, but didn't bother to introduce anyone— that would take too much of his valuable time. "Good. We're all here. Let's get started." Everyone rushed for a seat. Lindsay was left standing near the door.

"Ms. Hawthorn has something important to tell us," Carl snarled in her direction.

Lindsay was hesitant, unsure of what to do or where to begin. She drifted towards the head of the conference table near Carl's seat.

"Come on Ms. Hawthorn. We're all very busy. What is it you have to say?"

Lindsay glanced around the room at vacant eyes, then down on Carl. She gritted her teeth and began. "We all work for the US Government, particularly the Secret Service. We should all have the same objectives. Why is there such hostility towards me?"

"That's it. Let's go, we're done here." Carl was livid as he rose to leave the room.

"No we're not, Mr. Director. I do have valuable information, and you should have the common decency and courtesy to hear it."

Everyone else froze in their tracks, and turned to look at Carl. None of them had ever challenged his orders before.

Finally, Carl relented. "Do you, or do you not have tangible evidence in the assassination attempt?"

"Yes sir, I do."

"OK. You have two minutes to tell us what you know." And he sat down. Everyone else, except Lindsay did the same.

"Thank you. It won't take that long."

Everyone shuffled in his or her seat. Lindsay began explaining what she knew and how she knew it. She showed them the FAX, explained the "Body Count Discrepancy Theory," and concluded by repeating her opinion about Richard Feinstein—he was framed, and had nothing to do with the attack.

Four minutes passed and no one else said anything. Then, one agent after another began firing questions at her. She fielded and answered them more calmly now. They were interested in her story—and were leaning towards believing her. Eight minutes past, then ten. Lindsay continued answering questions. Carl Worthington just sat there listening and watching everyone else.

Then a lull as the questions dried up. Lindsay delivered the final blow. "You will, of course contact Air Force One and warn them not to land at Heathrow?"

Lindsay's stare at Carl was fierce. Carl blinked first. "Tom, contact Air Force One immediately and divert them to Paris."

"Yes Sir." Tom rose and rushed out of the room.

Carl was limp in his chair, arms dangling at his sides as Kelly knocked lightly on the door before entering.

"Mr. Worthington, there's an attorney on the phone who wants to speak to you."

"About what?" he barked.

"Sir, he says he represents Richard Feinstein."

Carl shot a glare at Lindsay, and then turned his attention back to Kelly.

"Have him hold until I get back to my office." Carl bolted out leaving everyone else just looking at each other.

CHAPTER TWENTY

Carl Worthington's Office
Washington, D.C.
Tuesday, Early March
10:43 a.m.

Carl neatly stacked the papers and reports he was studying when Kelly buzzed to remind him, "Mr. Weissman is still holding for you on line 3." Carl had procrastinated as he tried to avoid conflicts he knew he couldn't win.

Reluctantly Carl punched the flashing button and started quickly, "Mr. Weissman, what can I do for you?" No greeting; no excuses for the delay; no small talk; all business.

Startled, "Uh, yes, hello. My name is Harvey Weissman."

Carl cut him off. "I know who you are. What do you want?"

"What an asshole." Harvey thought to himself. He regained his composure.

"I represent Richard Feinstein. He wants to surrender to the authorities, but I am concerned for his safety. I will guarantee the surrender if you will guarantee his safety."

"Feinstein is wanted for the assassination attempt on the President, and for the deaths of over a dozen people. We will be careful, but I can't guarantee his safety."

Harvey got bolder. "Can't, or won't?"

"Now look here Mr. Weissman, don't you dare challenge my integrity." Harvey heard the spittle slam into the speakerphone.

"I don't give a damn about your integrity. All I care about is my client. If you can't, or won't guarantee his safety, then Richard will not surrender, and any additional bloodshed caused by your agents, private citizens or the police will be on your hands. I'm sure the Washington Post and the New York Times would be interested in how you are handling this tragedy."

"Don't threaten me you puissant mouthpiece!" The roar was so loud Harvey had to jerk the phone away from his ear.

Harvey was furious and almost hung up on him. One last try. Steeling himself, he continued as calmly as he could, "Mr. Worthington, we both want the same thing: justice. Richard Feinstein is willing to turn himself in so that he can clear his name and get on with his life. That's all there is to it."

Silence from Carl.

"Richard was framed. If your investigation hasn't discovered that fact yet, it will in due course, and Richard has information to prove it."

"I am aware of a possible frame-up, but there is little proof." Carl was calmer now. This was possible corroborating evidence to Lindsey's earlier story. This could turn into a real disaster for the Department and Carl himself. Carl hesitated as he pondered how to protect his own position as Director of the Secret Service.

Harvey started to speak, hesitated, then decided to pursue the frame-up line later.

"How about this? I will give you an address, you send some agents and Richard surrenders to them. That way he is not exposed to any danger from overreacting police officers or gun-toting private vigilantes."

"Will he just make a statement, or does he have any evidence other than his own self-serving interests? And, why should I believe him anyway?"

Harvey was exasperated and boiling again. "Mr. Worthington. My client was framed. He does have information for you that will put your investigation on the right track. Richard had no involvement in the attack on the President. He was not responsible for any of it." Harvey was not yet willing to divulge anything more.

"An alleged Frame-up is for a judge and jury to decide."

"Yes it is Sir, but first you have to apprehend someone, get an indictment, and then go to trial before a jury can make such a decision. You haven't even gotten to step one yet. Better still, you can avoid a trial entirely and the embarrassment of bringing charges against an innocent man. Surely you realize that whatever Richard knows will come out at a trial, and the consequences to you and the government won't be pleasant." The tide rapidly shifted. Harvey was now almost gloating. Carl was still pissed.

Carl tried to salvage his position. "It is a Federal Offence to hide a witness and withhold evidence in an ongoing investigation. I can arrest your smart ass and see how you survive in jail."

"I am aware of that, Sir. However, my obligations to my client are far superior to whatever might happen to me."

Harvey had encountered many government officials over the years, but had never met anyone like Carl Worthington. "What a real jerk" muttered Harvey to himself.

Neither man spoke as their minds churned trying to sort out the last few minutes of confrontation, and determine what to do or say next. Precious time passed.

Harvey heard the buzzer in Carl's office, then hushed words that sounded like "...One has diverted, Sir."

Harvey waited. Carl spoke first. "OK, Mr. Weissman. Give me the address and I will personally take Mr. Feinstein into custody. I'll bring several other agents with me."

"And you will guarantee his safety?"

"I will have a dozen agents with me in four cars. I assume you will be at this address escorting Feinstein, and you can come along to the Marshal's office with us. Is that enough of a guarantee for you?"

"Yes, it is, but I have a few more conditions."

Exasperated, "What else do you want?"

Harvey was thinking rapidly. "No police lights or sirens, no press, and no prior notification to anyone. Don't even tell the agents coming with you where you are going or mention Richard's name until they are in route. I want your word that no one other than these agents will know about Richard's surrender until after he is safely locked up in the Federal Building. Absolutely no leaks, Mr. Worthington. He also gets a private cell."

Carl hesitated momentarily. He actually was impressed by these demands—he would have made them himself. "All right. I agree."

"Good."

"What's the address?"

"Not over the phone."

"For G-d's sake, this is a secure private line to my office."

"My line might not be secure, Sir."

"Then how the hell am I supposed to know when and where to pick him up?"

"I will send a messenger to your office. The messenger will have the address and a written copy of the agreement we just made. The messenger will be instructed to have you sign the agreement before handing over the address."

"Now you've gone too far." The roar from Carl was intense.

"I am only protecting my client's interests." Harvey remained calm.

"Bullshit. You don't trust me." Even louder.

"Sir, I have never met you. Therefore I have no reason to trust or distrust you. I am just taking no chances with my client's personal safety."

Time was wasting. It made no sense to continue arguing. "OK, send your messenger over."

"Someone will be there within 30 minutes"

Carl hung up abruptly and didn't hear Harvey say "Good bye, Mr. Worthington."

Harvey scribbled some notes and rushed into the spare room that served as an office, and where they kept the computer. Richard and Suzanne followed. No one spoke. Harvey flipped a switch and gizmos and lights whirred and danced as the machine sprang to life. Harvey was thankful he was computer literate, or he couldn't have gotten the agreement prepared in time if he wasn't. He also knew that an agreement like this would probably not hold up in any court of law, if it ever came to that. He also knew that Carl Worthington could arrest or detain the messenger until the address was divulged without signing the agreement. He had no choice but to rely on Carl Worthington, hoping he would keep his word.

Harvey pecked away with two fingers, but made few mistakes. Within minutes, the one paragraph agreement was completed. He quickly added a line for Carl Worthington's signature and date, and then scanned the document on the monitor one last time. He was satisfied. He smiled at Suzanne and Richard, and then hit the Print button with the mouse pointer. The Laser printer whirred and spat out a neatly printed official looking document.

"Richard, this will help insure your safety. Carl Worthington, the Head of the Secret Service has agreed to sign it before you surrender. Read it so you'll understand what is going on." Harvey handed the document to Richard, who read it slowly and carefully. Suzanne read it over Richard's shoulder.

Richard shrugged and handed it back. "OK, I surrender. Then what? Even if I prove I was framed, I will always be guilty in the eyes of someone. You know there are people who still don't believe we landed men on the moon. They think it was all Hollywood Camera Tricks. And what about that poor guy falsely accused of the Olympic bombing in Atlanta? He's still tarnished even though he was really a hero. Many nuts won't ever believe I am innocent either."

"I agree with you, and I've been working on a plan for that as well. Suzanne, can I talk to you alone for a minute?"

Richard watched them go into the other room as he sat in the computer room alone. He was less scared, but only a little.

CHAPTER TWENTY-ONE

Cockpit of Air Force One
50 Miles from Heathrow Airport
Tuesday, Early March
10:58 a.m. Washington, D.C. Time

Ron Conklin, the Secret Service Agent in charge aboard Air Force One knocked on the Cabin door. Randy Schmidt, the co-pilot reached around and opened the door. "Hey, Ron. What's up?"

"Just got a call over the secure line from Secret Service Headquarters."

"Yeah, what do they want?" asked Peter Harding, the pilot as he turned to face Ron. Harding was an ex-Marine F-14 Fighter pilot who spent 10 years with Delta before being offered this job by the Secret Service. Harding flew the last three presidents all over the world.

Everyone knew that Headquarters only called when there was some sort of emergency. All routine transmissions came through field agent's radios. This transmission was different.

"We're ordered to divert to Paris."

"Paris? Why?"

"Headquarters said the orders came from the top: Worthington himself."

"You're sure about this? Is there a chance this is a mistake or misunderstanding?"

"Yeah, I'm sure. No mistake."

"OK, I'll contact ground control, give them the news and get new vectors."

"Ron watched as Harding fiddled with some dials and adjusted the small microphone on his headset. "This is Air Force One. Come in Heathrow Control"

Everyone waited as Harding listened for confirmation of the connection.

"We are currently at 520 knots and 32 thousand, heading for Heathrow. Air Force One will not be landing at Heathrow. I repeat. Air Force One will not be landing at Heathrow... That's affirmative. Request vectoring to Paris. ... Got it, Heathrow. Executing right turn now. ... On course to Paris, climbing to 35,000, ETA 37 minutes. Thanks Heathrow. See ya next time." Harding cocked his microphone back up and turned to Ron. The co-pilot watched the instruments as the huge plan gently and smoothly changed course.

"What else do you know, Ron?"

"Nothing yet. They just ordered me to divert the plane immediately. I'm going back to tell the President first, then I'll confirm with Headquarters that we're diverted to Paris, and try to weasel the reason out of them. I'll keep you posted." Ron ducked out and was gone. The pilots returned to their logs, switches, dials and controls.

President's Quarters, Air Force One
Heading to Paris
Tuesday, Early March
11:08 a.m. Washington, D.C. Time

"Thank you for seeing me, Mr. President."

"Don't be so formal, Ron. We've known each other a few years now."

"Yes Sir."

"Well? What is it, Ron?"

"Mr. Worthington has ordered us to divert to Paris. I don't have all the details yet, but I will keep you informed."

"Damn."

"Have we diverted already?"

"Yes, sir, we have. I notified Capt. Harding a few minutes ago. Procedures, Sir."

"I understand. There must be some other scare that Homeland Security, the Secret Service or FBI has uncovered."

"That would be my guess too, Sir."

"Of course. Thanks for the info. When will we be in Paris?"

"About 35 minutes, Sir."

"All right, Ron. Keep on top of this."

"Yes Sir. I will."

North of Heathrow Airport
Tuesday, Early March
11:13 a.m. Washington, D.C. time

Rafiq ripped off his headset and threw it down. Luis was watching with one eye on the TV Monitor and the other on Rafiq. Luis didn't look up from the monitor.

Rafiq slammed his fist on the flimsy table where the radios were set up. A leg cracked and the equipment tumbled off. Sparks flew, and crackling noises filled the otherwise still air.

Rafiq paced back and forth. He rubbed his chin, wrung his hands, and kept pacing. Finally he stopped in front of Luis and stared directly into his eyes. If nothing else, Rafiq was intimidating.

"Bring the RPV back," he barked at Luis.

Luis froze. "You're kidding?"

"Bring the RPV back. Air Force One was diverted to Paris. The Imperialist Leader is not landing at Heathrow. Bring the RPV back."

Luis knew Rafiq was angry and flustered. He had never repeated himself before.

"That's crazy. I can't land this thing. I barely got it in the air. Landing it is impossible, not to mention dangerous with all those explosives packed inside."

"There will be no attack on Air Force One today. I cannot just leave it in the air and let it crash wherever it runs out of fuel. We need it for when the next time comes."

"Why not let it crash? You don't seem to care who gets hurt."

Fire flew from Rafiq's eyes as he glared more intently at Luis. "I don't care how many Americans, or their friends the British people, die. I do care that the authorities will examine every little piece and might trace the RPV back to Abu'l. Now land that RPV or I'll kill you where you stand."

Luis returned to his controls with renewed urgency and intensity. He had his doubts, but decided to practice some simple maneuvers before attempting to land the plane. After all, he had watched pilots take off and land RPV's dozens of times.

"I'm going to practice a few things first, just to get the feel of landing."

"Make it fast. We don't have a lot of time."

Luis tried a right turn. That went well. He lost a few feet of altitude, but the RPV was flying in the direction he wanted. Then he tried a left turn. That too he performed as if he were an expert. Next he tried a shallow descent from about 400 feet up. Luis pushed the joystick too fast and the RPV went into a steep dive. The monitors showed the ground rushing up toward the tiny plane. Luis instinctively pulled the joystick the other way, and the RPV responded instantly by climbing back up. Luis delicately moved the joystick back and forth until the RPV was flying level.

"What's going on? Why haven't you landed the plane?" snarled Rafiq.

"I almost crashed the damn thing. I told you I couldn't do this."

"You must, or you will die." Rafiq was breathing over Luis's shoulder watching the monitor. Glancing back, Luis noticed that Rafiq already had his hand inside his coat—where he stowed his gun and an enormous hunting knife.

"Where is the RPV?" barked Rafiq.

"Heading away from us now. I do have it flying level."

"Turn it around and land it. No more games. Just do it."

"I'm trying." Luis started a very gentle right turn. He watched the flight gauges carefully. He was losing some altitude as he made the turn, but guessed he would still have the RPV at about 275 feet when it was finally pointing at the makeshift runway.

Then, there it was. The camera in the nose showed the RPV headed in the general direction of where Rafiq, Luis and the Driver were standing. Luis leveled the wings and very gently pushed the joystick forward. The altitude began decreasing, but the tiny silver flying bomb wobbled and jerked from side to side as Luis frantically tried to control the descent. As the plane got closer, Luis could sense he had better control than the monitor suggested. He found the narrow runway on the monitor and tried somewhat successfully to keep the near end of the gray concrete ribbon generally centered on the monitor screen. He remembered that the real pilots did exactly that when they landed the RPV's.

"OK, here she comes." Luis's remark made Rafiq look up to find the RPV heading for the runway just as Luis said. Rafiq fixated on the RPV. He watched as the shinny wings rocked rhythmically and the nose tilted up, then down, then up again. Rafiq kept watching. The driver joined the survey of the sky. No one moved a muscle except for Luis's hand pushing the joystick around trying to guide the plane in for a landing.

Luis only watched the monitor and the altitude gauge. He was sweating, and wiped droplets from his forehead. Those he missed dripped into his mouth. They were as salty as he knew human tears to be. He tried unsuccessfully to ignore his fear.

Luis started the countdown. "Altitude—One Hundred feet." The RPV was clearly visible about a thousand feet away.

"Seventy-five feet." The fuselage glistened in the sunlight; the RPV was less than 500 feet away. The entire plane could easily be seen. Rafiq and the driver stared.

"Fifty Feet." Luis was still struggling to keep the wings level and the nose pointed at the runway. It was very hard to do. Luis sweated more profusely.

"Twenty-five feet… Fifteen feet…G-d dam it." Luis jerked the nose up as the runway image on the monitor slipped out of sight to the bottom-right.

"What happened? Why didn't you land the plane?" Rafiq was all over him again. His olive colored face was crimson with anger. The once-hidden gun was pointed inches from Luis's left temple.

Luis focused only on the monitor and didn't see the menacing weapon.

Luis spoke as he fought the controls to guide the RPV back around for another try. "It would have crashed. I couldn't keep it lined up with the runway. The winds from the right keep pushing it to the left. I've got to get a feel of how to compensate for the wind or it will miss the runway again and crash."

"Try again. This time bring it down—wind or no wind. No more tricks." Rafiq clearly didn't trust Luis, but none-the-less looked up at the trees to see the leaves swaying.

Luis ignored the threat. He concentrated hard on what he had to do. He realized how much his hand holding the joystick was shaking. He tried to settle his nerves as the plane made a gentle banked turn around back towards them. Luis lined up the nose with the runway again, but pointed the nose slightly into the wind. This time he started at 50 feet.

"Fifty," he announced, sweating.

"Twenty five... Fifteen... Ten..." All eyes were on the RPV.

A gust of wind swirled bits of paper and dried leaves—and battered the RPV off course again. This time it was too late. Luis froze, lost control and the RPV slammed into the rear of the limousine parked fifteen feet from the side of the runway. The fireball erupted into a towering inferno, sending shards of metal hundreds of feet into the air. Bodies were dismembered; all three men died instantly. No one felt the agony or any pain. The blast could be heard several miles away, and the ensuing plume of smoke was seen from the Control Tower at Heathrow, and from several planes already in their landing patterns.

Emergency crews were immediately dispatched from Heathrow and local Fire Stations. At first, the Air Traffic Controllers thought a plane under their watchful eyes had crashed. A frantic quick scan of the radarscopes confirmed that none of the planes under Heathrow Air Traffic Control had crashed. The cause of the explosion was unknown, but clearly the fire was a hazard for other air traffic until it was controlled. Fire-fighting equipment was dispatched. Police and ambulances were summoned and converged on the scene, all guided by the control tower from their vantage point 300 ft above the vast runways of busy Heathrow

Airport. All air traffic was temporarily rerouted away from the explosion site. Initially, no one knew if there were any injuries or deaths, and no one expected to find survivors of such an explosion if anyone was unlucky enough to be nearby. Three people were nearby, and no one did survive.

Several squad cars were within minutes of the explosion site and immediately raced to the scene. A quick survey of what looked to be the wrecked small plane and a limo, plus the remains of at least two bodies, maybe three were too much for the Patrol officers to handle on their own. They called their Captain, looked around some more and then settled back into their cars to wait for their superior to arrive. There was nothing they could do for the victims.

George Hamilton arrived with sirens blaring and lights flashing. He only bothered to shut off the engine and siren before bolting from the vehicle. The door remained open.

The Officers that were the first on the scene jumped out of their cars and met Hamilton as he looked around in dismay. No one ever confused this George Hamilton with the famous Hollywood actor. This George Hamilton shared no physical resemblance or characteristics with the American. This Hamilton was not tall, dark and handsome. In fact everything about Captain George Hamilton was different, except perhaps they were about the same age.

Rodney Collins and Bert Graham quickly and professionally briefed their Captain. Hamilton listened intently as he continued to look at the wreckage and dead bodies. Nothing was immediately recognizable—just bits and pieces that gave hints at what they might have been before being blown to smithereens.

When the briefing was over and Hamilton's questions answered, Officers Collins and Graham braced themselves for the impending orders from their boss. There were no witnesses to what actually happened, only the aftermath. Everyone there at the time of the explosion was now dead. Only one body seemed to be in mostly one piece, so Hamilton ordered Collins to search him for any identification. Collins complied. No identification on the body.

Hamilton ordered a search of the area to see if anything could provide some clues. The Limo was a charred heap with a door blown off and the rear end scattered in a fifty-foot radius. After about an hour of searching the nearby bushes, another Officer found what looked like a burned suit coat and handed it to Hamilton. With gloved hands, Hamilton found the remnants of three Passports: one American, and one Iranian. The third passport could not be easily identified. No names on any of the passports were legible, not even a picture or the sex of the owner could be deciphered. Forensics would have to try and identify the individuals to which they belonged. The charred passports were bagged and tagged.

Hamilton's Cell Phone buzzed. A quick glance and he went ashen. It was the hospital. Hamilton's wife of 43 years had been admitted three days ago after her Breast Cancer had returned. This call could not be good news. The Doctor in charge of Francis Hamilton's care knew the Hamiltons well: he performed the double Mastectomy and oversaw the subsequent Radiation and Chemotherapy Treatments three years ago. He understood that Captain Hamilton was not to be disturbed unless it was an emergency.

Walking briskly away from the other officers, Hamilton flipped open the phone and after a cursory greeting, just listened. "Captain, Francis has taken a turn for the worst. She is not responding as we had hoped. I am very sorry to tell you this, but in my opinion she may not survive the night. I suggest you come back to the hospital as soon as possible."

Her parents were long gone, and Francis was an only child. Their own daughter had died of Cervical Cancer six years ago. George Hamilton was the only living relative France had left. Hamilton made an instant decision.

"Collins!" shouted the Captain. Collins strode over holding the beginnings of his report.

"Francis has taken a turn for the worst. I'm going to the hospital. You take over here. It looks like a bunch of tourists playing with Big-boy toys that went wrong. Take it slow, but be thorough. Brief me when you're done here."

"Will do, Captain. Hope everything goes well with your wife." Collins suspected the end was near, but tried to be supportive.

* * *

Officer Collins dutifully wrote his Report, noting the lack of apparent criminal activity. It was concluded that a Remote Control airplane of about a 6 feet wingspan powered by a gasoline-type engine could accidentally explode—especially in the hands of inexperienced or careless operators. There was no other evidence, so that was the most likely conclusion.

Neither the Heathrow authorities, or even the US Embassy in London was aware of the reasons for the diversion of Air Force One, so the US Ambassador to England was simply instructed to monitor the investigation surrounding the death of a US Citizen in an apparently accidental explosion and then report the findings to other US officials. It took several weeks, but the remains of Luis Ramirez were eventually identified through dental records and DNA testing. The State Department was notified as required by procedure, and eventually the information was discovered by the Secret Service—by accident. The State Department clerks had not been informed about Luis Ramirez and were not looking for him. To the office workers processing what appeared to be routine paperwork on an unfortunate death of an American citizen, this was just more routine stuff—unpleasant, but none-the-less routine.

Once alerted, the Secret Service then began their own investigation and with dogged determination traced the bits and pieces of the RPV back to Sterling and Associates. That took another 23 days, mostly because the scraps collected at the explosion site were not being treated as evidence in a criminal or national security investigation. To the ones initially investigating the accident in London, this was just an unfortunate case of three men doing something careless or stupid that caused an explosion and subsequently their own deaths. Nothing necessarily criminal about that.

CHAPTER TWENTY-TWO

Downtown London
Tuesday, Early March
2:16 p.m. Local Time

Mahara had spent a few hours wondering the streets of London window-shopping. Occasionally she would browse the racks of elegant stores. She even tried on a few skirts and blouses, but decided not to buy anything. She had never bought anything expensive from such fine stores entirely by herself. An Islamic man had always accompanied her and paid for whatever she wanted in Iran. She knew about money, but was not accustomed to having any of her own. But now, Luis had given her a few hundred dollars. She had no idea how to spend American money in London.

She ate lunch at a cute café, ordered a salad and water. Eating slowly she tried to figure out what Luis was doing and why he was treating her so badly. She knew her place in a Male-dominated society, but Luis had always treated her better than that. She couldn't think of anything she might have done to upset him. The nice lady that waited on her in the café helped with the money exchange, keeping quite a large tip for her trouble. Mahara never suspected anything. Eventually, she just decided to go back to the hotel in the evening. She wondered if Luis would be any different when she got back. Would he even be there? She changed her mind about the hotel—she was hungry again.

Mahara decided it was late enough and hailed a Cab. Something else she had never done by herself before. "Do you know any restaurants here?" she inquired of the cabbie in broken, heavily accented English that was hard to understand.

Normally, this cab driver made little conversation, especially with foreigners that were hard to understand. Mahara was different. She was young, alone and drop-dead gorgeous. The cab driver felt an urge to strike up a conversation with this beauty. Who knows where it might lead.

"Are you staying at a Hotel?" he inquired, hoping for a "Yes."

"I think Hilton Inn. Is that right?"

"Perfect. There is a great little Pub a few blocks from that hotel. Want me to take you there?" His accent was common British.

"Please, yes. You take me." Mahara meant the Hotel. The cabbie selfishly interpreted her response as the restaurant.

Twelve minutes later, the cab rolled to a stop in front of a row of older buildings, each attached to the other for the entire block. The sign cantilevered over the door protruding out to the street said "British Pub and Ale House," but Mahara couldn't read it at all.

"I'll take you in and help you order, sweetie."

"This not Hotel." said Mahara slowly as she surveyed the street.

"No. This is the Pub I told you about. Let's go inside."

Mahara wasn't astute enough to pick up on the obvious flirtation.

"OK." She said tentatively, not sure what to do.

They went in together. Heads turned to stare at this petite, elegant stranger accompanied by a scruffy cab driver everyone in the Pub knew as Nathan.

The hostess seated them at a small table near the back. The entire restaurant was pretty dark. Candles illuminated little oases of light on each table. Others continued to glance in their direction. Mahara didn't notice the attention she was getting from the male patrons. Those with female partners suffered, but largely ignored the stares and glares from wives and girlfriends sitting across from them. Some of the women poked their male companions in the ribs or kicked their shins when the staring lasted more than a few seconds.

"What do you want?" slurred a rumpled waitress not very eager to take their order.

"Two Beers." answered Nathan. Mahara didn't understand any of this, but kept quiet anyway.

The waitress turned on her heel and stomped off to the bar without a word.

Nathan decided to become bolder. "Where're you from, sweetheart?"

Mahara maintained a blank face.

"You speak English?"

No change in Mahara's expression. However, she was starting to feel uneasy.

The restaurant was fairly loud, but conversations from nearby tables could be heard.

The large TV mounted on the wall behind Nathan's left shoulder was tuned to the local afternoon news, as was all the others in the room.

Abruptly the screen flashed and splashy graphics proclaimed, "This is a major breaking News Story."

The bright colors caught Mahara's eye, and she turned to watch, even though she didn't know what was going on.

The graphic faded to a shot in the newsroom where a well-dressed, very proper British Reporter stared directly at the TV camera.

"We have breaking news to report. There has been an explosion at a remote location just north of Heathrow Airport. The cause is unknown, but there are reports of casualties. Preliminary reports from the Police indicate that there are three people dead. One might be American; the other two are tentatively identified as Arabic, possibly Iranian or Egyptian. Positive identification has not yet been made."

The reporter's face dissolved to a scene of destruction. Police cars with flashing lights were parked in a chaotic manner; fire trucks, long hoses and firemen suited for battle with the flames were busy doing their jobs.

A cutaway shot showed men in white uniforms loading a large black plastic bag into the back of an ambulance.

"What happen?" Mahara was scared. There were no real clues that this could be Luis, but, she instinctively feared the worst.

Nathan glanced up at the monitor on the far wall. "Some sort of explosion, I guess." He didn't care.

"American, yes?"

"Look Sweetie, I don't know. I wasn't listening."

Mahara was sure she heard the word "American." Now she was visibly frightened.

"We go now. We go to hotel."

Several envious male eyes darted in their direction, only to be met with more kicks and harder jabs from their female tablemates.

Nathan looked around and grinned. "Sure, Sweetie. Whatever you want." Nathan had a different idea about what the next few hours might bring. He had never been laid by a slim, beautiful woman before. All the women he was infrequently intimate with were overweight and sloppy—just like himself. His eyes twinkled with the images that danced in his mind.

Nathan threw a few British pounds on the table and helped Mahara from her chair.

Men continued to stare, wishing they were in Nathan's shoes. More kicks and jabs from the females, low moans and sheepish looks from the male patrons.

CHAPTER TWENTY-THREE

Hilton Hotel
London, Enfland
Tuesday, Early March
4:48 p.m. Local Time

The cab slowed to a stop at the entrance to the Hilton Hotel. Nathan quickly realized that if he was to go into the hotel for an extended period of time he couldn't just leave the cab unattended by the entrance. Jerking the cab into gear, he rushed to an open parking spot about a hundred feet away and parked.

Nathan rushed around the cab to open the door for Mahara. Holding out a hand, he helped her out, locked and shut the door. Turning smartly, he guided her towards the entrance with a bounce in his step— anticipating a glorious screwing from this beautiful stranger.

The glass doors slid open silently as they approached. Nathan slipped his arm around her tiny waste. Mahara was startled. She was taught not to allow anyone to touch her without her consent. Only Abu'l, Luis or anyone Abu'l gave her to was allowed that privilege. Nathan ignored her squirming and tried to keep her close as he guided her to the elevator.

"What floor are you on, sweetie?" he smiled, trying to be friendly, and hoping to distract and calm her.

"You no touch me." Mahara protested loudly as she continued to twist and push at him.

The Hotel plain clothed Security Guard, Roger Huffington, looked up from his paperwork to see the commotion. He immediately recognized Mahara—who wouldn't notice her? He didn't know her name, but he did know she was a guest at the hotel with one or two other gentlemen. He had never seen the man she was with before.

Roger intercepted Nathan and Mahara before they reached the elevator. "May I be of assistance?" he inquired, bowing slightly and looking directly at Mahara.

Nathan glared at him. "The young lady is with me, and I am escorting her to her room."

Ignoring Nathan, Roger addressed Mahara directly again, who was now tugging on Nathan's arm trying to get away from him. He was too strong. She couldn't break free. "Is this man with you? Are you taking him upstairs with you?"

Mahara looked at him quizzically. She only caught a few words. "I with Luis. I go to my room and wait for him." Her broken English was hard to understand, but Roger sensed she did not want this man near her.

Addressing Nathan, "Can I see some identification, sir?"

"I don't have to show you a damned thing. I'm going upstairs with the lady and you can't stop me." Total defiance.

"Are you a guest of this hotel, Sir"

"That's none of your business."

"Sir, yes it is. Only guests are allowed upstairs. I am with Hotel Security and I can keep you from going where you are not wanted or authorized inside of this hotel. Now show me some identification or I'll call the Police and have them ask you the same question."

"The Lady is a guest and she invited me up to her room."

Addressing Mahara, "Did you invite this man up to your room?"

"I with Luis." Mahara didn't understand any of this, so she repeated herself.

Turning to Nathan. "Are you Luis?"

Seeing no way out, "Fine" uttered Nathan angrily, but not letting go of Mahara.

Mahara gave one hard shove, and freed herself from Nathan's grasp.

"Sir, if you don't show me some identification or proof that you are staying at this Hotel, I can't allow you upstairs with the lady."

Turning back to Mahara, who had moved several steps away from Nathan, but not much closer to Roger, he continued "Would you like me to escort you to your room?"

Mahara was hesitant and said nothing.

As sincerely as he could, "I'm with Hotel Security. I am here to help you any way I can." Roger offered as he showed her his identification.

Mahara still didn't understand all that was going on, but did realize that Roger posed less of a threat than the cab driver.

"You help me find Luis?"

"Yes, I'll help you find Luis. Is he your husband?"

"Luis my master. You help me find him, yes?"

Turning to Nathan, "Sir, you are obviously not Luis, and the Lady does not want you near her, much less up in her room. I suggest you leave the hotel immediately."

"Damn you, the little tramp invited me here. I'm going up there with her."

"No you're not. If you try, I will forcibly detain you and turn you over to the police. I'll give you one minute to leave the premises before I call the police and file charges against you."

Nathan was now visibly angry—jaw clenched, fists curled and ready to fight. When Roger moved closer to him and patted his chest, Nathan backed down, turned on his heel and headed for the exit. Roger was armed.

Both Mahara and Roger watched Nathan disappear through the glass doors, then Roger turned to Mahara and with a broad smile and a grand sweep of the arm ushered her toward the elevator. "I can escort you to your room if you want, but I think you will be safe now. What is your room number?"

That Mahara understood. "My room is 1214. I have key." She proclaimed holding out the plastic card proudly.

Roger knew that the Cabbie could have easily gotten into her room, do with her as he pleased and left the hotel before anyone knew about it, had he not spotted them in the atrium. "I'll show you the way." as he pushed the Up button. He, at least, could control his impulses for someone as desirable as she.

Once inside the room, Roger learned her name, and asked about Luis, but got little information. He figured out that Luis had left the hotel by mid morning and had yet to return.

Roger guessed Mahara was of Middle Eastern origin. Many of the guests in the hotel were. Few were from the Far East or South America. "What country are you from, Mahara? Egypt, Iraq, Iran, Pakistan, Saudi Arabia?"

Mahara recognized Iran. "I from Iran."

"May I see your Passport?"

"Rafiq has Passport."

"I thought you said you were with Luis. Who is Rafiq?"

"Rafiq make Luis go with him. I with Luis. Luis my master."

This was dizzying. Roger didn't want to get in the middle of whatever was going on, and he couldn't get much from Mahara. The language barrier was too much of a problem.

"OK, if Luis does not return within a few hours, go to the Iranian Embassy and they will help you. I'll be back in a few minutes with their address. You wait here for Luis."

"I wait."

With that, Roger rose and headed for the door. He would check out the registration for this room, look up the Iranian Embassy address, and bring it back to Mahara. What more could he do?

* * *

The next morning after a fitful night with only on-and-off sleep, Mahara awoke in an empty bed. Luis had not returned.

Mahara sat up straight in the bed, the sheet dangling from her bare breasts. She looked around and saw no one. No Luis. No Rafiq.

She slowly slipped out from under the sheet and searched each room, softly calling out "Luis. Luis." No answer.

The fear returned. She was all alone in a strange city. Then she remembered the neatly printed piece of paper the nice man left yesterday. After making sure she knew where it was, she quickly washed her face, put on a minimum amount of makeup, dressed and was ready.

Exiting the elevator, she spotted Roger across the vast lobby chatting with another couple. She approached him tentatively and waited until the couple left. Roger turned and saw her standing there looking as gorgeous as ever.

"Mahara, did Luis come back?"

"No. Luis not come back. I go to Embassy now, yes?"

"Well, without Luis or a Passport, you need the help of your own government. They know how to handle these situations."

"You help me go to Embassy?"

"I can get you a cab and give the driver the instructions. Do you have any money?"

Mahara thrust a handful of American bills at Roger.

"Is this OK?"

Roger saw several Twenties and a Ten dollar bill—there were many more. "That is more than enough."

Roger smiled and offered her his arm. Mahara took it gingerly and walked with him outside to the cabstand. The first one in line inched forward to save them a few steps. The Driver looked much better than Nathan, and Mahara noticed that immediately.

Roger met the driver as he rounded the rear to open the door for them. "This is a special guest of our hotel. She needs to go to the Iranian Embassy." He took the slip of paper from Mahara and handed it to the Cabbie. A quick glance, and the cabbie nodded.

"I know exactly where it is. It should be about 15 minutes in this light traffic."

"Fine. Take the lady there as quickly as possible, but don't break any traffic laws."

"Yes sir. I'll be real careful."

Mahara slipped into the back seat. Roger bent in, offered his hand and wished her luck. With that, the cab drove out of sight down the elevated ramp to the road.

CHAPTER TWENTY-FOUR

Aboard Air Force One
Tuesday, Early March
5:49 p.m. London Time

Doc was antsy. He hated not knowing what was going on, particularly when it involved himself. Ron Conklin had not reported back yet, so Doc pushed himself up and went looking for him.

As Doc entered the Passenger portion of the huge 747 from the private entranceway to the Presidential Quarters, he spotted Ron coming down the aisle towards him. "Ron, come back to my office and we'll talk."

"Yes Sir, Mr. President." They retreated through the door the President just came out of.

Doc slid behind his desk as Ron settled into a chair on the opposite side. Such meetings were routine for both men.

"What more can you tell me? Why were we diverted to Paris?"

"I was just coming back here to tell you, Mr. President."

"Good."

"I spoke with several of Mr. Worthington's top aides. There was a threat to shoot down Air Force One as it landed at Heathrow, Sir."

"Shoot down Air Force One? That's crazy. Who would try something like that?"

"Apparently the same people, or group that tried to assassinate you, Sir, but that is unconfirmed."

"Richard Feinstien?"

"We're not sure yet, but maybe not."

"How did Worthington learn about the attempt on Air Force One?"

"From the Project Manager on the RPV program. It seems Ms. Lindsey Hawthorn, she's the RPV Project Manager for the Secret Service, got a FAX from Feinstein's wife. That FAX came from someone on the RPV Team. We think his name was Luis Ramirez."

"What is Feinstein's involvement?"

"There may not be any, Sir."

Doc settled back into his seat. Both men just stared at each other knowing exactly what the implications meant.

Doc broke the silence first. "What information other than the note found in the trailer points towards this Feinstein guy?"

"That's the problem, Mr. President. There isn't anything else. In fact, Feinstein might have been framed."

"Just keep on top of this. We'll all look like bumbling idiots soon enough."

"Yes Sir. I'll brief you whenever I get an update from headquarters."

"Thanks, and try to prod them along if need be."

"Yes Sir. I will, Sir."

"OK. When do we touch down in Paris?"

"ETA was 6:01 local the last time I checked, and we should be ready to escort you off by 6:45. This was short notice. We had to make special arrangements and take care of some Security issues before we can let you deplane, Mr. President."

"I understand. What are the plans for Paris? Will we attempt London again today or try for tomorrow?"

"Air Force One will be refueled this evening. We're taking you to the Paris Windom Hotel overnight. Scotland Yard and the London Police are making preparations for our arrival tomorrow morning around 10:30. The Secret Service advance team is there already. They will have a huge ground security force all along the landing approach, and at least three helicopters and two small engine planes patrolling the landing pattern. If anything looks suspicious, we will know about it within seconds and abort the landing.

"Good plan. Thanks, Ron."

That was Ron's cue to rise, bid farewell and leave.

* * *

Secret Service Headquarters
Tuesday, Early March
12:11 p.m. Washington, D.C. Time

Chuck Simmons, one of the hundreds of Secret Service Agents working on the Assassination Attempt case came across something quite startling as he compared one list of names with another. Chuck quickly fired up his computer and did a little more digging.

Chuck rechecked what he was looking at. Nothing changed, so he picked up the phone and called his boss. The conversation was short.

"Boss, I found something interesting when checking Customs Logs."

"What'd you find?"

"Luis Ramirez used his passport within an hour after the Assassination attempt."

"Bring what you've got to Worthington. I'll meet you there in 5 minutes."

Both men hung up without any good-byes, each gathered some papers and headed for the elevator.

Upon arrival, both men were ushered into Carl Worthington's office immediately.

Bob Hopkins spoke first. "Carl, Chuck has some interesting information you should see."

Carl turned to Chuck "Show me."

Chuck handed some papers to Carl and started explaining what each page meant. "The Customs Logs show that Luis Ramirez used his passport shortly after the assassination attempt." Chuck pointed to a highlighted line on the printout.

"Where did he go?"

"Iran, Sir." Pointing to another page.

"Why didn't we pick this up before?"

"Ramirez took a private Jet. We only get routine Passport notices from the scheduled airlines, Sir."

"Jesus. Another G-d damn hole we have to plug."

"Yes, Sir. It looks that way."

"OK. What do we know about the private plane he took?"

"It is registered to an international Holding company. We're running down the officers and owners now. We should have more in about an hour."

"Keep digging. You may be on to something. Let me know when you have more."

"Will do." Both men turned and left the office. Carl jotted down a few notes, and was visibly annoyed that Feinstein was not the one using a passport to Iran. At least he was close—they both worked for the same company.

Within 25 minutes Bob and Chuck returned to Carl's office with more intelligence.

Again, no pleasantries. "OK. What do you have?" blurted Carl Worthington.

Chuck did all the talking. "The Holding company is a shell. There are several listed owners and officers. All Middle Eastern names. We have no information on any of them, except one. We think the others are mostly fictitious."

"Who is the one we know?"

"Abu'l Mahsin, Sir."

"Wasn't he a General or something in Saddam Hussein's regime? Is he in Iran now?"

"Yes he was a General. He dropped out of sight before Iraq fell. We think he is in Iran, but haven't heard anything about him for over a year—until now. We're checking further."

"OK. Let's keep this under wraps until I brief the President when he returns."

"Your call, Sir." Bob finally spoke.

Apparently Abu'l and his high-priced lawyers did not even think about the records kept by the Customs Department when the set up their plan to shield Abu'l. All those layers of corporate shells meant nothing when faced with a simple Passport record. That Passport was then traced to the Corporate Jet that whisked Luis Ramirez away. That Jet could easily be traced to Abu'l's main company, exposing Abu'l Mahsin himself.

* * *

Aboard Air Force One
Tuesday, Early March
5:53 p.m. London Time

Ron Conklin knocked softly on the President's cabin door. "Come in" was heard from inside the President's quarters. Ron turned the knob, entered and shut the door behind him.

"Mr. President. I have some more information for you."

"Good. What've you got?"

"I called a Lead Agent at Headquarters just to see if anything new has turned up. He was hesitant at first, claiming Worthington forbade everyone from talking to you directly, claiming some Chain of Command garbage. Apparently Carl wanted to brief you personally when you got back."

"Damn him. I'm the President. I want that information now." Doc's voice was louder and more irritable.

"That's what I told him, Sir."

"And?"

"He relented, Sir. He said he didn't care if he got fired. He agreed you need this information as soon as it is available."

"Good for him. Keep me posted if Worthington tries to fire or even reprimand him. I'll intervene if I have to."

"Yes Sir. Bob Hopkins, that's the Agent Sir. He'll appreciate that."

Doc scribbled a note. "What did he tell you?"

Ron relayed the same facts told to Carl Worthington about an hour earlier. Doc listened with keen interest, thought silently for a few minutes, then spoke firmly.

"I'll deal with Worthington when I get back."

Doc had been looking for a reason to get rid of Carl Worthington. He'd heard all the grumbling and knew of several long-time Agents who left the Department because they could not stand working for such a mico-manager. Some said he was an egomaniac. This was the last straw.

CHAPTER TWENTY-FIVE

Inside the Oval Office
Friday, Early March
A Week After the Assassination Attempt
10:14 a.m.

Doc and Sarge surveyed the room. The Directors of Homeland Security, the FBI, the CIA and the Secret Service were there. Everyone but the President was standing. Sarge spoke first.

"President Chandler is proud of the work done by your agencies. That hard work has uncovered a previously unknown Terrorist—a particularly dangerous person. The CIA has determined that Abu'l Mahsin does in fact live in Tehran, and is protected by Iranian officials. There is no possibility of Iran turning him over to us, or anyone else. Mahsin was behind the assassination attempt last week right here on the White House Lawn. Mahsin somehow accomplished that attack through a legitimate company, Sterling and Assoc. out of Orlando. He also may have been behind the attempt on Air Force one last Tuesday. Both investigations are ongoing. This information has not been given to the general public. Everything we have learned thus far indicates that Richard Feinstein had nothing to do with the assassination attempt. Carl and some of his agents have taken Mr. Feinstein into protective custody. The evidence points to a Luis Ramirez as the perpetrator, probably under orders from Mahsin.

Our problem now is: how do we handle the Feinstein fiasco. We jumped to conclusions, smeared Feinstein's name and face all over the TV and probably destroyed his life forever. Remember Richard Jewel? He was falsely accused of the Olympic bombings in Atlanta. His life still hasn't returned to normal after all these years. We can't go around treating American citizens like that."

Director Jenkins from Homeland Security jumped in. "Mr. Colbert, we had solid evidence against Feinstein. We all acted in good faith. The attack last week required swift action, and we did exactly that. What else should we have done?"

Doc answered the question. "How about checking the facts and getting some corroboration?"

Sarge waited to see if Doc would say anything else. When there was only silence, Sarge continued. "There is still much more to do, and more evidence to collect. Your agencies will continue with their respective tasks. We have to neutralize Abu'l Mahsin, find Luis Ramirez, and check out any other connections Mahsin might have with any other American companies or US citizens. Also, the President will address the American people and explain in detail what we have found out. The venue will be the weekly Press Conference at 1:00pm this afternoon. President Chandler will make a short address and then take questions. The Press has already been notified and I'm sure there will be many additional reporters present."

Gordon Krump of the FBI spoke next. "Is that wise, Mr. President? We will all look a bit amateurish and silly."

"Yes we will. But I won't continue this charade, or withhold information some reporter might uncover next week or next year, just to beat us over the head with it at some later date. You all, and myself included, screwed up by leaping on Feinstein within minutes of the attack. We're lucky to have uncovered all that we have. We'll run with that."

"What do we do about Abu'l Mahsin?' Carl Worthington was incensed. Carl wanted someone to pay.

"We locate and freeze his assets wherever we find them. That's what we do with all Terrorists, and Countries harboring Terrorists. Even Terrorists need money to carry out their agendas. Iran is already bottled up with international embargos and frozen accounts."

Doc stared directly at Carl. "There is also another announcement." declared Doc.

Everyone turned to Doc and waited.

"I have reluctantly accepted the resignation of Carl as the Director of the Secret Service."

Carl was stunned. The President hadn't said anything about a resignation to him. He couldn't think of anything to say, so he simply stood there with his mouth agape. His face turned beet red and every muscle in his body stiffened. Carl sensed he had better just keep his mouth shut.

* * *

The Directors had left, and only Doc and Sarge remained.

"When did you decide to get rid of Worthington?"

"In Paris. He is an ancient relic, a notorious micromanager, and a fat-ass jerk. His time has long since run out. He can let everyone think he resigned."

"Your call. I couldn't stand him either."

Changing the subject, Doc continued, "Worthington's agents say that Richard Feinstein has a lawyer. We need to negotiate some mutually acceptable way of handling Feinstein. We can't physically protect him indefinitely, but we have some obligation for his safety when we do free him. Get in touch with his lawyer and see what we can work out. I just hope he doesn't threaten us a gigantic lawsuit."

"Feinstein's lawyer is Harvey Weissman. I think he's a criminal attorney, which makes sense since we accused Feinstein of a criminal act." offered Sarge.

"Let me know what you work out."

* * *

"I appreciate you coming to the West Wing so quickly, Mr. Weissman" as Sarge extended his hand and ushered Harvey into his spacious office.

"I have an obligation to my client. But, thank you for the invitation."

212

"I understand. Please be seated" replied Sarge gesturing to a nearby chair. "Can I offer you a drink? Coffee? Anything you want."

"Coffee. Black. One sugar if you don't mind"

Sarge pressed a button on his phone. A cheerful female voice said "Yes, Mr. Colbert."

"Patricia, please bring us two coffees. My usual, and the other black with one sugar for Mr. Weissman."

"Yes, sir."

Sarge walked across the room and settled into the sofa opposite Harvey. "I'll get down to business. There's no way around it."

Harvey studied him intently but didn't respond.

"I share the sentiments of President Chandler. He is very upset about the troubles that Mr. Feinstein found himself in because of the official investigation of the attack on the President last week. The US government is prepared to compensate Mr. Feinstein handsomely, provide new identities for Mr. Feinstein and his family, and escort them to any location they wish to start a new life. That, of course is in exchange for Mr. Feinstein's silence and a clear assurance he won't file suit against the US Government or elected officials."

Harvey expected something like this, but he still wanted to nail everything down. No detail was too small.

"That's a good first step, Mr. Colbert, but my client deserves much more."

"I'm listening."

Patricia knocked gently. Sarge got up and went over. Opened the door, motioned her in and took the silver Coffee Service with a smile. "Thanks, Patricia."

She smiled back at Sarge and retreated through the door, closing it behind her.

Sarge set the Tray down and offered a cup, already prepared, to Harvey. Sarge took the other one and sat down carefully.

Harvey thanked Sarge, took a sip, set the cup on a nearby table and started the negotiation. "Let's start with the compensation. How much are you offering?"

"One million dollars, tax free."

"Unacceptable. And I remind you that Mr. Feinstein has instructed me to go directly to the Washington Post if you and I can't come to an agreement. So, how high are you willing to go?"

"How much do you want?

"Ten million dollars, tax free."

No hesitation. "My office can disperse up to Seven and a half Million without raising suspicion. I can authorize that amount immediately, and then make a second payment of the balance in three months. Is that acceptable?"

"Damn, that was too easy. I should have asked for 20 million." thought Harvey to himself. "That is acceptable. I'll set up an account and messenger the number this afternoon if we can agree on the other matters."

"Fine. What else do you want?"

It was obvious to Harvey's finely trained instincts that Mr. Colbert was willing and able to agree to almost anything to keep this government screw-up hushed up. Advantage Harvey.

"We agree that my client and his family be given new identities."

"Good. What about the relocation?"

"My client is willing to have your people relocate himself and his family, but once relocated, the US Government gets out, and stays out of his life. No check-ups and no handlers. No contact of any kind."

Sarge thought such a request was odd, but shrugged it off as a nit-pick. It didn't matter whether or not the Government kept tabs on Feinstein once this was all over.

"OK. We can live with that. Anything else?"

"One last item."

"Which is?"

"The government will not release any statements about Richard Feinstein. Nothing about the frame-up, his lack of involvement or his disappearance."

"We didn't plan to, Mr. Weissman. It is as embarrassing to us as it is upsetting to Mr. Feinstein and his wife. We will do our best to evade any such questions from the press." anticipating Harvey's next question.

"Then we have a deal, Mr. Colbert. When will all the arrangements be completed?"

"The new identity papers, passports and such, will take the rest of the day. You send me the account number, and I will electronically transfer the first payment immediately. I can have a plane available late tonight, sometime after 10pm to take Mr. Feinstein to Orlando where he can pick up his wife, and transport them both to a Caribbean Island."

"Which Island, Mr. Colbert?"

"Does it matter?"

"Yes, it does. Relocate them in Bermuda."

"OK, Bermuda it is. Any particular reason?"

"Richard and Sherrie honeymooned on Bermuda. The Island holds special memories" he lied. "And by the way, my wife and I will accompany the Feinsteins to Bermuda. Any problem with that?"

Sarge didn't care. "Sure, both of you can go with them if you want. Will you need a plane back to DC?"

"No thanks. We'll make our own arrangements. Not sure how long we will stay."

Both men rose simultaneously and shook hands. Both knew the other would keep his word.

CHAPTER TWENTY-SIX

Luxury Penthouse, Tehran, Iran
Thursday, Early March
A Week After the Assassination Attempt
2:26 p.m. Local Time

Abu'l Mahsin listened to a top aide explain the latest report. "We have had no contact from Rafiq in two days. The imperialist President Chandler did go to Paris instead of London as we originally were told. The pig went back to London from Paris the next day and landed safely. International news reports say he is returning to America today."

The emergency diversion of Air Force One, the failed attempt to land the RPV, and the fate of the three assassins went unreported in the international press. Abu'l and his henchmen had no way of knowing what actually happened. So, in his normal bigoted and distorted view of the world, Abu'l made decisions devoid of any compassion or realism. He didn't really care about the lives of those who worked for him, and not hearing from Rafiq didn't faze him, except for the failed attempt to kill the President—again. Another attempt would have to wait.

Abu'l knew he didn't have the manpower in place or any sort of Plan for another attack any time soon. Such preparations for success in his Secret War would take time—and more money. Abu'l had both in abundance. He also realized, surprisingly though, that he could not keep

Mrs. Post a captor any longer. There was nothing to be gained by doing so. William Tyler Post, the Speaker of the House would not soon be President of the United States, and would not have the power and influence Abu'l craved.

Abu'l ordered the release of Mrs. Post, and instructed his aides to put her on a commercial flight back to Washington, DC. Abu'l had been careful to ensure that his name was not directly linked to her kidnapping and detention. He never visited her, and had instructed her captors to never mention his name. Even if the United States launched an investigation, they would only turn up no-name terrorists with tenuous ties to any known terrorist organization.

Abu'l would never learn what happened to Rafiq, Luis, or Mahara. He didn't care and wouldn't spend any time or effort to find out. Starting another Plan for his Secret War was all he cared about—and getting pleasure from his girls, of course.

* * *

Friday, Early March
A Week After the Assassination Attempt
12:49 p.m. Local Time

Harvey rushed home from his meeting with Mr. Colbert. He called Suzanne from the car and told her to meet him there by 1pm. She was getting out of her car as he pulled into the driveway. They hurried inside together.

"Did you contact Chuck Simpson?"

"Yes, and he was in a foul mood." Replied Suzanne as they shed their coats.

"What did you tell him?"

"When I asked for a favor, he said that his Golf game was suffering anyway. He missed the cut by a stroke. His putter failed him."

"So he can help us out?"

"Yes, he will help. He will fly his plane to wherever we want."

"OK. I told Mr. Colbert that Richard wants to go to Bermuda. So Chuck needs to meet us there."

"When?"

"The Government Jet will leave Andrews with Richard aboard around 10:30 or eleven tonight. They will pick up Richard's wife in Orlando by 5am tomorrow, then on to Bermuda."

"Wow, that's quick."

"The government is wiggling out of this mess as quickly as they can."

"I'll say." Suzanne opened the Fridge to retrieve a coke.

"There's more."

Suzanne paused in mid-gulp to look inquisitively at Harvey. "There is?"

"Yes, we are now millionaires—or at least we will be in a few days."

"We are? How?"

"Richard agreed to a 25% contingency fee if I could negotiate a settlement with the Government. The settlement is for Ten Million."

"You're kidding!"

"No I'm not. The funds were transferred to our account in the Bahamas this afternoon. I'll give Richard his money as soon as he and Sherrie are settled. This is my biggest fee ever, and the first one over 1 million."

Suzanne plopped down in a kitchen chair, dumbfounded.

"And we're going on vacation." Harvey sat down beside her and held her hand with both of his.

"What?"

"We're going on vacation. We deserve it."

"Where are we going?"

"We're accompanying the Feinsteins to meet Chuck in Bermuda tonight."

Suzanne started to rise. Harvey dragged her back down.

"Harvey, how can I leave my job on such short notice? What about your other clients?"

"We'll only be gone a few days—maybe a week. Your boss owes you some time off, and I'll get Paulette to cover for me."

"Who's Paulette?" Suzanne was skeptical and suspicious because she knew so little about Harvey's law practice.

"She's the new young lawyer who took over the vacant suite next to mine a few months ago. We're both solo practitioners, so we agreed to cover for each other if need be. I already called her. Now you can call your boss."

Suzanne was still anxious. She didn't like last-minute surprises. "I can't get packed this fast." She protested.

No need to pack, we can buy whatever we need there. We're rich, remember. Start acting like we are." Harvey joked.

Suzanne laughed and bent forward to give Harvey a great big kiss. Still embracing, Harvey pulled Suzanne up and led her to the bedroom. They had a few hours before they had to leave for Andrews Air Force Base.

CHAPTER TWENTY-SEVEN

Orlando Executive Airport
A Week After the Assassination Attempt
Saturday, Early March
4:16 a.m.

Sherrie Feinstein was waiting impatiently, arms encircling her huge belly. A sweater was draped haphazardly on her thin shoulders as she tried to ward off the early morning chill—53 degrees is chilly for Orlando. The two FBI agents had escorted Sherrie from her home to the airport in the dead of night. Sherrie was initially a little skeptical, but eventually agreed to go with them after Harvey called and spoke to her. She had yet to speak to Richard. Harvey and Suzanne both felt that it was best to wait for an in-person reunion, given Sherrie's condition.

As the small Lear Jet rolled to a stop near a deserted part of the Hangers at the far end of the complex, Sherrie became excited. Her fidgeting, ringing her hands and general nervousness alarmed the agents, especially Agent Linda Covens. The older male Agent, Lester Goodwin was concerned in a grandfatherly way. Their orders were only to bring Sherrie to the airport and take her to this particular location. She could bring one small suitcase. The agents were told that an FBI Lear Jet with Tail Number N3425 would be arriving between 4 and 4:30am, and they were to allow Sherrie, with her suitcase to get on board. They knew nothing more—nothing about Richard. Nothing about where the Jet was headed next. Nothing about who else might be on the plane. Both Agents recognized the Feinstein name, but said nothing, and kept their suspicions to themselves. Both had been involved in Witness Protection Programs before and knew that confidentiality and secrecy were paramount. They would just do their assigned job and put this whole matter out of their minds when it was over. There would be no reports written, no briefings to superiors, nothing except that the file would be closed and sent to a secret location deep within the bowels of the FBI file storage area. No one would ever read the file or see it again.

The agents glanced up at the Tail Number—it matched. Sherrie could board and their assignment would be over. The door just behind the Pilots opened smoothly and Suzanne stepped out. Harvey stood in the doorway blocking visibility into the plane. Suzanne extended her hand to Sherrie, who took in with a weak shaky grip and an apprehensive look on her face.

"Sherrie. I'm Suzanne Weissman. My husband, Harvey and I are expecting you."

Sherrie had been warned not to mention or use the Feinstein or Richard's name until they were safely on Bermuda Soil. After that time, it wouldn't matter anyway because they would have assumed new identities by then. "Nice to meet you both" as she feebly waved at Harvey, who returned the gesture.

Suzanne spotted the drab colored suitcase next to Sherrie. "May I help you with that?" as she bent to pick it up.

"Thank you." replied Sherrie as she patted her belly. Sherrie turned to the two agents. "Thank you for your kindness." She hugged them both and then turned back towards the plane. After all, she had spent the last six hours with them and had developed some kind of bond.

With a sweep of her free hand, Suzanne indicated that Sherrie should climb the four steps built into the open door. Suzanne followed lugging the heavy suitcase. Harvey stepped aside just enough to allow Sherrie and Suzanne to pass. The door smoothly closed immediately after Suzanne was inside. The engines whined louder as the pilots made their preparations for takeoff.

Richard lunged forward and swept Sherrie into his arms. Neither spoke. Both cried. They just silently embraced. Neither wanted to let go of the other.

"Please take your seats and buckle up, folks. We're cleared for takeoff." declared the pilot, Captain Arnold Fisher. Morgan Fields, the pretty lady co-pilot was fiddling with levers, knobs and dials as the engines roared to life. Their Flight Plan was from Orlando non-stop to Bermuda, and the Pilots only knew they were transporting four people—no individual passenger names were listed on the Manifest.

Suzanne helped Sherrie into the luxurious seat next to Richard. The Seat Belt Extender was already in place. Sherrie buckled the belt snuggly around her hips, carefully avoiding her Baby Bump.

Within an hour they were far out over the expansive Atlantic Ocean. Richard and Sherrie held hands as they marveled at a spectacular sunrise. Bermuda and the rest of their lives were just over the horizon.

* * *

Harvey handed the new Blue Passports to Richard along with new Social Security Cards. Richard and Sherrie looked at their new names, then at each other. Harvey continued the orientation. "Richard, your Passport photo shows you with a full beard and mustache." as he pointed to Richard's fake set. "Wear that when we deplane in Bermuda. After we get you settled, start growing a real beard and mustache." Harvey intentionally did not mention that Bermuda was not their final destination.

Harvey and Suzanne sat behind Richard and Sherrie. Both couples held hands, snuggled, kissed occasionally and were happier than either recalled in recent memory. The flight was smooth and uneventful. There were lots of snacks and drinks in a nearby cabinet and refrigerator. The conversation was easy, quiet and short, whenever there was any.

* * *

The Customs Officer was quick and efficient. He looked at each Passport Photo then the face of the person it belonged to. All four were easily recognizable as being authentic. The few personal items and Sherrie's suitcase were searched by another Officer. Nothing illegal was found. A swift stamp on each Passport, and they were all legally in Bermuda.

The FBI Jet was summarily refueled and given permission to return to the United States. This was just another one of the dozens of trips that they had flown all over the world.

* * *

Once inside the terminal, Harvey and Suzanne started looking around. Suzanne spotted him first. "Over there," she pointed. Chuck Simpson saw them coming and waved.

"Good to see you, Chuck. We're all here. Let's get going."

No introductions. They just turned as a group and followed Chuck down a flight of stairs to another White Jet—a Gulfstream this time. Neither Richard nor Sherrie asked any questions. They trusted Harvey and Suzanne, so they just went along.

Once on board and settled into wide seats, Harvey asked Chuck "Did you file the Flight Plan yet?"

"Yes. I'm scheduled to play in a professional Golf Tournament in Europe next week, so we will land in Paris. I told the Gate authorities you guys were friends just checking out the plane. They don't care, and the tower won't know if you four were or were not cleared by customs. You were right Harvey. There's no way we could have pulled this off in the States."

Richard and Sherrie looked at each other, then back to Chuck and Harvey. They had no clue about the elaborate deception going on for their benefit.

"We're not home free yet. What's the Plan for Paris?" inquired Suzanne.

"I think we can just go through Customs as any tourist might. They don't care how you get there or from where, only that you have a valid Passport when you arrive."

"How do you know that?"

"I've flown to Paris a dozen times in the past 4 or 5 years. They never checked anything except my Passport. The few times anyone asked how I got there, I just told them. No one ever tried to verify my answer. So, we just say you came on my plane from Bermuda going on Holiday in Paris, and that's all."

"OK. That should work. We all have our own Passport." agreed Harvey.

Sherrie was excited about Paris. Little did she know—Paris also was not their final destination.

* * *

Getting through Customs in Paris was a breeze. The only issue was Sherrie's obvious pregnancy. The Customs Officer asked in broken English if she had permission to travel in her condition. He was concerned about how a problem with an expectant American Woman might impact the French Government. Sherrie thanked the Officer for his concern and lied that her Doctor said it was OK to travel for another two weeks. Harvey was quick on his feet and continued the charade. He explained that they planned to return to the States in ten days, joking that if they didn't take this trip now, they would have to wait 20 years when the child was in college. The over worked and underpaid Officer was satisfied as all five nodded in agreement. Suzanne actually chuckled.

Chuck excused himself from the small table where they were having a quick bite to eat. "Gotta file my flight Plan." Richard and Sherrie thought he was off to wherever the Golf Tournament was being held.

Richard had heard of Chuck Simpson. Obviously he was good enough to be able to afford a Jet. He had seen Chuck's name on several Leader Boards while watching televised matches, but didn't know if he had ever won a Tournament. "I play a little Golf myself—about a 12 handicap. Where is the Tournament?" asked Richard, trying to be friendly.

"It's a qualifying Tournament before the British Open next month. I have to play to qualify for the Open. The top five get an invite."

"Good luck."

"Thanks," looking at Harvey, who just smiled.

The Qualifying matches actually start next week, giving Chuck plenty of time to finish what he started in Bermuda. Chuck was filing a different Flight Plan.

Chuck returned in less than 45 minutes and announced "We leave in an hour."

Richard and Sherrie missed the "We" part.

"Well, it was a pleasure meeting you, and not just because you are a professional Golfer. offered Richard, rising and extending his hand.

"Thanks."

Harvey piped up. "There's something else we need to tell you both."

Richard sat down. Sherrie wrapped her arm around Richard's shoulder and waited for Harvey to continue.

"Paris is not your final destination." was all he would say.

"If not Paris, where are we going?"

"We'll tell you when we are in the air. The walls may have ears. We have to be careful. Trust me. You will not be disappointed."

"I guess we have no choice. You both have done so much already; we can wait a little while longer." Richard and Sherrie exchanged quizzical looks.

"You do have a choice, but if you trust me to get you both out of this safely, then sitting tight for another hour is the best alternative."

"You're right, Harvey. I shouldn't second-guess you and Suzanne."

"This has been quite an adventure, but we're close to the end."

* * *

Everyone took their same seats on the Gulfstream and buckled up. The Tower instructed Chuck to get in line behind five other planes waiting for clearance to take off. Richard and Sherrie held hands. So did Harvey and Suzanne as they waited their turn in silence, lost in their own thoughts. The only sounds were the low hum of the engines and the occasional muffled chatter between Chuck and the Ground Controllers.

The climb to 32,000 feet was leisurely and smooth. Chuck maneuvered the Jet expertly as he executed the commands from the Air Traffic Controllers in Paris.

Harvey was the first out of his seat. Suzanne joined him as they stood before Richard and Sherrie, smiling broadly. "Your baby will be born in Tel Aviv."

Sherrie's right hand flew to her mouth—the other encircled her belly. Tears ran down her cheeks. Richard's mouth was open as he just stared at a grinning Harvey Weissman. Suzanne bent to hug Sherrie and offered her a tissue.

"You are no longer Richard and Sherrie Feinstein. That life is behind you. Your new one lies ahead. We, rather Suzanne has arranged for a modest apartment, nicely furnished. She has also contacted a doctor to monitor Sherrie and assist with the delivery when the time comes. Richard, if you want to work again, I can arrange that with any number of Israeli Defense Contractors. Your skills and experience are very helpful for Israel's defense."

Richard was still speechless, and just sat—almost dumbfounded. No one had ever helped him so much before in his whole life.

* * *

As the sleek Gulfstream descended towards the Tel Aviv airport, Harvey leaned forward and squeezed Richard's shoulder. "Welcome home, my friend. Welcome home."

Also available from PublishAmerica

A DEER IN WINTER
by Michelle Ordynans

A Deer in Winter is an inspiring story of survival. It's the semi-autobiographical tale of a young woman's odyssey as she escapes from an abusive home, endures homelessness in the cold of a New York winter, and survives sexual attacks and harassment. In the meantime, she continues her last term of high school while secretly homeless, in constant fear of being discovered and returned to her abusive household. Through it all, she sets her sights on meeting her ultimate goal—graduating high school and attending college in the fall so that she can eventually rise above her troubled background and build a better life for herself. All the rituals of daily life must be negotiated: how and where she sleeps each night, in the rain and snow; how she gets food; how she cleans herself and her clothes; and how she spends her evenings. Along the way she works, makes friends and boyfriends, and explores the fascinating sites of New York City.

Paperback, 206 pages
6" x 9"
ISBN 1-4241-6999-2

About the author:
Michelle Ordynans was born and has lived in New York most of her life, with her early childhood in Florida and a few years in Israel. She is married and has two grown children and several pets. She works with her husband and son as an insurance broker in New York City.

Available to all bookstores nationwide.
www.publishamerica.com

TUNNEL OF DARKNESS

by Rose Falcone De Angelo

Why are some people given the ability to see into the future or communicate with the dead? Is this a gift or a curse? The visions come uninvited and change an ordinary world into one of marvel, turmoil and sometimes fear. This is the story of Bernadette, whose psychic powers begin at the age of ten and carry her into the strangest places.

Paperback, 241 pages
6" x 9"
ISBN 1-60474-153-8

About the author:

Rose Falcone De Angelo was born in New York City's east side to Italian immigrant parents. Rose moved to Florida in 1986. She is the author of a book of poetry, *Reality and Imagination*. At ninety-one, she is the oldest published poet in the state of Florida and has intrigued all who have the privilege of knowing her. She is currently working on her memoirs.